Songs To Dream By

Stories by Adam Moderow

Ten|16
PRESS

www.ten16press.com - Waukesha, WI

For information, please contact:

www.ten16press.com
Waukesha, WI

Editor: Jenna Zerbel
Art director: Kaeley Dunteman
Cover designer: Ashton Smith
Interior designer: Kaeley Dunteman
Author photo credit: Erin Kuntzelman

For every kid who
brought a book to recess.

Table of Contents

For Juliet
and Willow

A Song To Dream By

Vic Martin never dreamed of the fire; he dreamed of the smoke. He knew the fire was around him, though, like it had been every night for the past month. It was part of the scenery—not welcome, but accepted. Understood. It was the smoke that surrounded him. It was the smoke that trapped him and cut off his path if he tried to escape. It was the thick cloud that scrambled the layout of the house. It was an airborne grit that pulled every drop of moisture from his body, leaving his eyes stinging and his shouts little more than muffled croaks. It was the gray, billowing body that chased him farther and farther away from her voice.

Vic's eyes awakened, but his lids refused to open. If they opened, there was a risk that once again they'd let in the smoke, and it wouldn't be a dream this time. If they stayed closed long enough, maybe Vic would be able to fall back asleep and remain oblivious as to whether the smoke had found him again. Yet, the smoke was waiting for him in his dream as well, but at least that was the smoke he'd already survived. That smoke already took what it wanted. Vic's

-1-

quick, shallow breaths—barely enough to tickle the ends of his nostrils—didn't detect any heat, so his eyelids cautiously opened. They'd learned what to expect from the room over the past month, but they still didn't trust it to be there.

A brick wall tinted blue by a night-light. A collection of milk crates keeping the meager wardrobe off the old wooden floor. A crib holding ten-month-old Diana, who was a sleeping bundle—for the moment, anyway. A narrow alcove—the only break in the four walls other than the door—holding the toilet and sink. Vic's eyes were the only thing moving about the room. Beyond the crib, there was a door bordered by a band of red light seeping in from the fire exit sign in the hallway. The hallway led to a stairwell. The stairwell led to a bar. *Mystic Blues.*

Home.

Marina didn't stir. She was as silent and still as the rest of the room. Vic couldn't see her, but the lack of movement from the other side of the mattress told him all he needed to know. It was better that way. Marina didn't like to talk about the fire. Knowing that Vic could only dream of the smoke had done little for their marriage.

Dr. Kouris had said trauma could do that. He'd said talking it out can make sense of the chaos. Once, Vic had asked him if it mattered that it was a one-sided conversation.

"It's important to express ourselves to our loved ones," Kouris had said then. "That's what makes them our loved ones. Even those who have passed. They can't answer, but they can still allow us to express our grief."

Vic didn't ask him if it mattered that, sometimes, Marina answered.

The red running around the door called to Vic, but he didn't move. The room was still, and he had no reason to change that. Logically,

Vic knew that a sign hanging mere feet from the door was the only reason for the outline—it was not fire. The smoke would always be at the edges of his mind, though, and whatever primal parts remained from his cave-dwelling ancestors could only hear the edges.

Survival instincts still were not enough to draw him into action. If the glow beyond signaled some sort of intruder, why should he draw them in prematurely? His appearance in the hall would not change any minds or intentions. Even if an intruding force visited the room, what was there to take? The entire reason the family had found themselves here was because they had nothing.

At ease with the uneasy stasis, Vic relaxed back into the mattress and closed his eyes as carefully as he had opened them. The outside world plunged into suspense as his fear insisted that the smoke would find them again if he didn't keep watch. His mind showed him the smoke becoming a solid form with limbs and claws. A creature coalesced from it, devoid of features but brimming with power. It turned toward Vic, and he opened his eyes.

A moment passed, and Diana whimpered from her crib.

Vic leaped into the ready position and waited for the next signal from his daughter. She cried a little louder without opening her eyes. Vic scooped her up in his arms and began the calming ritual they'd agreed upon. A slow rock in the crook of Vic's arm, and Diana calmed. Yet, she wouldn't go back to sleep unless there was a song. Vic ran through the catalog in his mind and selected one that his students used to love. He had originally learned it at summer camp for one of those comradery-building tricks the councelors used to implement. He had then stolen the technique for his own classes. The song was catchy, rhythmic, and repetitive to the point that you could sing it forever, which the elementary kids would often test for themselves once they'd left his classroom.

When Diana was first born, Vic had spent weeks running through every silly song and nursery rhyme he'd collected in his years as a camp counselor and elementary music teacher. Some of them he hadn't sung in years. One or two he had looked up to make sure he had the words right. When he'd found one that Diana took a liking to, he taught it to Marina, but she always preferred Vic singing them. Diana never seemed to care who was singing, though. She just liked the song.

Vic began the song in a hushed voice so that only he and Diana could hear. It only took three verses before Diana slumped again and could be set back in her crib. She'd be good until morning now. Something about either her age or the dark, quiet room ensured that she would only wake once per night. It was always once, though. She liked to check in.

Maybe she had dreams like he did. Maybe some part of that night—the fire and the smoke—had stuck in her memory, preventing her from enjoying her evening rest. There were nights that she didn't seem capable of getting into a deep sleep. She would shut her eyes, slow her breathing, and go limp, but the feel of the mattress and the absence of Vic's embrace was enough to bring her back to the waking world. Some nights, it seemed as if something was waiting for her in deep sleep—that place of dreams—forcing her to stick to the shallows, where she could be quickly roused. With enough patience, though, the length of a song would do the trick to take her deep, where she couldn't so easily bob to the surface. If only Vic could sing himself into that level of sleep.

Sometimes he didn't get there in time, and no song would soothe that particular beast. On those nights, all Vic could do was stare into the boundless void that was his screaming child and wait until she tired herself out. This, he thought, was what it meant to confront true powerlessness. Diana's despair became an unstoppable force. It would barrel ahead until it ran out of energy. The choice was to either hold tight or be destroyed by it.

Most nights, he got to her in time, though.

Vic returned to the mattress lying on the floor, folded the covers around himself, and shut his eyes. The smoke did not come immediately, but it hovered around the edges of his mind as he slipped after Diana.

"She loves your voice," Marina lobbed from the opposite side of the bed.

"She loves yours, too." It came out on impulse.

"I can't sing like that anymore."

Vic swallowed the lump in his throat and sighed himself to sleep.

Vic had tried to go back to the classroom. None of his personal instruments had survived the smoke. There were plenty of options in his music room at the school, though. The instruments were all decades old and heavily abused by the students, but regular maintenance, which brought a sound back to its proper voice, was part of the joy. An instrument in his hands could unblock the dam. Any built-up pressure or clutter would flow out in a steady series of notes and chords, adding order to the immediate world. He had tried to go back. He'd lasted two days before he was asked to reconsider.

The school year was almost over. They could treat it like medical leave. Vic was no good at work when his home was so uncertain. He'd insisted that his work, the music, would be the best way to regain some of that stability, but administration wouldn't hear it. The fire and the family required his presence. And the other teachers said his songs had gotten too sad.

Greg Kiernan, a student's father, owned a few buildings downtown and offered to put the family up in one of them. It was a brick room in the basement that used to serve as a green room-slash-crash pad for the entertainers that had passed through. The building hadn't been occupied in a decade before Kiernan bought it, and nobody had seen the inside of Vic's new room in twice as long. But it was a room. It had running water and electricity. Best of all, the brick made a fire seem unlikely.

Kiernan had been working on refurbishing the building and offered Vic one of the disused corners. In exchange, Vic helped with the grunt work, clearing out the rooms Kiernan hadn't gotten to yet. Some of the corners hadn't seen light—let alone a broom—since before Vic had hit his first piano key. Kiernan said it was nice to know the building was occupied during daylight hours. Vic was happy to have something to occupy himself with, since school wasn't an option anymore. With Diana at daycare, the days tended to get too quiet. It made Vic nervous to not hear her fussing.

The building had been a pseudo jazz club back in the 1920s (or what passed for a jazz club more than two hours away from Chicago and surrounded by cornfields, anyway). Kiernan had tried to recreate the same aesthetic, and to his credit, the patrons seemed to like it so far. It struck Vic as a theme-park version of a jazz club, but it was the roof over his head for the moment.

Mystic Blues had only been open to the public for a few months when the smoke chased Vic into the basement. The ground floor had been spruced up first so that it could start making money while the other floors were brought into line. The second floor had a big open ballroom that Kiernan was hoping to use for wedding receptions. The third floor was a small lounge with an attached office. Rumors claimed that more than one illicit organization had operated out of there back in the day. Vic's new home in the basement was the part few people knew about, and it was last on the renovation schedule. Of course, it was also the floor that required the most attention before Kiernan could make money off of it.

It was in one of these undiscovered chambers that Vic found himself for the day. The door wasn't locked, but it didn't open readily, either. A little shoulder pressure, and entrance was earned into a room that could have been the same one he'd slept in the previous night, were it not for the animal remnants, scat, and otherwise. The room felt like there was a leak somewhere—a little too much moisture in the air. Vic slid his mask into place, partly for the sanitation and partly for what his experience with the musky rotten smell had taught him would be waiting inside the room. A fresh lightbulb in an ancient socket helped him see things a little more closely.

First, there was an old couch that had been well worked in by what Vic hoped were mice. A dresser with a mirror stuck in one corner. Vic would move that to his room later in the afternoon. The toilet could've used some attention, but that was a job Vic would leave for the plumbers coming in a week. He'd told Kiernan that he would clear the junk, but when it came to plugs or pipes, he was out. Vic turned and noticed an object stuck between the wall and an arm of the couch. It was thick at one end, narrow at the other, and long enough to fit a guitar. Vic felt as if he had been lost in a foreign country and finally caught a glimpse of a sign in his native tongue.

He hefted the couch enough to free the case, feeling the feet crumble from the sudden demand. Vic set the case on the couch. It was old, judging by the scuffs and level of dust, but instrument case technology hadn't changed a great deal in the last century. The latches were rusted, one of them was missing a screw, and they opened with a stiff squeak and sudden clack. The instrument inside the guitar case wasn't a guitar, but it would do. Given the situation, it was certainly an appropriate instrument.

For a moment, Vic was seven years old again, rummaging around his grandparents' attic. He had pulled a similar instrument out of that high, hot place and found his project for the summer. "Nobody in the family plays," his grandpa had insisted. Vic decided in that moment, the family needed a banjo player.

It needed new strings but otherwise felt solid enough to take a tuning. Vic inspected the neck, checked the frets, and felt around the head. He'd need to add a new bridge and a couple hardware bits to the repair list, but there was nothing missing that he couldn't scrounge together. The simplicity of its design was one of the reasons the banjo had become popular in communities lacking much else to begin with—communities trying to imitate what had been taken from them with whatever discarded items they had at hand. Banjo is a humble instrument. Banjo is an instrument for the desperate.

For the first time in a month, Vic did not think about smoke or all that he had lost. The banjo might not hold a tune for more than a few notes, but it would hold his attention for the afternoon. As a matter of history, the banjo had long offered escape for the oppressed people who created it. Banjo is adaptable. Banjo is a path to freedom. It had always been a loyal friend to Vic.

If nothing else, Kiernan could hang it above the bar. Maybe it could add some credibility to Mystic Blues.

The strings were new, but the sound was old. The folks at Watson Music were excited enough to see Vic again that they didn't even charge him for the strings. Then again, they didn't get a lot of calls for banjo parts, so they might have just been happy to get them off the shelves. Opening the door to that shop was like opening a door to the disused family cottage. It didn't come easily or smoothly. but once it was open, the memories became a tactile part of the air.

Vic hadn't used a claw hammer regularly in a few years (the kids had thought banjos were too old fashioned), but the tunes quickly came back to his fingers. Simple ones at first, the kind any respectable player would know. *Cripple Creek, Old Joe Clark, The Boatman*, and even a version of *Twinkle, Twinkle Little Star* echoed through the brick basement of Mystic Blues. The banjo held itself together and settled more and more into tune with each verse.

Banjo is an underutilized instrument. It had never gotten the publicity of guitar or even bass. Guitar always has iconic players who use the sound to lead listeners into grand experiences. For the majority of folk, the most iconic banjo player is Kermit the Frog, and the only experience they expect is "Deliverance."

There's also a class system to any instrumental ensemble. Much like a high school cafeteria, you only need one glance at the group to know the hierarchy. Guitarists, trumpeters, flautists, violinists— you get to the top of any of those sections, and you're set. Not many first chair trumpets will hang out with the banjo player. First chairs are more likely to be with the tuba player, or even the third chairs, than the banjo player. Playing banjo is a good way to secure some solitude early on. Vic had always liked that. Saxophone was the instrument he had played for the band. Banjo was the instrument he had played for himself.

Vic's playing escaped its brick studio and meandered up the stairs, bringing Greg Kiernan to his basement abode.

"You convince the school to give you a loaner?"

Vic stopped playing but held the instrument tight. "Huh, no. I, uh, found it while cleaning out one of the rooms yesterday. Must be from one of the acts back in the day. Probably 1950, if not older. I had Watson help me fix it up a bit. Didn't think it would play at first, but it's a sturdy piece."

Vic hadn't realized how much he enjoyed the instrument. He took a moment to find his breath as his fingers started finding their way back into the key that they had been playing with.

"Thought you might like something from the old days. It'd look pretty great hanging above the bar. I had to know what it sounded like, though." Panic played an interlude inside him as Vic realized that he had offered to part with the instrument. It was strange, considering he had only just found the banjo, but it'd been so long since he held an instrument of his own. Now, offering to give it up twisted his stomach into a loop.

Greg thought a bit as Vic's fingers continued to pull a tune from the banjo in question. Vic knew the tune had a name, but it wasn't one logged in his memory.

"Tell you what," Greg said. "Why don't you hang onto it. An instrument like that should be played, not displayed."

A sigh of relief left Vic's body. "Thank you, that's very kind."

"Well, yes and no." Greg cut Vic short like a businessman trying to maintain his dominance. "Comes at a price . . . " He drew it out a little more than necessary. "Play. Play for me and the patrons tonight. Give us some background, some atmosphere. It may look good above the bar, but it will do more if it's in use."

"I'm not so sure it will." Vic stopped playing and propped the instrument against Diana's crib. "I don't think I'm the musician you want."

"I heard you when I was coming down here. You're good. Better than the jukebox, anyway. People love live music."

"Sure, but they also love music that makes people feel good.

Music you can dance to, or at least smile to. You know what the school said about my playing, and that's why I didn't finish out the year."

Greg considered this for a moment. "Do you know what Steve Martin says about the banjo?"

Vic felt that he did, somewhere deep down, but he couldn't find the words. "Steve Martin says a lot about the banjo."

Greg laughed at the obvious cover. "'The banjo is such a happy instrument. You can't play a sad song on the banjo; it always comes out so cheerful.'"

"The healing power of banjo? That's your suggestion?"

"Looks like it. Plus, I could use some entertainment for the regulars. Sheryl, my wife, will be here. Let her watch Diana for long enough to see if I'm right about this." Greg stood straight in preparation to leave. "So, I can count on you being upstairs tonight?"

"Sure. I don't think it'll work, but I owe you at least that much."

Greg smiled and nodded before heading back through the hallway. Vic grabbed the banjo from the crib and began working through as many tunes and improvised licks as he could remember. Every note, every tune continued a journey that dared him to keep up. Maybe Steve Martin was right. Even the slow, more somber pieces had a spring running through their bars. As Vic followed these notes and watched his fingers relearn the instrument, his empty sadness responded. It didn't disappear, but it did sit back, as if it too wanted to see where the song would lead.

The crowd wasn't expecting music. Not banjo music, anyway. There was no setup, no sound system, no announcement. Vic simply grabbed a seat with his back to the wall, pulled out the instrument, and started playing. Greg had told him to be background music, atmosphere. So, he tried his best to stick out no more than the light fixtures or framed black and white movie posters.

Sheryl held Diana so she could see Vic warming up, but then it was time for bed. She usually went to sleep pretty easily. Putting her back when she woke up, however, was the trick.

The first few songs went unnoticed, which was a good thing. Vic's fingers had a bit of stage fright. As he became more comfortable with the gig, so too did the audience grow comfortable with his presence. He received casual glances at first, and barely audible applause from one table after a song. Based on the dramatic way he pointed, one man in a denim jacket was asking Greg if Vic was supposed to be doing what he was doing. Once the introduction was over, the crowd settled back and accepted the new accent on their evening.

Once Vic let his fingers take the lead, he found himself paying more and more attention to the crowd. There was nobody that Vic recognized but nobody out of place, either. They had all been there before, or in places similar to Mystic Blues. They all knew how to carry themselves, what and how to order. A few were admiring the exposed brick that Greg had left up around two of the walls—for those who want to feel like it's a dive bar while ordering their overpriced glass of chardonnay. A man in flannel was perched on a stool, running his hand along the bar. Vic watched him try to catch the eye of everyone that passed so he could ask about what kind of wood they used.

Most of the crowd, though, was simply trying to have private drinks around their dimly lit tables—a world to themselves, surrounded by other worlds. The lights didn't prevent them from seeing the other patrons, only simply discouraged them from wandering too far beyond their base.

Near the end of the hour that Vic had agreed to, he started to wander through some chords and stumbled on a song from his childhood. A simple song from summer camp. A song that had bounced around the dining hall every summer until you could feel the music binding the staff together. A song that had been one of his students' favorites and was now regularly implemented to soothe Diana to sleep. Catchy, rhythmic, and repetitive to the point that you could sing it forever.

The lyrics ran through Vic's mind, but he didn't sing. His role was to be the background. Louder and louder, they played between his ears. Different verses, different versions of the song; he could almost hear them echoing through the lounge.

Then he realized he *could* hear the lyrics. The patrons had recognized the song and started singing along. At first it was only a few well served mumbles, but table by table, the entire space had joined in. They were all twelve years old again, away from home and clinging to the unity afforded by nonsensical words set to an elementary chord progression. As long as the song held, that group of people would hold together as surely as if they were blood. They were unified, joyous, and at peace. The only world that concerned them was the poster-clad walls, the drinks in their hands, and the music around them.

The song couldn't hold forever, though. Vic came to the end of the verses he knew. The last note faded, and so did the stupor the lounge had taken part in. The audience slowly shook off the feeling, and Vic began to pack up. Outside of a few donations that had been thrown into the battered case, there was no evidence of his performance five minutes after it was completed. A nod to Greg behind the bar was returned, and Vic descended the stairs to his one-room home.

Sheryl greeted him at the door. "Sounded great, even from here," she said. "Diana started snoring about twenty minutes ago. I think the music helped."

"Best review I've had all night." Vic thanked her and entered the room like a teenager sneaking home after curfew. The banjo let out a whisper in open "G" as he laid it across the milkcrate dresser. He froze, waiting for any sign of movement in the room. Diana let out the slightest snore, but she maintains its rhythm. Safe at this stage, Vic removed his shirt and crawled into bed.

"How did it go?" Marina mumbled.

"It went well." Vic couldn't see the point in any other description. The night had been a novel experience. He hadn't had such a loose, organic performance since the coffee shop gigs in college. He'd first met Marina at one of those gigs. Any lightness he had felt from the performance vanished as Vic acknowledged that he couldn't share the music with her anymore.

Marina offered no follow-up question, comment, or otherwise. There was only a stillness in the air and a chill in the sheets. Even Diana stopped her snoring, acquiescing to the tense tranquility.

"Would you like to hear one of the songs?" Vic knew she would refuse. Part of him thought that was why he asked. It was the polite thing to do, but playing a song for a dead audience was a performer's nightmare.

"It would be lost on me."

Despite his premonition of the moment, Vic felt his heart drop. With Diana sleeping, he wouldn't have played anyway, but once upon a time, he and Marina would have risked it. Once upon a time, music had been the fabric of their world. Collaborative and critical, Vic and Marina had found each other lost between notes. Now, the only sound they shared was the eternal whole rest that this part of the music prescribed.

Vic rolled to his side, took a breath, and released himself to sleep.

He heard Diana rustle before anything else. He was halfway to that other world of dream and illusion when the soft friction of her pajamas against her mattress crossed through part of his brain. His body didn't move until her voice—still getting acclimated to the world—shot out. A cry, and then silence.

"Maybe it will pass," he hoped.

A cry again, and Vic climbed out of bed. He stood by the crib and began a mumbled song. It was earlier than normal. She might just have been having a nightmare. It shouldn't take long to get her back to sleep.

The cries only got louder. Half an hour later, her lips quivered with the soundwaves she was producing. There was such power coming from this small creature. Power that had no source other than the raw void of impulse. She had been fed, changed, and held. Vic found himself slumped against the brick, staring into the tiny void that was his daughter's wail at a complete loss for what to do next. His thoughts stumbled from one point to another, never confident in where they were, why they were there, or where they were going next.

"Play for her." Marina's voice penetrated through the child's plea. "You've tried everything else."

Vic hesitated to release his child but set her in the crib and replaced her with the banjo. His mind was still an incomplete jigsaw puzzle as Vic let his fingers strike where they wished. He couldn't focus long enough to select a song, so his brain reverted to the last one he had played—the song he had sung for her in the past, the song he had played that night for the bar. A slow, catchy tune that relied on rhythm and whimsy to lock with the audience.

Diana's cries lowered in intensity, and her eyes opened enough to watch Vic's fingers in the dim red light sneaking in from beyond the door. She turned to her side and focused through the bars on her father and the odd device in his hands. She still emitted a whine and a moan that bounced around the room, but finally they came at decreasing intervals. A few more bars into the song, and the banjo was the only sound still moving about.

Marina and Diana were both silent. They both collapsed back to their starting lines, as still as the night around them. Vic finished the verse and put another one into motion with a steady decrescendo. He struck the last note and froze. He listened for any sound of disturbance reinvigorated, but after a minute of holding his breath, he released. Diana was still staring at him, but the look was distant. Maybe she was sleeping with her eyes open, Vic mused. He put the banjo down once again, and after passing a glance over Diana, he curled up in bed. The fuzzy world of dream welcomed him.

The smoke came for him again, but he didn't wake.

Diana didn't call for the rest of the evening. Her eyes never shut, though. She watched and listened through the night and took in the new world.

Diana was still watching when Vic brought her to Watson Music to have the banjo properly inspected. She was an observant little girl and seemed fascinated by the strange shapes and colors that lined the walls. The brass instruments shone in complicated spirals. The string instruments hung on the wall like tribal artifacts. The percussion section sat in the open, waiting for anyone to come knock it around. They all had their unique sound, too. The regulars took turns demonstrating for the small child, who was the most attentive audience any of them had had in a long while. For the better part of the afternoon, Vic and Diana experimented with the different sounds and ways of producing them. Vic started fantasizing about Diana's first instrument—what he could teach her before she ever started music class. How young was too young to start talking music theory? Which instrument would call to her?

No matter the instrument, it would start as an inert lump of material—skillfully crafted in most cases, but incomplete. A musician picks it up, and from nothing, they bring a sound to the world. A rip in the air allows this new collection of sensations to coalesce in a space undeserving of it. Music is more than sound. All the senses can be activated by the right instrument in the right hand.

Vic and Diana finished their tour. Diana didn't offer much in the way of feedback, but sometimes focused and appreciative ears are all that is needed.

"It's a nice piece," Noah, the owner said behind the counter. He carefully handed the instrument back. "Surprised it still holds together, but these things were made with a different quality back then. Meant for life on the road. And I see those new strings are treating you well." Noah looked at Diana, her head resting on Vic's shoulder. "And aren't we the little musician? Are you going to join your daddy on the road?"

Diana didn't respond, mostly because she was ten months old and couldn't form coherent thoughts yet. She simply stared back and questioned Noah's sanity with one eyebrow firmly raised.

Not to be deterred, Noah reached behind the counter into a box that had seen better days. He pulled out a small wooden rattle painted yellow on the rounded end. "For when your daddy needs backup."

Although he didn't know it, the rattle was nearly identical to one that had been lost a month ago. Claimed by the fire. Diana, like her father, was rebuilding her collection.

Vic recognized it and felt the impulse for a tear or two but found that nothing came. "Thanks, Noah. That . . . That means a lot."

"Don't mention it. Hook 'em while they're young, right?"

"Heh . . . right." Vic swallowed the moment. "Hey, thanks for looking at the banjo. Whether Diana backs me up or not, it's looking like this thing might have a second life. And not just as decoration." Vic smiled and nodded goodbye, one hand on the banjo, and one hand holding Diana to his shoulder.

"It's good to see you making music again, Vic."

"Thanks. Feels good."

Mystic Blues was still quiet when they got back. Employees arrived and took chairs off tables. The lines were checked. Counter tops were wiped down. Greg dodged in and out of the main room, making sure that nothing had gone sideways since the previous night.

On one of his trips, he caught Vic's attention and directed it toward a chair set up against the back corner with an instrument stand next to it. "Last night was exactly what this place needed. Any time you're willing, that seat will be open for you."

Vic looked at the chair and adjusted Diana in his arm. "You want me to play tonight, don't you?"

"If it's not too much trouble," Greg said through a salesman's smile.

"Diana. I don't have anyone to watch Diana tonight."

"Keep her up there with you. It's not a loud place, it's only an hour, and music is supposed to be good for developing minds, right? Sheryl told me your little one seemed to like what she heard last night." Greg shrugged at the simplicity of his own reasoning. "Besides, I can always have Becky watch her at the hostess stand."

Vic began forming a polite declination in his mouth. Before it could emerge, his mind tripped over itself, and he started rethinking his position. Diana did enjoy music. She'd had a great day. Vic would like to play. There could be worse things to appear on stage next to him than a cute baby.

"If she starts getting grouchy, the gig is over."

"Of course." Greg patted Vic on the shoulder and pinched Diana's cheek. "Folks will love it." He left with a smile.

Vic set to work on the impromptu stage. He spread a blanket, and then another. It may have been freshly renovated, but at the end of the day, it was still a bar floor. He looked back and grabbed a stack of cardboard boxes. If there was one thing he had plenty of, it was cardboard boxes. He took one that had brought in the evening's new wine bottles and opened it up so that it was just an "L." Vic took the two pillows he owned and propped them against it. Diana could sit up on her own, but some nearby support was always welcome. With the rest of the boxes and a generous amount of duct tape, Vic made a simple wall in case she decided to wander. It probably wasn't the safest playpen, but it would suffice for the hour. The setup would have made Marina nervous, but that didn't make it wrong.

By the time he was done, it was about time to start playing. He set Diana in her new kingdom, complete with her new rattle. He put a coloring book and some crayons in there as well, but he had a hunch that they wouldn't see much action. Diana watched him set up and ignored the audience members walking by trying to catch her attention.

Vic began to play and was happy to see an immediate audience response. Part of it was certainly Diana. It's hard not to smile around a baby, especially one that's not yours. When she began shaking her rattle in time with the music, the crowd only fell more under her spell. Maybe Steve Martin was right about the cheerful nature of banjo—especially with baby backup.

In direct challenge of that thought, two men stumbled in with sloppy assertiveness that you usually don't find outside of fraternity row. Their party had started much earlier in the day. Greg told them as such and asked if they would maybe like a glass of water with their next round. Language that Vic had been hoping to keep away from Diana was exchanged, and finally, Greg asked them to leave.

One of the men turned to go but decided instead to grab an unoccupied stool and see if he could get it through the front window.

He could.

Vic stopped playing and knelt in front of Diana. The crowd, already peripherally aware of the commotion, stretched to the walls to build distance between them and any future glass shards. Greg shouted something to one of the workers, and the crowd watched the new show to see how this sudden tension would resolve. The stool tosser—noticing that he had made himself the main event—grabbed another stool and swung it around himself, preventing anyone from getting too close. His friend hadn't planned on this development and started trying to talk his friend down.

Vic didn't register any of the building standoff. He was trying to stop his head from spinning as he crouched around his daughter. He could feel his adrenalin preparing him for action, making him breathe hard and deep, but no action seemed wise. That's when he smelled the smoke. As his heart and lungs pulled in more oxygen to prepare for battle, the burning stink found its way into his brain.

Vic blinked his eyes and tried to shake the sensation away. It only got stronger, until he could taste it. Vic scanned the room in a panic but saw no flame. No smoke. There was no convincing his mind that it wasn't real, though. Somewhere, he knew the smoke was waiting.

The crowd was stuck watching the disturbance unfold. Arms made threatening gestures. Mouths moved rapidly. The hostess, Becky, was saying something into the phone. But none of the sounds made it through to Vic's ears. All he could hear was his accelerating heartbeat.

Through the cloud in his mind, Vic heard a single voice break through. Rather than overpowering the obstruction in his ears, it sounded as if it came from underneath. It was within his mind already. The voice was slight but strong. "*Play,*" was all it said.

Vic once again tried to clear his mind. Now wasn't the time for new voices.

At the front of the bar, a brave patron tried to calm the stool-wielding gentleman and was rewarded with a shot to the stomach. Vic froze. He knew he should get Diana to safety, but his limbs were stuck in place, huddled in the corner around his makeshift playpen.

"*Play,*" the voice in his head said again. It was stronger and smooth.

Vic forced his arms to reach for his child but found his fingers wrapping around the banjo's neck instead. It was like trying to force a magnet out of alignment. Vic pushed in one direction, but his arms were pulled in the opposite.

"*Play,*" the voice invited again. Vic's fingers began moving before his brain told them to. As notes coalesced, the smoke receded from his senses. He saw Diana, looking up at him, rattle in hand. Vic focused on her and let the song come out.

It was not a song he recognized, but it seemed to stick to a logical progression as he bum-diddied his way through. It was a quiet comment on the intensity of the room at first, barely noticed. But it quickly grew. Vic kept his eyes on Diana in her pillow corner, but all the other eyes came to him.

He kept the tune going as he turned to face a still crowd. The normal audience, the intruders, and even Greg, Becky, and the rest of the employees were looking at Vic's humble stage. It was the same feeling of unity as the night before, but somehow more. Somehow, less. There were no words to join in, so maybe the music had to do more of the work. Without the texture of the words, though, emptiness sat near to the room.

Vic didn't play any louder, but every competing sound disappeared all the same, consumed by the new auditory predator in the ecosystem. The individual notes started to break down in Vic's ears. He could identify their individual components and shared logic even as the specific combination of notes came off the strings for the first time. A shiver jumped from his spine into his shoulders—whether from euphoria or terror, Vic couldn't tell.

The song ended and hung for a moment like the stench of burnt popcorn. The crowd blinked itself back, and one by one, they started to gather their things and wander out the door. Nobody looked at the glass or the window frame it used to occupy. Nobody said a word to one another. The two intruders seemed to have been drained of all aggression. They walked outside and sat on the curb until a squad car came. Greg and his employees wandered out as well, mingling with the crowd, even though nobody could quite remember why they had come out in the first place. Everyone left.

Everyone except for Vic and Diana.

Vic reviewed the empty room, but there was still nobody there. He wasn't sure how much time had passed since everyone walked out, but the crowd had left. The ones responsible for the window had been taken away. Greg had boarded up the window and locked the door without even a glance at Vic, still onstage, trying to make sense of anything that had just happened.

Vic turned to gaze upon his daughter. She looked back at him with an expression he had never seen on her face before. It was reason. It was the face of an older person, not of one still in diapers. He crouched toward her again, their eyes never breaking from each other.

He set the banjo beside them. Diana reached her tiny hand out and gently pulled it across the strings, bringing a "G" into the silenced room.

"That was . . . that's . . . how . . . " Pride and confusion fought for dominance. Vic's floundering thoughts were interrupted by the sudden presence of the smoke. Like before, it leaped through his nose and sent his brain into panic. He looked around the lounge, but it was no longer the lounge. The chairs and tables were still there in silhouette but without so much as the pretense of tangibility. The walls were beyond perception as every space became filled with a rippling dark. It coiled around Vic, circling as it had before. For a moment, he felt the heat, tasted the carbon, and heard Marina call out. This wasn't the smoke infecting his new world; it was the smoke reminding Vic of what it had already done. He was there, trapped by the smoke. The smoke that anticipated every escape route he saw. The smoke that remained in his head, clouding his thoughts. The smoke that reached out and grabbed for him.

Vic frantically looked for anything different and came to Diana, still sitting on the floor in front of him. She had never been in any of his delusions before. If she saw the smoke, she didn't show it. Her posture was relaxed, and her eyes still rested on Vic.

The heat and smell faded. Thick ribbons of smoldered air converged behind Diana. A dense shape formed—a tall shape, maybe eight feet, with willowy limbs. The borders of the shape refined, and Vic realized that the shape stretched back farther beyond his sight. All he saw was the grasping end of an appendage larger than the room could contain. The controlling end of this appendage never appeared. It stayed shrouded in distance and darkness.

Vic looked back at Diana to avoid getting lost in the depth of the manifestation. She was the only unchanged anchor in the room. Focusing on her meant he couldn't be afraid. He couldn't teach her to fear what wasn't there. Even though every part of his body was telling him it was real. The smoke couldn't reach him because he had to be strong for her.

"This is a pure fear. It left you with nothing but yourself." It was Vic's own internal voice that said the words, but Vic was not the one who thought them. The thinker was somewhere beyond the smoke's edge. There was a different timber to it, but Vic knew this was the voice that had told him to play. This was the voice that had told him to play the crowd away.

Vic froze. The hallucinations had never been this intense. They'd never spoken to him before. They had never thought *at* him before.

"Is that emptiness why you sent the child away?" Vic's mind asked him.

Vic's brain fumbled for anything coherent, anything away from the voice that was his own but not. "What child? She's right here." The words were mumbled and confused.

"No."

A hole opened in Vic's stomach as questions flooded through him. His mind was compromised enough with every moment that Vic stayed on his feet, instead of dropping to his knees as the rest of his body begged him to.

"Wha . . . no . . . That's not . . . where . . . "

"*She is where I was. She's where all minds go when not contained by the physical. The land of essence. The land of dreams. You sent her deep enough that she became untethered from herself. She's a curious girl. She wandered and found me. I wasn't supposed to be found. Yes, you sent her very deep. I followed her trail back. She still dreams elsewhere.*"

Words formed like uprooting a tree. "I . . . I don't understand."

Silence for a moment. No speaking, thinking, not even the sound of breathing. Then a scene played before Vic's eyes. There were three people in rags on a beach. Dusk hid their features in dim light. They began playing string instruments that Vic did not recognize. Vic couldn't hear the music, but the shadowed figures played around what could have been a large whale carcass that had washed up on the beach. A whale with a willowy paw lying beside it. As they played, the carcass was set on fire.

An aura—an emotion-adjacent quality—radiated from the creature that Vic began to suspect wasn't a whale after all. An inevitability. A promise of perpetual motion and presence. It would not be stopped. It was a boundless void hiding behind the trappings of the world. Vic could only gaze into its dimensions. There was nothing to do but hold tight and hope for a glimpse of sunlight before being returned to the void.

The flat colors revealed by the flames melted together and spilled out in every direction. There were no longer players, nor the beach. There were islands of color hanging unattached among other similar drifting objects. All of the islands were fluid, changing shape like the water that astronauts drink in zero gravity. Vic noticed a collection of green and gray that he thought must have been the whale-like thing. It didn't have the shape of the creature but had the same feeling. It radiated the same emotion, the same sense of intention and inevitability. Vic moved toward it, though his limbs exerted no effort.

The grouped colors around him shifted and flowed, each responding to their own current. The closer he got to the whale creature, the more his skin tingled. It was like stepping closer to the edge of an enormous canyon. Proximity increased dread exponentially while eliminating the ability to turn away. Vic's legs curled under him. The motion would have normally resulted in kneeling, but his level had not changed as he continued to be drawn toward what was decidedly unlike any whale he had encountered before.

Other colors continued to swirl around but at a distance. Vic came to a stop at the edge of the whale creature, now so large that his vision could not contain it all at one time. His breathing became shallow, and his head refused to stay still.

An amount of time passed. Vic lost any sense of how much. Shapes and colors streaked by. Some crawled. It could have been a minute, or it could have been centuries. His brain had shut down every cell that wasn't dedicated to taking in the entirety of the form before him. Even his heart and his lungs only occasionally convulsed, presumably to remind Vic that he was still alive, despite every sign to the contrary. His ears began to work at some point as a fog of sound rolled in. It was only then that Vic became aware of the silence he had been contained in since the hallucination began.

Two parts of Vic's mind reactivated in quick succession. First was recognition of the sound. It was vague and quiet, but he would recognize it anywhere (apparently). It was a song he had heard and played too many times—at summer camp, in school, for Diana, and for the bar.

The second thought that registered was recognition of one of the other color forms. Again, it was formless, but it emitted a feeling, an emotional aura that Vic knew without being able to articulate how. The new shape approached closer than any others had. It was light purple with green and blue speckling through it. It seemed to Vic that it had its own internal radiance. Of course, any father would think such of his daughter.

Diana's essence floated to rest beside the whale creature, and a moment of regard was shared between them. Then the whale moved with shocking speed back the way Diana had come. Vic was dragged along and forced to watch his daughter shrink into a speck of light in the darkness. There was no sound beyond the music, but Vic felt a wave pass through him that could only have been Diana's cry.

The vision ended, and suddenly Vic was looking at his room in the basement of Mystic Blues—the room that Vic and Diana shared, accented by the faint red light sneaking in from the door. Vic had never seen the room from this angle, though. He recognized the bars in front of him. Yet, he had never seen them this closely before. He had never seen them from the inside. On the outside, he saw himself—his thin, tired body as it had sung Diana to sleep the previous night. As it had sung what he'd *thought* was still Diana to sleep, that is.

The song stopped, and his surroundings shifted once again. Vic was back in the smoke-free lounge, looking at the still unblinking body of his daughter, and presumably the creature that had infiltrated her. She . . . *it* looked back and took a deep breath. Vic stumbled a few feet to the left and vomited against the wall.

Questions and exclamations erupted from him in panicked, halted breath.

"*You still don't understand.*" The invader spoke from his daughter into his mind. "*Let me show you.*"

Vic's arms moved independently—one for the child, and one for the instrument. He was aware of the scenery changing, but this time because he was moving through it, not because it was moving around him. His mind couldn't process in real time until he was back in his room, looking at his daughter. Now sitting on the bed, he glanced at a sleeping Marina.

"*Her container was destroyed by fire while she slept. She wasn't deep enough, though. She is still tethered.*"

The smoke came back from every corner of the room, and the creature inside of Diana once again had presence. Vic's head throbbed, and he collapsed against the doorframe. His fingers found their way to the strings of the banjo and produced a collection of notes that should never be placed together. The sounds fought each other in a systematic chaos. Vic's ears wanted him to stop, but his fingers kept playing, bringing his head closer to peace with every note.

Vic found the strength to open his eyes, only to find Marina melting into a translucent shadow of color—burnt orange, purple, maybe red near the end. She lifted her head to look at Vic before her lines faded and she became little more than a shapeless splash of color against the back wall. Vic called out but couldn't find his voice. Her form vanished, and Vic's fingers became still.

Once again, the weight of silence fell upon him. Marina's voice no longer echoed in his ears. Of course, it had been a month since her true voice had been heard by anyone.

The room was cold and empty. There was a feeling of emptiness, like when all the furniture is removed from a room. The banjo became heavy, or maybe Vic became too weak to hold it, and it slid to the ground with a weak tone. The smoke retreated to where it had come from. The creature in Diana's eyes looked at Vic across the red tinted vacuum of a room.

"You understand now."

It wasn't a question. The being inside of the child still didn't use her mouth to communicate. It was simply a voice in Vic's head that emanated from the body of his daughter. The voice of a creature that could make him hallucinate the smoke and fire that had taken his wife and forced the remains of his life into a brick basement, which he didn't think he would ever get out of. Vic's heart was audibly faster than it should have been. He forced his breathing to even out and gestured toward where Marina's shadow had been. "Where did she go?"

"I've answered that question."

"She's in that place with the colors? That place you were in, where Diana is now? Was that heaven?"

"That word has no meaning. Don't worry about where they are. We won't be going back there."

Vic discovered a spring beneath him and rose to his feet. "Wait. I thought you said that's where Diana is. How am I going to get her back if we aren't going there again?"

"You're not."

Vic wanted to be distraught, but his body wasn't fluent in emotion anymore. It processed slowly. The words made sense, but only as words, not as an idea with meaning. It was the difference between dots on a page and the music they might become.

Vic sat again. "I didn't know what I was doing . . . Was it me? Was it the banjo?"

The child's body blinked, the only recent sign of life. *"I like your instrument. I've never heard anything quite like it before. It has a pure sound. Simple. Quaint. But there is nothing special about that particular instrument, nor is there anything special about you. You were the right musician, with the right trauma, with the right instrument, at the right time. You were part of the right combination of factors. It didn't have to be you, but it is you. In this moment, you are my messenger. You will bring the people to me. Through you, I will reclaim them."*

"'Reclaim them.' What's that supposed to mean?"

"Remember, I know your fear; I know you. You were a teacher, a conveyer of new information and vision. Help me teach. Help me reintroduce a world view that hasn't seen the sun since before anyone can remember."

It was all getting to be too much. The temptation to pass out waged a respectable battle inside Vic's mind. He couldn't leave yet, though. Vic shut his eyes firmly, opened after counting to three, and reassessed the scope of his new world and the small figure of his daughter, who might have been an ancient dream creature.

"Who . . . " Vic began. "Who is it that I'm helping?"

"Names give too much power. My label is beyond your ability or caliber anyway, Vic. If it helps, though, you can call me Diana."

"I very much doubt it will."

"Good. Hold onto that feeling. It will be useful later."

Vic was able to form the beginning of a question before the smoke and heat surrounded him again. The creature had brought him back to that night. Marina had been screaming from the bedroom—the bedroom he wouldn't get back to. Diana, the real Diana, had whined in his arms. His vision blurred as the smoke wove its way inside and forced out tears. He might have been able to fight it. There might have been enough time. But Diana didn't have the time.

His feet had decided for him and carried him down the stairs, lit by the encroaching flame, and through the front door of the house that he would not make it back into. Marina's voice had been drowned out by the roar of the monster consuming the house. The dark of night was replaced by the living glow. Vic had gazed into the destruction before him, pleading for an opening to show so that he could get in or she could get out.

Nothing.

The glow gave way to a thick darkness, darker than the surrounding night. It billowed slowly and heavily, like tar that had figured out how to fight gravity. It expanded wider than the house and rose like a bear stretching to its full height. Gradually and then all at once, the walls and floors disappeared.

As Vic searched for a sign, the child in his arms became pliable and molded to his arms. She rapidly lost weight, until she was hardly putting any pressure on his arms at all. He looked, and Diana had become her dream form—a mix of color and light, void of confirmed shape. The transition completed itself, and she floated away, far from Vic's reach and the chaos of the scene around them.

That part of the memory was new. Vic had lived this nightmare before, every night since the original incident, and not infrequently during the days too. He knew the chain of events. He knew the colors and feelings. Reliving it was torture, but the repetition had created calluses. With nothing new, he had built up a tolerance. This part was new, though.

"No, I saved her. I did that part right. She was right here! I saved her!" He had only been able to protect one of them, but he knew he had been able to do that much. It was the only thing he had been able to do.

He shouted his continued objections to the collapsing house until his mouth refused to form words anymore. Dry from the heat, he gagged on the persistent smoke. He looked in every direction for the swirl of light purple with green and blue speckling, but he found only darkness highlighted by fire—and the smoke, growing larger and reaching towards him.

The smoke and heat dissipated in an instant, and Vic found himself shouting into the brick so loudly, the reverberation made the banjo sound. He stopped when his own screams hurt his ears and fell onto the thin mattress in his dark basement home.

"Fear is a pure emotion. It is unhindered. When you are in fear, you are your purest self. When you are in fear, I know you do not hide anything. I know you are a loyal messenger. Fear is how we can most plainly communicate. I was not the tragedy that happened to you, but if reminding you of that night allows you to serve, so be it."

Vic was still out of breath from the memory. "I will get her back. If I could send Diana away, if I could play her into that place of dreams, I can bring her back."

A smile stretched up the left side of Diana's face. *"As the one who sent her away, you will think that. Cling to it. Foster the hope that you're right. And as long as you do, you will be in fear. Fear that you are wrong."*

Words didn't come. There were no bearings for a situation like this, and Vic found himself drifting loose in the breeze. He slid to the ground, grabbed his banjo, leaned against the crib, and began to play.

The smoke came again but slowly. He recognized the presence of the thing inside his daughter guiding the smoke and putting his fingers on the next correct fret. If it could have calmed the raucous crowd from earlier as an impromptu performance, imagine what it could do with practice.

"*A new perspective,*" the creature whispered in his head. "*An old perspective. My perspective.*"

Vic's mind wandered away as he gave himself to the song. The song was all he had left. In some neglected part of his mind, he chuckled. It was a sad song. It was a sad banjo song. But he wasn't sad in the playing of it, because he was the one playing it. The song was all he had left. And that was enough to start with.

I will find a way to bring Diana back, the secret corner of his mind thought. *Because I am the musician. I have the song.*

For the next two weeks, the door to Vic's bedroom did not open. Greg and several workers tried to force it, but no key or crowbar had any power over the entrance. Most people thought that Vic had taken his daughter and moved to another town. They needed to get away from what had happened. Vic locked up when he left and didn't tell anyone. It was an old building, so some of the locks were rusted and stubborn. Late at night, however, when he was closing, Greg could almost make out music coming from the basement.

For the next two weeks, Vic practiced and refined a song that had not been heard by anyone who wasn't now dust. He practiced under the tutelage of the smoke and the creature possessing his infant child. He practiced and hunted for a way to bring his daughter back to his world.

Time passed within the room, but neither Vic nor the creature inside of his daughter were concerned or aware of it. They no longer existed on a plane governed by time. For them, time passed like a fly buzzing nearby, noticeable for the mild irritation but ultimately irrelevant.

Vic was consumed by the new song. His breathing, his heartbeat, and even the occasional clearing of his throat obeyed the new rhythm possessing the room. The sound filled his stomach. The smoke filled his lungs. His eyes saw flashes of what had been and what would be. He rarely knew which was which. All Vic could surmise was that the flashes were what the creature wanted. What the creature intended. It was a broken world. The creature had been sent to the land of dreams by those men on the beach for a reason. Vic had stumbled into bringing it back. Giving Vic hallucinations and possessing a child were the least of its abilities. Vic could see the future the creature intended to create—dark, full of smoke, and desolate.

Vic always emerged from the flashes to find that they had taken place between notes. The smoother the song became, the more detailed the flashes were. The less of himself he felt coming back to the world.

Then he saw the face of his daughter. The face of his daughter that was not his daughter. His instinct was to shut his eyes and try to reenter the flashes of the broken Earth. He'd rather look at the apocalypse than the daughter he had failed. But Vic knew it wouldn't work. He knew the creature inside his daughter wouldn't allow it. The creature needed him to see Diana—be close enough to hold her but frozen with the knowledge that there was nothing he could do.

The creature had told him fear was a useful, pure emotion, but it was just one. Throughout their rehearsal time, it became clear that despair and madness were just as useful to the dream creature. While Vic was sustained somehow by the music, the smoke inhabiting Diana fed off the increasing void Vic felt inside.

After a while, Vic preferred Diana's face to the broken Earth flashes. Even if her face was animated by smoke, it still reminded him of who it used to be. And secretly, who he would make it again. It was all he had to sustain himself through eternal rehearsal. That, and the song. It may all have been part of the creature's plan, but what else was there?

The song didn't repeat. Vic was never quite sure what happened in the next bar, but if he followed the smoke in his head carefully, the notes seemed to become music. Oppressive music. Enveloping music. Music that Vic would have liked to not play.

He'd tried a few times. Vic had tried to stop playing the song during the first few hours, or days, or weeks—however long it happened to have been. He'd tried playing the song wrong, playing a different song, playing nothing at all. Each attempt to change the song had been met with shooting pain throughout his body—a shock along every nerve beyond his hands. His hands were too valuable.

It wasn't really an individual song. The longer he played, navigating through the smoke and pain, the more Vic realized it is more of a style of playing. There was an emotional intentionality behind the notes and timing.

After a few painful experiments, he could intuit a path that felt like his decision. He wasn't sure if he was making the music with any sensibility besides pain avoidance, but gradually, Vic had decided where the music should go, and it became the correct path. At first, it had been only a note at a time, but slowly, he could produce entire phrases without so much as a wink from the puppeted body of his daughter.

The time came when the smoke brought him to a stop. Vic picked up Diana, and with the banjo slung over his shoulder, they left the room for the first time in two weeks. They ascended the crumbling brick stairs and made their way to the main room. Tables were occupied, pleasantries were exchanged, and the wait staff scurried around the pods of people like fish avoiding rocks in a stream. Vic quietly made his way to the corner of the room, where an unoccupied chair still waited. He set Diana down before sitting himself, and then he began to play.

The tune started subtly and simply, barely touching the air. As the notes inched their way across the room, glances in Vic's direction increased, but none stuck. Nobody recognized the old man with the scraggly gray beard. The song was pleasant enough, though. Maybe it was some kind of outreach that Greg was trying—bring some down-on-his-luck musician in to play. From the looks of him, the player could use a sandwich for his troubles. A shower wouldn't hurt either.

It wasn't until someone noticed the child sitting on the banjo case that anyone maintained their glance. The child stared back with eyes that didn't blink and a face that didn't emote. In the dim lighting of the lounge, her eyes gave off a slightly green radiance. Most of the crowd chalked it up to a trick of the light and generous service from behind the bar.

Greg noticed the commotion. He began to walk toward the man but stopped. The crowd seemed to be enjoying it. The song had an interesting quality. Might as well see where it went. Maybe this guy could replace Vic. Greg thought for a moment that this guy might even look a bit like Vic—in forty years, anyway.

Vic only saw the outlines of shapes far off in his periphery, as well as the smoke between. He listened to the smoke and followed the style it had laid out for him. The shapes beyond gradually stop talking, making the smoke easier to follow. Making it easier to focus. Making it easier to change directions.

As he had done before, Vic started only with the occasional note, slowly building into a measure here, a phrase there. He didn't stay on the variation but expressed it long enough to be confident in what came next. It was a subtle variation. It shouldn't have been noticed until he was gone.

During the eternal weeks of tortured practice, Vic had concluded two things.

1. The ancient creature inside of his daughter would never be done with him, not until it reclaimed its once monstrous form. Vic didn't know how it intended to do that, but he did know that it would involve him playing for countless subjects until they were ready to feed the creature with their will and despair. Vic had sustained the creature until now, but its appetite was growing. It would start with the audience tonight and consume more and more, further and further until the creature was sated.

2. He couldn't call Diana back. There was probably a way, but Vic had only been allowed to learn how to send a mind into the dream world. He didn't know how to call one out. Even if he did, how could he make sure Diana found her way back to herself, or that she would be the only one present when she arrived? Diana would remain a swirl of color until he could figure out how to call as well as send.

"Play," he whispered to himself.

Being careful to stick to the style the smoke had dictated, Vic transitioned into a formal piece. A song with lyrics he didn't invoke. A song he had sung and played countless times before. A slow, catchy tune that relied on rhythm and whimsy to lock with the audience. Repetitive to the point that you could play it forever.

Music, like any magic, is directional. It isn't an area effect; there must be an intended audience. There is spillover, but the full scope of the performance is only for those whom it is directed at. Vic wove the pattern that the creature inside of his daughter expected, even with the change in song. It was the audience that had changed.

Vic didn't know if he could play the creature back into the dream world. Vic didn't even really know how it had happened the first time. Vic did not play for the ancient creature attempting to reestablish its dominance. He played for himself.

The silhouetted shapes, the smoke, and even the sound of his own playing faded, and for the first time in over a month, Vic went deep. Vic felt the notes moving around him until eventually, he felt nothing. Nothing but the pseudo presence of the other shifting clouds of color.

Whatever it was—this creature that had Diana's form—it would have to find another player. Maybe it could, or maybe it couldn't. It had said there was nothing special about Vic. It wasn't Vic's concern anymore. All Vic was concerned with was finding the swirl of light purple with green and blue speckling. He would call out her song until he found her. Catchy, rhythmic, and repetitive to the point that you could sing it forever.

An Exchange:
A Hollow Brook Story

They sit in the car. It isn't their car. Well, it *wasn't* their car. Forty-five minutes ago, before the men parked and hid among the parking lot improvised by the crowd of a high school baseball game, it became their car. Before then, it had been someone else's car. It might have been your car. If you once drove the kind of neutrally-colored sedan that you could never find after leaving the store because there were at least three other identical cars in the lot, there's a better than average chance that this was your car. If you once left your nondescript car unlocked in the parking lot of a dentist's office because you thought, *Hey, who would be wandering around a dentist's office parking lot at six o'clock on a Friday night?* this story may solve a minor mystery for you.

If it was your car, apologies. You won't find it. You wouldn't want it back anyway.

The two men are in the car for specific—but importantly different—reasons. Those reasons are why they're parked near a baseball game that they are not attending. The high school's ball field sits across from a small, white rental house with a gravel driveway and poor street lighting. It's a cheap house, given that it's located so close to the field. That's why the woman that the men in the car are waiting for is renting it.

The garage is open but full of boxes, which is why the past-its-prime Jeep is waiting in the driveway. The house sits on a narrow lot of land that was left over after the other houses had staked their claim. The house to the west is home to a chain-smoking woman who hasn't left the house in seven years, and her husband who leaves every day. The house to the east is owned by a retired preacher with a trick knee and an affinity for daffodils.

The men know these things from a week of surveillance.

You know these things because I just told you.

I know these things because I will live in that leftover house with its limestone basement and U-turn kitchen. Not yet though. Our story must take place first. The rent will still be enticingly cheap.

The man who stole the car is also the driver. He has one arm propped on the steering wheel as he watches the house for signs of a particular movement. He switches his focus from the house to the ball game. The coaches turns the lights on as night settles in, making the two men and their ill-gotten transportation fade more deeply into the twilight.

The home team is winning. That too would direct attention away. Actions don't have to be hidden if the observer is focused elsewhere. A bright spotlight or a dynamic double play is all the excuse needed for nobody to see what is about to happen.

The man in the passenger seat is not watching the game or the house. His attention is on the puzzle he pulled from the several he kept in his small leather-bound notebook. Cryptograms. Coded messages relying on recognizing patterns and making the proper exchanges until a jumble of letters becomes a complete thought. They are rhythmic. They move with logic. They are therapeutic. They occupy enough of his attention to prevent his mind from wandering.

Any newspaper the passenger came across was relieved of its puzzle. The passenger then saved them in his book until they were required. It wasn't why he had been given the book, but sometimes an object can have multiple functions. Multiple identities. The passenger prefers the newspaper puzzles. They decode to silly jokes and puns that any grandfather would roll his eyes at. "In preparation to be banished from his nation, he bought some stuff at the deportment store." Things like that. He could get the same thing through a dozen or more apps on his phone, but the passenger prefers the scratching of a pencil.

The puzzle he completed before getting into the car that is not theirs did not contain a funny pun. It had not been cut from a newspaper. That puzzle had been given. That puzzle had been assigned.

The driver has an identical notebook, but there are no puzzles in that one. In their time together, the driver has always been the last to open his notebook. Some people have a good memory and don't need to take notes. The passenger doesn't think that describes the driver, though.

"*I* becomes *U*," the passenger mutters to himself. He fills this piece of the puzzle in and looks toward the house. The driver's attention is directed back to the house, and a light goes off.

"Here she comes," the driver says. The two exit the car, leaving the ball game behind. They walk up to a woman with a coat that looks too warm for the season. She was heading toward the Jeep parked in the driveway.

The woman doesn't look surprised by the two men approaching at the beginning edge of night. The men each have a lapel pin on their blazers—like an owl's haunted eyes scanning for a sign of prey. The men each hold up small leather-bound notebooks with the same mark on the cover. She knew those eyes were hunting for her. She hoped to get to the grocery store before they found her, though.

The woman pulls her coat tighter. "This is how it happens," she says, and it's somewhere between a statement and a question. The driver and the passenger nod slightly in confirmation and lead the woman to the backseat of the car that wasn't theirs until it was.

The men tie the woman's wrists together but not particularly well. The woman knowing that they don't want her to move is more important than any actual restriction of movement. They blindfold the woman and put another length of cloth around her mouth. It's better if she doesn't see what will happen over the course of the night. There is nothing she can say that will change the itinerary now.

The two men, the woman, and the vehicle that is like so many other vehicles leave Cleveland Avenue as a double is sent bouncing around right field. Nobody at the game sees the car leave.

The driver drums on the steering wheel in precisely the way that the passenger has asked him not to. It is a tic that comes out when he is bored or having trouble understanding something, which is a little redundant where the driver is concerned. "Management acting funny around you lately?"

"No more than usual. You know how she is."

"Sure, but . . . more so."

The passenger pulls out his notebook and opens to his puzzles. "That thing with the windmill developers was closer than expected, I think. Sounds like there are still some unanswered questions. Mayor

Kane is still learning how the winds blow, it seems. She's not comfortable yet with what we do. Or what she *thinks* we do. She has people testing us. Rumor has it, she has someone meddling in our work."

"Our work," the driver dismisses with a huff. His tapping slows to a stop as he turns onto the next road.

"There is always something new." The passenger finishes the puzzle. He already knew where it was going, but it was important to follow through. Sometimes the solutions surprise you.

The woman in the back seat, who is trying to be comfortable with the middle seatbelt, does not attempt to say anything. Although the night centers on her, her role is now object, not participant. If anything, the challenge of the night is reclaiming her agency, her right to participate.

The two men, the woman, and the vehicle drive to The Dining Car, a diner made to look like the inside of one of the many dining cars that used to pass through the railyard the next block over. Both the yard and the diner hold on by the simplicity of their design and the lingering patrons looking for the taste of a "better" time. The two men know the truth. There are no better times. There are simply times before you know, and times after you know. The Dining Car has the best eggs benedict in town, though.

The parking lot is a square, surrounding the restaurant. The owner repairs one side every year—meaning, there is always a freshly paved side and a side that patrons try to avoid. The west end of the parking lot is an embankment leading up to a highway. It's all about location. The access road to the west also has a car wash that hasn't been open for business in over a decade. On the south side of the parking lot, there is a Wendy's. There is a vacant lot to the north, where a hotel was consumed by fire a number of years ago. It did not burn down. It was burned down.

The car comes to a rest in a spot along the highway closer to the vacant lot than the Wendy's. This side was paved last year, so it's still reasonably smooth. This is the quietest side, as it is the farthest from the front door. The only people who come to this side of the building regularly are the employees on their smoke break. And they don't get any farther than the picnic table placed next to the plain gray door below the single floodlight.

"We're going to grab a meal," the driver says. "I get a nervous stomach. We shouldn't be long."

"*Mmmlllmmmrrr*," the woman says, forgetting her role.

"Because you're smart enough to know that this gets worse for you if you aren't here when we look out the window."

The woman can't tell if the passenger is looking at her while replying.

The driver stares after his partner for a moment before turning to the woman. "Right. You must realize who we work for. Imagine how easy it will be for us to find you if we need to. Easier than it was this time." He isn't entirely sure what that claim means, but it sounds like something that would be said if he were watching this scene in a movie.

The doors shut, and the woman is left with the dry ambience of the car. Occasionally, a semi rumbles past on the highway, but mostly she can only hear the muffled gravel crunch of other cars passing around the parking lot. Nobody notices her in the back of the car. Nobody wants to.

Inside, the display case pies tempt the driver, but the men are seated before he can survey the options. It wouldn't really matter anyway. There are the ones filled with pudding and the ones filled with fruit that's so saturated in preservatives, it might as well be pudding. The men sit in a window booth so the driver can watch the car and the passenger can watch the diner. Waters and menus are delivered. Food is ordered. Coffee is poured.

The menus are edited with sticky notes.

The coffee is fair.

The men didn't come for the coffee.

The diner smells like diners should—butter, lingering cigarettes (even though they haven't been permitted inside in years), and unstable comfort. Nobody comes to a diner after dark because their home life is comfortable. A diner lets them play at coziness, though. Around the right areas, there is the note of overzealously applied disinfectant as well. It's a place of refuge and camaraderie in anonymity.

"Read any good books lately?" asks the driver.

"Yes." The passenger does not return the question. He knows the answer.

The passenger feels the weight of his notebook in his left jacket pocket. There are other things in the notebook, but the puzzles are what his mind drifts to. Pulling them out now, however, would be unwise. Too many questions. It would be rude too, but that's a secondary concern.

A bacon cheeseburger and fries are placed in front of the driver. He will smell like grease and fat for the rest of the night. Eggs benedict for the passenger. The two eat in relative silence, their minds focused on what is about to happen. Different things.

The driver disassembles his burger, applies some of every condiment available, and reassembles his creation. He leans over and rips off the biggest bite his jaw will allow. The passenger cuts into his egg so that the yolk can run. He uses his English muffin to soak it up so that every bite will have some of the flavor. It also makes the yolk less likely to drip on his jacket.

Outside, the woman who cannot see, speak clearly, or move in any meaningful way considers how she left the house. She mentally retraces her steps from when she went to leave that night. She had meant to go to the grocery store. She was out of asparagus. She grabbed her reusable bag. She pulled her jacket off its hook. It's a little warm for this time of year, but better that than not warm enough. She turned the lights off on her way out. She had turned the stove off after using it to prepare dinner. The door was locked. The garage door . . .

She didn't shut the garage door. She would have done it from her car, as is her habit. But she didn't make it to her car. She made it to this car. The door to the house was locked, so it might not matter. Nothing to do about it now, anyway. Maybe, nothing to do about it ever.

As the men finish their meals, a bus boy comes by to take their empty plates. His eyes fall to the geometric lapel pins on the men's jackets as he stacks the dishes into a manageable tower and places them in his gray bin. A dishrag falls from his back pocket. He moves back to the kitchen without picking it up. Inside the dishrag, there are three dots of mustard. Or is it four? No, it's three, the driver decides. The other mark is something else. The driver nods to the passenger. The passenger nods back.

Outside, the driver goes one way, and the passenger wanders another. For the first time in longer than it should have been, the passenger looks at the moon and its uncountable background of stars. The night sky as it is every night. The night sky as it is only on this night. The passenger breathes in the chilled and contaminated ground-level evening, imagining how far up he would have to get before it tastes clean. He stares deeper into the art installation that is the expanse before him. The sky, the stars, the vague glowing brushwork against the darkness—it all strikes him as overpowering in its simplicity.

The passenger returns to the car. The woman is still there, unable to see, unable to speak intelligibly, and limited in movement.

"You understand what is going to happen tonight?"

The woman nods slowly.

"You understand what your role in this is?"

The woman nods more slowly.

"You understand that what will happen, the way it will happen, and that it has to happen that way."

The woman nods once.

The man nods and opens his notebook to his puzzles.

The driver returns with a small brown package, roughly the size of a shoebox, tied with string. The box does not contain shoes. There are markings on the lip of the lid that could be misinterpreted as scratch marks. Both men know how to read the marks. Both men know better.

He shows the box to the passenger, who acknowledges with a nod. The driver puts the box under his seat. "They've got a new dumpster. Took me a bit to find it."

"Change is always disorienting." The passenger returns to his puzzles. "*H* becomes *S*," he mutters.

The driver, the passenger, and the blindfolded woman drive beside the train tracks, which run along the river to the industrial part of town. Every year, there is an innertube race down the river. There are occasionally races along the train tracks as well, although those aren't municipally sanctioned.

There are factories, warehouses, and loading platforms, most of which are owned by one family. The factories make things to put in the warehouses before they are loaded on trains and pass The

Dining Car on their way beyond the city limits. This city creates but does not retain. The city is stagnant. That's where the notebooks and lapel pins came in. Someone must watch. Someone must know. Someone must keep things in motion.

The car pulls into warehouse number three. The bay is open, so they don't have to park outside. Nobody is watching, but it's best to stick to the shadows anyway. There is a car differently similar to theirs. It is a different car—different company, different color even—but they could be mistaken for each other by anyone disinclined to pay attention.

The warehouse is an eight-bit cave filled with small, pixelated walls. Stacks of what could easily be mistaken for shoeboxes of different sizes have created brown canyons that stretch and intermingle through the two-story space. Many of the peaks pass beyond the light fixtures hanging from the ceiling. The light is shuttered and redirected by these walls, making it difficult to tell how far back the canyons run.

The men know what is in some of the boxes, but not others. Some of the boxes they do not know the contents of by happenstance. Some boxes they do not *want* to know the contents of. Some boxes, they want to not know the contents of.

Management waits for them, leaning against the hood of her car. She scrolls through a phone, making notes in her small leather-bound book. When she sees the new car pull up, she drops the phone into a box that could be mistaken for a shoebox. She ties the box in twine and tucks it under her arm.

The two men walk up to a safe, respectful distance. They indicate toward the blindfolded woman, who is still sitting in the back of their vehicle.

Management waves the box vaguely at the woman. "Very good." The woman does not wave back. "I don't like complications," she continues, gesturing around the room with the box. "Kane doesn't know. She thinks she does, but she doesn't. Doesn't accept our presence. She doesn't believe the stories her father and grandfather told her. Now she is complicating our work. I was hoping for an easier transition than this."

The three look around, each assembling the pieces in a different order, at a different pace.

Management looks at the bound, gagged, and blindfolded figure in the back of the car. "I don't like complications. Simplify the situation."

"Very good," says the passenger.

"I understand," the driver says. He doesn't, though. He rarely does.

"Did you get a chance to solve today's puzzle?" Management asks. The driver is confused only for the moment it takes him to realize the question isn't for him.

"I did," the passenger answers.

"I'm still lost on a point or two. It doesn't seem like it should end where it's heading." Management starts scanning the ceiling like she sees a bat.

"At some point, it becomes the only place it can go."

"That's the rub, innit?" She looks disappointed. Whether it is because of the conversation or her ceiling search is unclear. "There are only so many letters in the alphabet," she agrees with a chuckle to herself, still not looking at anyone on ground level. Management crosses to the woman in the back of the car and unties her hands she can give her the box with the phone in it. The woman does not fight. Management leads the woman to a wall of boxes. "Follow the wall and exchange this for another. You have ninety seconds."

The driver, the passenger, and Management watch the woman feel her way to a spot and swap one package for the other. The new one is heavier than the first, but smaller. She turns around and discovers that she can see light on the edges of her blindfold. She follows the light until she runs into Management again. She hands off her new box.

Management takes the box, smells it, and gives it a gentle shake. Something soft but heavy thuds inside. "Huh," Management says, making a note in her book. She leads the woman back to the car and ties her hands as they were before. "You know why you're here," Management tells the woman. "You know who we are. We will get what we need from you. The exchange goes more smoothly if you're willing, but it will happen no matter what."

Management closes the door behind her.

"Well," she says to the men. Management gives the passenger an envelope made of blue construction paper. "He'll be out tomorrow. My guess is, you'll have to move within forty-eight hours." She turns to her car and drives away.

The passenger stuffs the crafted envelope behind his notebook.

"Why doesn't she ever give me the assignments?"

"Because you're the driver." It isn't the truth, but it's close enough to a friendly jibe that the driver doesn't think much further about it. They return to the car and the woman, none of them noticing the squirrel bouncing along the canyon of boxes.

The men guide their car into the settling dark of the evening. Night moves slowly, providing ample time for citizens to run from it. But once it has fully asserted itself, its omnipresence is unquestionable. The chilled darkness absorbs some sounds and accents others. It's a good time for sneaking about.

"Do you ever worry you won't finish those?" the driver asks the passenger.

"No," the passenger says, completing another crypto puzzle. "Pair-O-Keats," he mumbles to himself. "That was a good one."

Silence stretches between the two, different than the quiet of the night. The passenger senses it is the silence of his part of the conversation not being filled.

"I don't worry about not finishing them. If you solve each letter properly, the solution is a necessary outcome. If you're only focused on the ending, the pathway there can get sloppy." He has not helped the silence. "Besides, they're pretty easy once you understand the patterns."

They cross the south train tracks and head north, past the old high school, whose entrances are still labeled *boys* and *girls* in the brickwork. A block later, they pass the new high school, where the entrances are less obviously labeled.

They pass the second oldest house in town, the one that looks like it was built to be haunted. They pass the new orthodontist's office. That place is haunted.

They pass Castinetti's. Their pizza is good, but not good enough to warrant the lifestyle the owner seems to enjoy. The men know where the extra revenue comes from and how it relates to the 11:18 delivery every Tuesday. The owner isn't ruffling feathers, though, so Management has never asked them to pursue it further. One of the boxes in warehouse number three is waiting for the day Management's orders change.

They pass the north railroad tracks and the edge of the town proper. There is a mile-long stretch that separates the town from the lake community. (*Lake* should probably be in quotes. *Community* as well.) It's a collection of considerate strangers surrounding a nicer-than-average spillway. Within that mile, there are the highway access points, a concrete supplier, and the wetlands.

They stop the car at the wetlands and get out. The ground squishes a bit in the damp night. The light from the car is chopped up by the reeds bordering the small pond. Chirping frogs jump in and out of the glow. Beyond the light, something larger than a frog takes cover and watches, trying to decide if the new arrivals are predators or prey. Its time is not yet, but soon.

The wetlands preserve is a quiet place, besides the frogs. Any place set up to preserve nature usually means that low human activity is the best policy. It's a place teeming with life—but not the kind of life that could report what is about to happen.

"All right, get her out," says the passenger. The driver opens the door and guides the gagged and blindfolded woman out. The driver stumbles a little. He doesn't stumble on anything; he simply stumbles. His feet do not move in proper relation to the physical environment.

The woman does not try to escape. She could, and successfully, but she doesn't. She waits through the moment it takes for the man to regain his footing, unsure of what caused him to lose it in the first place. She has a guess, but it relies on him being aware of the future. Or possibly aware of the present. Neither of those options seem likely.

The driver aims the woman in a direction following the headlights of the car. The driver did not remove her blindfold, but she is able to see a slight glow around where her nose pushes the fabric out. Still, the sureness of her steps in this uneven terrain—with almost no visibility—impresses the passenger. He chose well.

"Walk," the driver says, and the woman shuffles in small steps on the muddy ground. She can smell and hear water nearby but does not know how close it is. If it weren't for the persistent chirping of the frogs (spring peepers, if she had to guess), she might have a better sense of the layout. The ground gets harder as she moves from the mud to the hardpack grass, indicating a well-trodden spot. She stops, given that it seems like this is what the spot is for.

The passenger, who is still beside the car, pulls out a knife. It is not stained, but it is well used. The wear of the handle is deep, and the way he holds it speaks to their familiarity. The two have taken good care of each other.

The woman hears one of the men begin to approach. She breathes normally, loosens her shoulders, and bows her head slightly. She is ready. As ready as she can be. It won't be pleasant, but she is ready.

The driver halts suddenly, within reach of the woman. "What is that?"

The woman feels her heart skip a beat and then compensate with a double-time follow-up. She knows what it is. It couldn't have been heard. It wasn't meant to be seen.

"What is what?" the passenger asks, closing the distance to the other two.

"Wha . . . That movement. There was a ripple at the edge of the water."

The woman sighs.

"That's a trick of the moonlight."

"No. It . . . moved . . . Where?"

The passenger sighs.

The woman reaches out with her formerly bound hands and grabs the well-worn handle that the passenger is presenting. The price of admission.

The driver stares across the water. He continues to stare, but it becomes less intentional as his body accepts what has happened and begins to shut down.

The woman follows the pull of the knife as the body begins to fall. The passenger helps guide what was the driver to the ground. The spot of bent grass where so many exchanges have taken place. The passenger twists the driver so he won't die with his face in the mud.

The last thing the driver feels of note is the passenger's knife being reclaimed. The release of pressure is pleasant before it is uncontrolled.

The last thing the driver smells is decomposing fish and lakeweed. He doesn't know it, but that's what the smell is.

The last thing the driver hears is the passenger's voice. "You complicated things."

The last thing the driver tastes is a piece of bacon that's been caught in his teeth since The Dining Car. He has been working on it ever since and only just got it free. Soon, when the car light is gone, the creature that is larger than a frog will taste it. It has been tracking the smell of grease and fat coming from the body since it arrived.

The last thing the driver sees is the moon and its uncountable background of stars. He hasn't looked at the night sky in a long time. In these fleeting moments, the sky, the stars, and the vague glowing brushwork against the darkness all strike him as overrated. It's mostly void.

"I'm sorry," the passenger says. It isn't to the driver. He is gone. It isn't to the woman. This was her choice. He leaves the words to be absorbed by the wetlands and overcome by the watching frogs and any other attentive senses.

The woman, who has removed the blindfold and gag, bends to pick up the cloth that recently bound her wrists. Well, it *appeared* to bind her wrists.

The passenger removes the lapel pin from what used to be the driver, rises, and stares over the water. "This is where it begins. This is where it ends if you're lucky."

He walks to the car. The woman follows. The passenger sits in his seat, so the woman gets behind the wheel. After a gesture from the passenger, the woman reaches under her seat and pulls out the small box that started the night in a dumpster.

"It is an unpleasant business. The city needs us to do the unpleasant business. Looking forward to working with you." He hands over the lapel pin.

"The same to you."

From the box, she removes an untouched leather-bound notebook with a vague owl design on the cover. She opens to the first page, puts the date at the top, and makes a quick note to herself about the past ninety minutes.

"Where to now?" she asks.

"We should do something with the car. I don't know where it came from. It isn't mine."

The new driver considers and then takes the car back to the ball game. She leaves the keys in it so that it may become someone else's.

For Al

A Moment of Time

I t was either perfect or unimaginative design governing the waiting room of the Longmont branch for the Temporal Travel Agency. It could be perfect, because it accommodated the turnover flow of the business. Nobody was ever left standing, but the room never felt empty either. Of course, some of that crowd management might have been due to the predictable nature of the business.

Malcolm was leaning more toward a lack of imagination, though. In the times he had been in the waiting room, the same chair was always empty. He had come in for a medical exam, psychological evaluation, scheduling, and rescheduling due to a bug that was going around the high school. Sometimes, the waiting room was only half full; sometimes it was near capacity. One time, Malcolm had come in five minutes before closing, and there was only one other person there. No matter the population or arrangement of empty chairs, however, there was one chair that was never occupied. The light pink cushion was well preserved, with no rips or stains like some of the other chairs, but it wasn't an object built to be pristine. It was an object for use. It should have been given a better location. There shouldn't be a chair directly under the television screen.

Why would they put a chair there, other than because they lacked imagination enough to know that this chair would never be used? If you were inclined to watch the screen while waiting, you wouldn't sit there, because then you couldn't see. If you wanted to do anything besides watch the screen while waiting, you wouldn't sit there either, because everyone would be staring at you while you read the outdated newspaper on the side table. The only reason someone might sit there would be because there was no other option, and they would be grumpy about it the whole time. Bad customer service. Unimaginative.

Malcolm wondered if that particular chair ever got lonely or envious of the other chairs. That single quirk in design may have isolated the chair, but it also made it the most interesting thing in the otherwise monochromatic room. Maybe that was the point. Other than Malcolm, nobody seemed to be concerned with the extra chair. It made the room look like every other waiting room. A commonplace to trick the brain into thinking it was a common place. As if time travel would ever be commonplace.

"How much longer do you think it'll be?"

"I don't know. I'm not scheduled for another seven minutes, so I'd say at least that long." Malcolm smiled in what he hoped was a sly way.

"Right. About that, you could have told me we were going to get here half an hour early." It was an old exchange between the two, but it never seemed to bother either participant. Maggie had never willingly been early for anything in her life. On time, sure. Rarely late. But *early* was a foreign concept to Maggie.

"In the five years that you've known me, when have I ever not been early for anything?"

"Just because you're too anxious to show up at a respectable time doesn't mean the rest of us have nothing better to do than sit around waiting rooms." Maggie pushed her deep sea colored hair out of the way. She had just thought of a point and couldn't tolerate distraction. "You do realize that this is the one time you could have been late, right? It's a time travel agency. Time is the one thing they have plenty of."

"It would still be rude to show up late," Malcolm said with a laugh. He turned and glanced at the voucher in his hand. *Longmont High School Social Studies Honor*. Every year, the top three graduating seniors in the department were given a chance to travel back in time. Time travel for an aptitude in history seemed a bit on the nose, but if the administration had been creative, they would have never gotten involved in running a high school. Maybe they should have gone into designing waiting rooms.

"By the way," he said, turning back to Maggie, "thanks for coming with me." The Temporal Travel Agency treated the process like a medical procedure. There had to be someone ready to take you home afterwards. Apparently, the travel process could have some dramatic effects on hand-eye coordination. Malcolm had also been told not to eat before the trip.

"Don't mention it," she said with more compassion than she intended. "To be honest though, I just wanted to see the inside of this place. Considering what's behind those doors, the waiting room is unimpressive."

"It's the wrong size too."

"What?"

"Nothing. Didn't your dad run a visit last year? I thought he went to visit his old chief or something."

"He did," Maggie said with a roll of her eyes. "I didn't come with though. It was a work buddy thing. It sounded like they had a bet riding on it at the plant. I don't know if he won or lost, but he was quiet afterwards. Kept to himself for a week or so. Still hasn't talked about it with any of us."

"That's what I mean. It's nice to know that there will be someone waiting for me. I don't know if I'll be totally myself when I get out."

"You'll be fine. You know when you're going. You know what you'll experience. There shouldn't be any surprises for you. It's not like you're visiting some historical battle or spying on what really happened at Roanoke. You're going to a concert. It's not even a concert you need tickets to! It can't be that traumatic. Why are you visiting this guy, anyway?"

"He changed my life." It came out of his mouth more simply and without the gravity that Malcolm had expected.

"I thought you said you'd never spoken to him? If it weren't for you, I'd have never heard of this guy. I know you love that song, but how can he have changed your life? Is he family or something?"

"In a way." Malcolm smiled sadly and looked to the tan carpet for words. "How many people do you think you have met in your life?"

Maggie scrunched her forehead for a second. She loved when Malcolm started arguments with offbeat questions like this. She could rarely follow him all the way through the maze that he laid out, but it was always an interesting journey. He was the only one at school who talked like that. It got annoying quickly, but at least it was unique and genuine.

"I wouldn't know where to begin to guess."

"I read somewhere that over the course of years, the averages works out to one or two people per day. If we say one and a half people a day, that gives us about five hundred and fifty people every year. Let's just say five hundred so that I can do the math in my head. Five hundred different and new people every year that pass through your awareness. Even if we take away the years we can't remember—say ages one to three—you and I both still have fifteen years of meeting people. Conservatively, that's about 7,500 people that each of us has met independently."

"You've spent a lot of time thinking about this, haven't you?"

"A little bit," he said with the guilt of a five-year-old cookie thief. "Of your 7,500, how many would you say that you have fallen in love with in the first thirty seconds?"

"Is this the part where you tell me you've fallen in love with someone in the past?"

Malcolm laughed despite his best efforts. Maggie was always good for that. "Seriously for a minute, I'm trying to answer your question. And I'm not even requiring romantic love. How many people have you met and, in that instant, knew they would be important to how your story got told. Is there anyone? Or can you at least imagine what that is like?"

"Yes. I guess, maybe."

It seemed to Malcolm that there was something off about the way Maggie's face had looked when she responded, but Malcolm passed on. He was getting to his favorite part.

"And when you first met that person, you knew. Even though you meet hundreds of people a year, a variety of different orientations and options that you have to navigate over time. In the space of a breath with that person, you knew. It changed things. Maybe that feeling lasted, or maybe it didn't. That's how emotions work. But in that moment, you knew something that changed you. You and that other person shared a moment that froze reality. Time was no longer a factor, for in that moment, you held an eternity.

"*This* song from *this* musician created one of those perfect moments for me. I want to see if I can replicate the experience." Malcolm gave a lopsided smile to Maggie as he caught his breath and watched for some sign that his words had registered.

Maggie held the stare before answering Malcolm's glance. "If I vomit in your shoes, we can still be friends, right?"

Malcolm turned back toward the carpet with the same sad smile on his face. He knew that Maggie understood what he was getting at, in part anyway. If only she didn't feel the need to hide it.

"How far back are they sending you?" Maggie was never comfortable with silence.

"Twenty-three years," Malcolm answered with noticeably less energy. "They were playing at the county fair. Big open area, mixed crowd but not packed. As you mentioned, I don't need a ticket or any money to get in. I'm hoping it will be a low-risk enough scene that I can stay for the whole concert."

"They will let me know how long, right? If I can duck out to somewhere that isn't this place, I'd like to know."

"Time travel, remember? Timing isn't . . . "

"Malcolm Brown?" A man with a clipboard announced the name to the nearly full room. He didn't like his job and made no attempt to hide this fact.

Malcolm raised his hand. "I'll be back," he assured Maggie and stood up.

"Make sure your wings are flapping right."

Malcolm gave a wink before walking through the door with the disgruntled bearer of the clipboard. "Walk this way," the man said and led Malcolm down a Sheetrock hallway. Not exactly the futuristic decor he had expected, but neither was the waiting room. "You will meet with one of our visit guides, Michael, who will give you the rules and set the final details for your visit before implementing your trip. You can address any concerns with him. Here is his office. Head in and have a good trip."

The gentleman—who had yet to take his eyes off the clipboard or change his inflection—turned and left down the hallway, back toward the waiting room.

Malcolm was left looking at a simple door, slightly lighter in color than the gray hallway. There was a small name plaque to the right that said: *Michael Davison: Temporal Visit Guide*. With no other option presenting itself, Malcolm took a breath, opened the door, and walked in.

♫ ♩ ♫

The office was centered around a small desk (which was one model removed from a folding table), a bookshelf filled with rows of color-coded binders (most of which hadn't been opened since they were placed), and three mismatched chairs (one behind and two in front of the desk). Malcolm tried not to think of Goldilocks. As the one chair behind the desk was occupied by a man in a gray suit with a red tie, Malcolm assumed that the man was Michael Davison, Temporal Visit Guide. His hair was short and held in place by an unnecessary amount of gel. Malcolm wondered how much force it would take to pop a balloon on the rows of rigid blades upon his head. How much lint did it collect?

"You must be Malcolm," came from the practiced smile on the man's face.

"Yes, sir."

"Great, I'm Mike. Have a seat. We'll go over some last-minute details, and then we'll send you on your visit."

"Okay."

"It looks like a pretty simple visit. You marked that your focus is time, rather than interaction, which is why we approved this concert at the fair for your scene." Michael seemed very experienced at talking to someone while shuffling through paperwork. It took a moment to realize that despite his friendly voice, his eyes never actually landed on you, the subject. Davison had this patter down and knew the rhythm. He was burdened by the repetition but found a bit of dance in these by-the-book, bureaucratic interactions. The color-coded binders had probably been his idea. Unlike the walking clipboard from the lobby, however, it looked to Malcolm as if Davison enjoyed the routine of the job.

"We don't have a lot of secured scenes for your target. The documentation just isn't there like it would be for something of more import, say presidents or celebrities. We have to be very clear when programming a visit about the scene and its security. More points of observation means fewer safe entry points, but it also means the entry points are more clearly highlighted for us on this end. Can't send you to a scene that we think is minimally populated, only to find out that there were cameras to capture a time traveler popping into existence." At this, Michael laughed strongly to himself. Yes, he enjoyed his job.

"Fortunately, we were able to put together enough documentation to ensure the security of the fair. It isn't a popular scene, and possible observers—tech or otherwise—are easy to avoid for your entrance and exit. Also, by the very nature of the fair, there will be a lot of strangers mixing with other strangers, so we are able to give you the entire concert. That's two hours plus a five-minute entrance and a five-minute exit cushion time. That comes to two hours and ten minutes that you will be on your visit, as well as how long you will be occupied. Who will be waiting for you when you return?"

It looked like Malcolm and Maggie had both been wrong about time not being a concern. "Her name is Maggie. She's in the lobby."

"Excellent. We'll let her know."

"This is time travel, right? Why can't you just bring me back the moment after a leave?"

"It was so much easier in the old days. We used to. We used to bring you back two minutes after you left, but it got so confusing trying to keep track of relativistic ages. You age when traveling at the normal rate, even if you come back a few minutes later. I think the government just didn't want to put up with the headache. So anyway, you will show up in a secluded spot of the fair and have five minutes to find a seat at the concert. It will be a big music tent, so you . . . Oh, I see from your file that you probably already know what the tent looks like. You grew up in the area."

"Yes, sir. But, I wasn't born yet." Nervousness crept in.

"*Hmm* . . . The rest of your application must have been top notch. They usually don't let first-timers play it that close."

Malcolm wasn't sure what Davison wanted him to say in response, so he simply floated a, "Thanks," across the desk and hoped it would be accepted. Davison stared for another ten seconds at Malcolm's paperwork before shaking himself out of it.

"Anyway, after the five minutes are up, you have a ten-foot radius. If you move beyond that range, you will immediately be brought back. When the two-hour concert is over, you will be allowed to move and find a secluded place to come back. Again, we can't have you just winking out of existence with everyone watching. We have enough trouble with the premature returners."

"You would just zap me back, right in the middle of things? What if people are looking at me?"

"We'd rather that than have you muck things up by interacting with the scene. People lose people in the crowd all the time. The mind plays tricks. It's easy enough to write off someone you think you saw just disappearing into thin air. Someone who comes up to you and tells you they are from the future, on the other hand . . . That is a little messier. If we have to call a cleanup crew on your account, your friend Maggie will have a lot longer to wait for you. Understand?"

Malcolm tried to think of something witty but decided it was not the time. Also, nothing came to mind. He simply tightened his mouth and nodded for Davison to continue.

"Your speaking will be highly restricted as well. Sorry, no singing along. You will have the basic complement of emergency words, but anything beyond that, and you are back here."

"How . . . how will you know the difference between sounds I make and sounds around me? It is a concert, after all." Malcolm didn't like interrupting; Michael was pretty far into the script and had found his rhythm. Still, it seemed like an important enough issue to risk needing to find a line again.

"We monitor you, not the situation. Those visitors looking for an interactive visit rather than one focused on time are the primary focus for this feature of our services. These are the visitors who end up as fast-food cashiers, bus patrons, or random citizens who ask for the time. These interactive visitors are allowed to speak, but only certain preapproved phrases in accordance with the script. Our system is designed for those kinds of situations. For your scene, you will simply have no approved phrases outside of the standard *yes, no, hello, goodbye, sorry*, and of course, the noncommittal grunt. Unless you want to pay the extra fee for voice modulation, so that no one in your old home recognizes your voice. Honestly, I am surprised that isn't already part of the deal."

"No. Minimum vocabulary sounds perfect."

"Good."

"Can I clap?"

" . . . You can clap."

Michael waited to see if there was anything else or if he could find his place in his notes again. Malcolm simply smiled back.

After clearing his throat, Michael resumed, "Please remember the philosophy behind this program: the only reason time visits work is the idea that people aren't paying attention. If we don't think we need to focus on something, we don't. You can't tell me how many steps it was from the waiting room to this office because you didn't pay attention. Nor can you tell me how many people were sitting in the waiting room before you came back here."

"One fewer than the number of chairs."

"What?"

"Nothing."

"The point is, it isn't any of your business to know those things. Even if you have a familiar face, clothes, or voice, all of that is out of place, and ergo, it is as irrelevant as the color of the carpet. We don't need to care about containing and categorizing that information. This situation is constantly acting in and upon the world and influencing the people in it. John Wayne doesn't notice any significant detail about his bartender. That lack of definition gives time visitors an opening to get close and see what the Duke smelled like without unraveling space-time. Subtlety is the key. Keep that in mind, and you'll do fine. Any questions?"

Malcolm thought for a moment before deciding against the tangents in his mind. He shook his head.

"Good. Sign here, please," Michael said, sliding an official-looking form toward Malcolm. "This is just a form saying that you have agreed to the terms and regulations of your specific time visit, and that should anything not go according to plan, Temporal Travel Agency is not culpable."

Malcolm signed the form and handed it back to Michael, who filed it away somewhere.

"It also says that I have gone over the standard paradox warning regiment with you, and you are fully aware of the hazards associated with traveling through time. Do we need to spend much time on that? Frankly, we're a little behind schedule."

Malcolm bit his cheek to not laugh. "No. I think I'm good. I've seen those movies."

"We've all seen those movies." Michael smiled and held the door open. "Now, if you will follow me, we'll get you prepped."

♪♫♪♫

Malcolm was led to a room with a series of lockers to the immediate left and a lonely-looking chair to the right that reminded him of the one in the waiting room. The new chair was nothing special. Rather, it was special in not being anything special. Where Malcolm had anticipated shining metal, tubes maybe, or at least a cord of some sort, there was instead a recliner—a maroon recliner with purple lining and a cup holder in the arm. The only peculiar thing about the chair was the fifteen feet of clear space surrounding it. The rest of the room gave the chair grandeur by keeping its distance. The first thing that crossed Malcolm's mind was that maybe grandpa was going to tell a story, and they wanted plenty of space on the floor for the children.

Beyond the lockers was a glass room built into the corner. The glass room was divided in two, one side filled with a terminal and several screens providing data on visits in progress. The other side was filled with air, apparently. Michael cleared his throat after a second or two, then asked Malcolm to pick a locker and empty his pockets into it. After leaving his trinkets behind, Malcolm was directed to the air room.

"First, here is your new watch. It is set to your destination time, which is displayed on the smaller of the two dials. Knowing what time it is, however, will not help you as much as knowing how much time you have left. The larger and more important dial counts down until the end of your visit. It will glow green during your five-minute transfer times and go dark during your core two hours." Michael handed the new watch to Malcolm. It weighed differently on his wrist than the one he had just stashed in the locker. "I can't tell you how nice it is that you're going to a time when nobody would think twice about a watch with a digital screen. Go back too many decades, and we have to get creative. Or everyone just wears long sleeves."

Malcolm couldn't tell if that last part was a joke or not.

"You may want to close your eyes for this next part." Michael smiled, made his way to the computer terminal room, and sealed Malcolm alone in the air room. Malcolm took the suggestion and noticed the sound of air being pushed through a vent somewhere nearby. By the time Malcolm realized the vent was actually two— one above and one below him—he felt cold pinpricks all over his skin, even through the clothed parts. It was like standing out in the snow for too long. The process lasted about ten seconds, until the snow stopped and the air became still.

"You can open your eyes now," said Michael's voice as he opened up the air room. "You are now covered in our patented Temporal Insurgent Concealment Kits—T.I.C.K.s. They're nanobots. Right now, they are forming a shell around your body, which will allow you to poke your way through space-time. They are a collective, each working on a small task to support the greater whole. Generations were spent thinking that time travel would involve a size and scale larger than could be contained on the planet. Turns out, we just needed a lot of really tiny bugs.

"These little guys are also how we monitor your visit. Before, you asked how we separate your sound from the scene. Well, this is how. The T.I.C.K.s passively record what you experience from your point of view, which will be available to you as a video file when you leave—for a nominal fee, of course. They are, however, active in their monitoring of you. If you violate any of the rules, the T.I.C.K.s will know an instant later. If you move more than ten feet, if you exceed your phrase bank, the T.I.C.K.s will detect it and bring you back. They are synced with your watch, both uniquely programmed to your trip. Therefore, they have all of the same restrictions that you do. At the end of your two hours and ten minutes, the T.I.C.K.s will bring you back, no question.

"Right now, they are mapping your body and clothes, creating a holistic network of communication among themselves. If you are hiding anything—if you stashed anything in your pockets or anywhere else, hoping to leave a clue in the past—forget it. The T.I.C.K.s have already included that in your map and will bring it back when you return. This precaution also prevents you from bringing back any souvenirs. It seems simple, but we still have people going after old baseball cards.

"The T.I.C.K.s also, let's say, *soften* your appearance. You're not going back that far, and you wore non-labeled clothes like we asked, so we don't need a costume change. But the T.I.C.K.s create a filter around you as well, so you always look passably neutral in your environment. Fashion may change rapidly, but the generic clothes people wear are a little more interchangeable across neighboring decades. Turns out, most people aren't paying that much attention to whether your clothes are in style or not. Certainly not at places like the county fair, at least."

As Michael finished and Malcolm stepped out of the air room, trying not to think about microscopic robot bugs crawling up his nose, the terminal next door started to beep.

"Oh," said Michael, lifting an eyebrow. "Somebody is early. Stick near me, Mr. Brown."

An instant later, the lonely chair on the other side of the room was not as lonely anymore. Malcolm was surprised to see that there was no flash, no smoke, no bending of the physical reality around the chair. One moment it was empty, and the next, it held a woman of maybe sixty years.

"That son of a bitch! I knew he was on a golf weekend when mom came to visit. 'A burst pipe at the courthouse' my ass. Took me fifteen years, but I caught him."

"Yes, Mrs. Perry," Michael began, walking over to the chair, "but one of your restrictions was to stay one hundred feet away from him. Time may have passed, but he was your husband back then too. We couldn't risk him recognizing you. The T.I.C.K.s can muddle your physical features but not that close up."

The woman stood and walked over to where Michael and Malcolm were standing. "Doesn't matter. I know now, and when I get home, he is going to look like a humpback whale—no teeth and covered in lumps."

"I'm sure he will, Mrs. Perry," Michael said, leading the woman to the air side of the glass room. "But first, we'll get those T.I.C.K.s off of you." He then walked back to the terminal and asked Malcolm to have a seat in the once again unoccupied recliner. "I'll send you on your way while she is cleaning off."

Malcolm sat in the chair while across the room, a blue light surrounded Mrs. Perry.

"Remember," cautioned Michael, barely turning from the terminal. "Subtlety. We are putting you where no one will notice you appear. Try to be somewhere similar when your time is up. If you are seen disappearing, it will probably be written off by the observer as their eyes playing a trick. Ghost stories come from somewhere. It could also lead to someone in the past changing their course of decisions and creating a reality where this technology never exists. Try to be out of the way."

Michael punched at the keys on the terminal, and Malcolm felt his body warming from the outside in. The T.I.C.K.s were opening the door. As the warmth spread to his core, Malcolm expected a flash or pop or some kind of clear border between now and then. There was none. In one beat, he was staring at Michael and the computer, and the next beat, he was looking at the heavily-carved slab of wood that served as a door. One sniff confirmed that he was in the restroom. Malcolm shook his head, stood up, and made his way out of the dark, damp cavern into the hay-dust distorted sunlight of a midsummer county fair.

♪♪♦♫

Everything was washed out in the setting sun, giving one last effort for the day. Or maybe it was just the shock to Malcolm's eyes from not being in the dark anymore. The smells hadn't changed much in twenty-three years. Deep fried anything, cattle and sheep being groomed for show, hay and gravel that led from exhibit to exhibit—the basic makeup of a county fair was a tried-and-true formula. Somewhere in the distance, the Tilt-A-Whirl started another run with a clacking sound that always made Malcolm nervous. He was tempted to see if the cream puffs tasted the same but thought better of it. He had a mission and only so much time in which to accomplish it.

Finding the music tent within five minutes wasn't hard; it was the biggest structure without any livestock. If you knew what to listen for, you could also pick out the band warming up.

Malcolm initially took a seat near the back, looking to play it as safely as possible. With showtime approaching and the tent less than half full, Malcolm glanced at his watch. The still-green display told him that he had a little movement time remaining, so Malcolm traded up for a seat a bit closer than halfway to the stage. He wasn't exactly following the subtlety rule, but this was a once in a lifetime opportunity.

Technically, it was even beyond the scope of a lifetime for Malcolm.

Malcolm watched the band doing last-minute checks off to the side of the stage. There was no "backstage," really. There was an open platform and a few speakers set up on the edges. The three-piece band stood in the back, looking noticeably younger than Malcolm remembered, of course. Phil, the bass player, was tightening his shoulder strap. Dinah, the keyboard and mandolin player (only occasionally at the same time), grabbed a fresh bottle of water. They all had singing duty, but she had a tougher set as the only female voice. And then there was Al. He nearly hit his head on the tent flap as he made some wide-armed joke to the sound technician. They had probably just met, but already Al was his best friend. Maybe it was the gray hair, maybe it was the wide smile that never left his face, or maybe it was the warmth that radiated from him, but nobody met Al without wanting to be his friend. Niceness fosters niceness.

With a signal from the technician, Al grabbed his guitar and nodded to the rest of the group. The band took the stage, introduced themselves, and started the show. The audience cheered—all twenty of them, these lucky few who had found themselves in the right place at the right time. Most of them would enjoy the show. They would recognize songs and support their friends onstage. It wasn't their moment, though. It was Malcolm's. He didn't feel more intelligent or perceptive than the folk around him, just luckier.

Malcolm sat in silence, or perhaps more appropriately, in refusal to intrude upon the sound that he had come for. He followed the notes as he had so many times before. The notes the audience was just hearing for the first time. Again, those lucky few.

Malcolm focused on the guitar player—the one who had started this, the one who motivated Malcolm's visit. He was tall and the dominant voice but held Malcolm's attention for another reason. He wasn't a dancer. He had a good voice but nothing mind-blowing, and his guitar skills were unpolished, though effective. There was no reason to pick this performer out among others, but Malcolm still found himself awed by the singer. It didn't matter that he wasn't the best and didn't perform with the greatest flare, because his small movements and the simplicity of his show had life to it. He was having fun. *They* were having fun, on that small stage covered in hay, playing simple tunes. All for an audience made up of relatives, the odd passerby who needed a shaded place to wait before the tractor pull, and at least one couple on their first date. And a devoted fan who would not be born for five years.

That was the part that was hard to explain to Maggie or anyone else. This wasn't his favorite band. This wasn't his favorite performer. It wasn't even his favorite song that they would play later on in the set. He had seen better bands, heard better singers, and listened to better versions of that particular song. But, in a moment, in the future, the combination of these imperfect elements would hit his ears at the right moment, in the right way, and create something

Malcolm had never experienced before. An isolated moment where nothing else had any relevance. It didn't make any sense that it had happened in the way it did, except that it had.

The band had played a few songs and was beginning to settle into the rhythm of that particular performance when a woman sat down a few seats from Malcolm. He was the only person for three rows of chairs, making her seat selection spark Malcolm's curiosity. His mind reflected on all of the movies and books he had read about time travel. This person had to be a distant relative of his, right? That's how the humor of time travel worked. What other possible reason could there be for her to sit so nearby? Malcolm looked at the woman and tried to figure out the mystery.

It wasn't his mom or either of his grandmothers. Nobody in the family broke 5'8" and this woman looked like she could touch the tent ceiling at a stretch. She wasn't a teacher, nor, as near as Malcolm could remember, even the wife of a teacher. He kept staring, trying to figure it out, until he was caught.

"Can I help you?" the woman asked kindly. She was in her fifties but had clearly taken steps to ensure that she didn't stop there.

"No, sorry," Malcolm said, shaking his head as if he had accidentally fallen asleep. Hopefully she would take that as an effective apology.

She smiled and said, "The music puts me in my own world too. I love when he plays at home after dinner." As she spoke, she indicated toward Al, the guitar player.

So that's who she is, thought Malcolm. He laughed and said, "Yes," for response, then turned back to the band. They finished their tune, and the audience applauded. The band took a few moments to prepare for the next song before striking a chord and beginning the intro. It was the song he had come for. The four-minute target of this entire journey.

"Oh, he loves this song," the wife said. "He says it's about traveling for a love and finding that you end up loving the act of traveling just as much. Seeking your love becomes just as appealing as the love itself. He says that's why he likes music so much. Music isn't leading to anything; it is a journey to itself."

But it does lead to something, Malcolm thought, glancing at the couple on their first date. *It leads to me.* His parents had told him the story of their first date many times. That's how he had first been introduced to the band, when his parents would play their music for him. They had told him the band played this song on their first date. They had taken Malcolm to the concert sixteen years after the moment they were in, where Malcolm had his moment. The night would be perfect for them. Maybe it could be perfect for him, too.

"Al thinks songs like this are for all travelers, because it is both the journey and the destination at the same time. I just think it sounds relaxing."

"Yes," Malcolm said, not really listening anymore. Her words were good but not the sounds he had come to experience.

As the intro finished and the lyrics began, Malcolm breathed in and knew everything about that moment. His mind held every detail of his surroundings, and it was happy with what it found. He was both perfectly relaxed and poised for anything. It was like the calm rhythm of wheels beneath you, or the doorway to another world of a loved one's hand on your arm. It wasn't his moment, though. The phenomenon wasn't repeatable. It was a beautiful moment, but in reflection, in nostalgia. Not because it made something more than the sum of its parts.

The remainder of the concert was something of a blur. The band played song after song, all of which Malcolm had heard before. All of which Malcolm enjoyed. None of which were able to bring about the moment he was after.

After the show, Malcolm sat waiting for his watch to change colors, taking one last look at the past. The wife stood up, they exchanged goodbyes, and she was on her way. As his wrist turned green, a thought occurred. Eleven feet later, Malcolm knew the plan would work. He walked up to the stage and waited to catch Al's eye. When contact was made, Malcolm gave a small nod of his head. Al stepped down from the stage, still standing nearly a foot above Malcolm, and stuck out his hand.

The two shook, and the singer smiled. "What did you think?"

Stuck for a reply, Malcolm shuffled through the allowed phrases. He said, "Yes . . . "

The singer laughed, involving his entire face. It was the kind of laugh that is usually reserved for grandfathers and Buddhist monks. "That good, huh?"

It was Malcolm's turn to laugh. The singer turned back to the stage to begin packing up from the performance. Malcolm took a quick glance around to see everyone focused on their own part of the end of the show. Malcolm really was nobody's concern.

"Thank you," Malcolm said. There was more, but it was muted in that moment.

Malcolm never found out if the singer responded or even turned around to his words. The moment Malcolm spoke, the T.I.C.K.s warmed once again, and the stage, the musician, the smell of hay—all of it was gone and replaced by the small room in the T.T.A. building and Michael staring back.

Malcolm was glad he didn't have to come back on his feet. The recliner made for a soft landing.

"You had less than two minutes left. You couldn't wait two minutes? I hope whatever you said was important." Davison must have had a rough two hours.

"It was," Malcolm said.

"Well, we're all still here. You must not have done too much." Davison put his hands on his hips and sighed. "There will be an investigation, you know. This was outlined in the paperwork. We'll probably find nothing, but if there is something out of synch with what our records show, you will be hearing from us again."

There was an element of threat behind Davison's words but not enough that Malcolm thought the outlined situation was very likely. It was going to be some extra work on the company's end, but there was nothing to find. He would be fine.

Malcolm stepped out of the chair, had the T.I.C.K.s removed by the blue light, retrieved his items from the locker, and followed Davison back to the lobby. He didn't stick around to say goodbye.

"Thank you for running your visit with Temporal Travel. Here is an access code. If you visit our website, that will give you access to the recording of your trip. It will be active for seventy-two hours for you to make any purchasing decisions. Oh," the receptionist said as a notification popped up on her screen. "We will be contacting you should any complication be discovered from the anomaly generated in your visit. Thank you. Please come again." The receptionist offered a smile that looked more painful than happy.

Malcolm smiled back and turned around right into Maggie.

"So, how was it?"

Malcolm thought for a moment. There were several different versions of the story that could be told. Only one was right for Maggie.

"He was taller than I expected."

"Figures."

The two exited the building and began to walk. "I'm glad to be out of there," Maggie began. "There was a chair nobody sat in the entire time you were in there. I'm pretty sure it's haunted."

"Probably a visit ended early," came Malcolm's absent-minded reply.

Maggie stopped. "You know, what you were talking about earlier . . . about a moment, an instant shared with people at the first meeting. That immediate connection and mutual awareness of that connection. I do understand that. I have had that."

"I know," Malcolm said. "I've seen those movies too."

The two traded a knowing smile as they began walking again. Malcolm felt his breath slow, found that the sound from the street was muted, and couldn't explain why the street they were on seemed brighter all of a sudden. He reached out and took Maggie's hand in his. It was the second time in his life that Malcolm owned a moment of time.

The Case of the Green Math

Investigation Log
Yet to be Titled Case (Green Math?)
Entry #1 | 11:30 a.m. | Cafeteria

It used to be that lunch was the prime time to collect leads without teacher interference. With a peanut butter and jelly in hand and a pudding cup in the waiting, suspects tended to let their guard down. Candy swaps happened in plain sight. The volume on the contraband phone would slip louder than normal. And the snitches had much looser lips when talking through a mouthful of potato chips. Most of the time, we'd let things pass. We could follow up later, once we knew who to watch. Lunchtime was a chaos of rule-breaking, and it was one of my favorite sounds in the world. That sound meant I was needed. That chaos got me out of bed in the morning. (Well, that and the smell of Mom's made-from-scratch waffles.)

But lunchtime had been quieter ever since the safety patrol started cracking down. Lunch wasn't a free-for-all anymore.

Lunchtime was exposed and lonely—like being out on the ocean, or the only kid who didn't hear the bell calling you in from recess. Everyone, from hallway bullies to honor roll students, was finding their way to detention for at least part of the day. Of course, I wouldn't know anything about that. Not anymore.

I'd caught a bum rap a while back, and the safety patrol decided I was bent. "Unworthy of the sash," they'd said. They knew something was fishy, but too many of them were happy to see me go. A single moment of weakness, and I was forced to live the rest of my fifth-grade year as a civilian. Even after I had spent all that time finding a brown duster that would fit me!

The name's Robert Denver Jr. My dad calls me Gilligan. I don't like to talk about it. Most everyone else around calls me Bert. That's how this case began, with someone calling out, "Bert!"

Mikey C. sat down across the table from me, interrupting my salami and onion. Mikey C. and I go back quite a ways. I used to get good information from him in exchange for looking the other way on some of his side projects—tips on forged hall passes, candy smuggling, and even kickball betting pools. Mikey was a smart kid. Too smart, maybe. He thought he was above the system. As a representative of that system, I took it personally. Even so, he kept me tuned into the pulse of these hallways. A pulse that still echoes through my ears.

Mikey C. looked terrible. He was tired and pale. He's always been more of the indoor type—not to mention his more than twitchy tendencies from his Sugar Bomb habit—but this was something else. It reminded me of the mumps outbreak of '17. We lost a lot of good people that spring. Mikey looked disproportioned and sweaty.

"Whatever you've gotten yourself into, Mikey, I wouldn't help you if I could. Not that I can, and we both know why."

I should mention, I don't like Mikey C.

"I've got nobody else. I can't take it anymore, and I figured . . . given your situation, maybe you would take the case. Try to get back on the force."

"Listening to you is what got me into my situation. I'm not too keen to repeat that mistake." I took a bite of my sandwich and held up what remained. "You have that long to convince me otherwise." It was only my first half, but he didn't need to know that.

He swallowed hard. "You know I've been serving a stint in detention?"

"They found your counterfeit doctor's notes, I heard. I also heard you claimed you'd been framed, as usual. Doesn't sound like anyone believed you, as usual."

"Right, well, I've done detention before. I know how to survive. But, it's different this time. The mornings are still the same. Mrs. Bennet has us do her math worksheets. But the afternoons are . . . weird, now that Went took over."

Mr. Went, the music teacher. Budget concerns and spacing issues meant he was also the afternoon detention monitor now.

"What, you don't like the music he plays?"

"The music is only part of it. The real issue is the math. He still has us doing these practice worksheets, but they're way different than Bennet's. They're made up of these symbols and equations I've never seen before. Nobody has. Some of them are numbers, some could be musical notes, but most of it is just nonsense. Come to think of it, though, most math starts to look like nonsense to me after a certain point. It's some kind of musical math, I guess. I . . . I don't know."

He paused, and I tried to make my sandwich bite last long enough to get awkward. He knew he was crossing into dangerous territory.

"You know I'm not the one you should come to with math concerns."

Mikey C. dropped his right arm on the table and pulled back his sleeve, revealing what looked like a math equation in green marker up and down his entire forearm. He poured some milk from my carton onto his arm and rubbed. The green didn't come off. Guess it wasn't marker after all.

"It's happening to all of us. We don't put it there; it just shows up. None of us know . . . "

"All right, Mikey. Let's get you to your afternoon appointment." Joe Wrigley stepped up and put a hand on Mikey's shoulder to walk him to his afternoon detention. Safety patrol duty. Good gig if you can keep it.

"Please, Bert. Find out what this is." Mikey C.'s eyes were wide and scared.

Joe started walking Mikey away but made time to hit me with a hard stare. I suppose that's as close to a pleasantry as I should have expected from my ex-partner. The two disappeared, and I made a couple decisions.

This case was serious. Mikey C. wouldn't risk coming to me unless he had no other option.

The other half of my sandwich would have to wait.

I wrapped it in my pocket after I completed these notes. Then I was off to talk to an old friend.

Investigation Log
Green Math
Entry #2 | 11:50 a.m. | Hallway outside of the detention room.

I made my way to the detention room. Through the window in the door, I could see Mikey C. and maybe half a dozen other detainees. Workbooks out and diligent work all around. It may not have been what he was hired to do, but it looked like Went had detention under control.

I couldn't quite make out what was scrawled on the chalkboard, but it didn't take much effort to notice the similarities between it and Mikey's new tattoo. I still couldn't make heads or tails of the characters, but that didn't mean much. I had a math tutor who'd once told me that solving a math problem was like solving a mystery. You followed the clues of the equation, paid attention to how they behaved, and the answer would present itself. I'm still waiting for the answer to present itself.

Joe was talking to Went. Neither one looked pleased. Went gestured to the door and grabbed a fiddle from his desk. (Maybe it was a violin. I can never tell the difference.) Joe, seeing that he had been replaced, turned and walked out of the room so fast, he almost passed me waiting for him at the door.

"What do you know, Joe?"

He turned with a smirk that I've seen too many times. It was the same smirk he'd had when we were interrogating suspects during the missing mystery meat case. One dead end after another. We'd tracked down leads for weeks and come up empty. We were in over our heads, and all we could do was smirk.

"Bert. This is strictly patrol business. *Civilians* should still be in lunch."

"Nice to see you too, Joe." And that was the truth. It wasn't Joe's fault I'd gotten kicked off the patrol; it was my own. Of course, he hadn't done much to stop it. "Something Mikey C. said got me curious. I thought I should make sure he got here all right."

"Careful. Following around Mikey C. is what made you a civilian in the first place. Keep hanging with that crowd, and people will talk."

"Safety patrol will always be talked about. We know that better than most." I followed him as he walked away. "That's the price of the burden that chooses us."

He stopped by the drinking fountain that hadn't worked since some third grader stuffed it with bubblegum during the Halloween parade. "Is that what this is about? You think if you find a case and solve it, you'll get back on the patrol?"

"No. I know same as you, the rest of the patrol will never see me with a badge again. I'm like last month's state tests; they're happy to be done with me. Mikey seemed worried, though, and I do have plenty of time on my hands lately."

Joe looked around, maybe considering his options, maybe seeing if there was anyone around to overhear our conversation. When he turned back, some of the humor and arrogance had left him. That smirk was back—the smirk that told me there was something deeper here, and even he wasn't sure what it was. "You know Mikey C. He's a Sugar Bomb freak. If he's not jittery from too much, he's crashed and hallucinating from not enough. Don't trust what he says. You know better than that."

He walked away, but I rolled one final question at him. "What do you know about the green math?"

He came back to me, quick and direct. Joe's finger was so close to my face, I had trouble focusing on it without going cross-eyed. "Stay out of that, Bert. Nobody knows anything about any green math. There is no green math, got it?" His words were quiet but sharp, like when your mom yells at you in public but doesn't want people to know she's yelling at you in public. "As a friend, I'm telling you to stay out of it. It's not worth risking what little you have left. Go study in the library and try to forget this whole thing." He left the conversation like the bell for recess had just rung.

Then the bell for recess rang.

In a way, I decided to take Joe's advice. I finished my notes outside of the library. Anyway, as long as I was there, and I had all of recess, I decided I might as well do a little studying. We would see what those old pages could tell me about green math.

Investigation Log
The Missing Equation
Entry #3 | 12:00 p.m. | Library

I have mixed feelings about the library.

As a detective, there are few places with a more concentrated collection of resources. It's a wealth of diverse information, and more importantly, it is a quiet place in which to work through it all. The chairs are firm and uncomfortable (I suspect by design), encouraging any research project to resolve itself as quickly as possible. Even if your eyes started to wander, they would be frightened back by the monthly student "art" exhibit.

The regular shelving and quiet atmosphere make the library a perfect location for covert research—or spying on those using the environment for more nefarious purposes. On the other hand, a library comes with librarians.

A librarian's job is to curate the collected knowledge and assist inquiring minds in their investigation. I have never met a school librarian who agreed with that description. They've all seemed much more interested in restricting my access to vital case information, encouraging me to follow wrong leads, and regularly blowing my cover when I've been "loitering in the 100s for too long and making everyone uncomfortable."

My nemesis in this arena is Ms. Markson. She has complicated more than one investigation and never once recommended a book I found useful. Despite my best efforts, I was never able to make her the subject of an investigation, either. She covers her tracks too well.

I walked through the doors, rounded the corner of the circulation desk, and there she was. The Cerberus at the gates of knowledge was standing there in her abstract painting turned blouse and a strong aura of superiority. Our eyes met, and without compromising the sneer on her face, she asked, "Can I help you find anything, Mr. Denver?"

"Nope." I didn't break stride or eye contact until my neck required it. I knew what I was after, where to find it, and that I couldn't afford to be distracted by whatever new book she was trying to push. I made for the 500s and hoped I looked like I was on class business. If you look like you have an objective, people tend to not bother you with their own.

The 500s are not where I usually find myself. The natural world never seemed to require much further investigation. The natural world makes sense. It follows rules. Its order is simple and obvious. It's people that make no sense. It's people who need to govern themselves with bells. It's people who require investigation. The 500s are also home to the mathematics books, for some reason. I didn't generally seek out additional math work if I didn't need to. Whatever the case requires, though.

I scanned the shelves for as long as my mind could take—about five minutes, if the school clocks are to be believed. I found a lot of characters and symbols that I couldn't understand, but nothing like what I'd seen on Mikey C.

Maybe it was context. Things out of context never look like they ought to. I once had a conversation at the park with a woman preparing for a hang-gliding expedition on an hour-long ferry ride before I realized she was my second-grade teacher. Context is tricky. Without its proper surroundings, a subject loses meaning.

Math was proving to be a dead end. If I'm honest with myself, I probably wouldn't recognize the right thing if I saw it. Like I said, I don't come to the 500s much—the math section specifically. I can count on one hand the times I'd come down that aisle.

I could count on one finger the number of times I'd been in the 700s. The Case of the Macaroni Van Gogh. Today doubled that number. After science proved inadequate, I turned to art. What I didn't find there told me I was finally on the right track.

It's not uncommon for these shelves to look empty. Students are required to check books out for classes, and continuing budget cuts mean there are fewer and fewer books to shelve. The ones that did remain were often older than anyone could remember. The Clinton presidency, at least. But there was nothing there. I stared at the shelves where music should be, and there was nothing there. Someone had the books. Someone was hiding the books. Someone was keeping the books from me.

At this point, I now knew two things.

1.) This went deeper than I thought. I might not be able to finish this investigation before recess ended.

2.) To know where to go next, I would have to talk to Ms. Markson.

Ms. Markson's desk was decorated with the kinds of cutesy knick-knacks and motivational posters that made you think she was constantly preventing a psychotic break. The shelf dedicated to kid's meal toys did not help the assessment. Maybe she should have spent some time around 150. There had to be something about what to do in the event of a midlife crisis there.

"Robert. The rude neanderthal in a trench coat. Will you allow me to help you today? We just got *Tucker's Trail* in. It's about a boy near your age. When tragedy strikes, he must take responsibility for his family during the Civil War."

She's recommended more or less the same book every time I've come in here. A boy like me coming of age against the backdrop of some world event that the author is trying to trick me into learning about. She got me once—before I knew better—with *Dance, Douglas*. It's about a boy who worked in his dad's butcher shop during the roaring '20s. Every night, he would turn on the radio and practice the Charleston while sweeping the floor. Will he ever find the courage to tell his dad he wants to get into vaudeville instead of becoming a butcher? Spoiler alert: yes. He tells his dad, his dad accepts Douglas's new career path, and then they dance the night away. See, it was New Year's, 1929. A great year to be a small business owner or an entertainer.

"No. I'm here on official business."

"Oh, I thought you were no longer on the force. Something about behavior unbecoming of an officer."

I wasn't surprised she knew. People like Markson make it their business to know the business of other people. "Let's call it unofficial-official business then."

Her eyebrows rose in skepticism. "If you're not here on patrol duty, you need a pass to be here without your class. Do you have one?"

Haha. She said *duty*.

But enough with distractions. I didn't have a pass, which meant I might only get one shot at the information I needed.

"Why are there two entire shelves missing? One wouldn't surprise me, but I didn't think even *you* could lose two whole sections of information." With any luck, her ruffled feathers at my "insubordination" would make her forget the pass thing. Blinded by indignity.

She crinkled her nose and put on a tight smile. It was a confident smile. A condescending smile. A "you're not as smart as you think you are, young man" smile. I hate that smile. "The entire point of a library is that the books move around. The democratization of information. If you spent half as much time examining this year's youth reading list as you do playing detective, maybe you'd know that."

"Oh, good. So, you know where your music books are."

"A teacher asked me to pull them for a special project, along with some from the mythology section."

"Let me guess. Mr. Went?"

"Not that it's any of your business, but yes. He said something about using them to keep students busy since he's monitoring detention now. Budget cuts, you know."

"I've heard. Can I take a look at them?"

"No."

I suppose I had that coming.

"Listen, there may be lives on the line. I'm just starting this investigation, but I can already tell this thing is big. Are you really going to be the one to stand in the way of justice? Are you going to be the one who lets something sinister creep into this school? It's just like that bird book you're always going on about. There's a mockingbird flying around this place, and I'm the finch who's going to kill it."

Good speech, literary reference, call to action. Should've been everything a librarian needed. Now for a strong close.

"Do the right thing. Help me protect this school. Let me look at those books."

"No."

I was a bit lost. That kind of speech usually works on TV. Maybe I should have read more than the cover of that mockingbird book. "But, I . . . um . . . "

"I can't let you look at those books because they were just checked out."

"I thought you said they were on hold."

"I said he asked me to pull them, so that he could have a student helper come pick them up. A student with a note from his teacher, I might add."

"When?" I asked as what she'd revealed sank in. "Which way did they go?"

"About a minute before you came up here." Then she pointed to the exit. "There's only one door to this place."

It occurred to me that that's probably a fire hazard as I charged through the door.

"Don't worry. Keep this up, and you'll have plenty of time to look at those books." I only caught some of that before I was out of earshot, but I'm pretty confident about what she probably said.

I didn't see anything in the hallway, so I headed toward the detention room. It used to be the sewing room—still had all the tables with the machines built into the top. Home ec. had been cut a year ago, but the machines hung around.

My gut stopped me, and I don't think it was just the salami finally settling. Markson had said that a student picked up the books. I had a good bet as to who that representative was.

I changed direction and headed to the teachers' bathroom one hallway over. The teachers don't use it because it shares a vent with the boys' locker room. Well, Mr. Roth, the art teacher, uses it, but we always figured his nose didn't work anymore after years of chemical exposure. You can't hang around that much paint, glue, and glitter all day and expect your nose to still work properly. He wasn't a threat though, because he whistled whenever he walked the hallways. Based on his repertoire, he might have been going deaf too.

This nearly abandoned bathroom has come in handy in my career. Joe and I had made a deal with a custodian for a spare key. It was a quiet place to think, hide, or stash material in the ceiling tiles. As far as I knew, there were only three people who used that bathroom, and I didn't hear any whistling.

The door was unlocked when I got there. He was standing on the toilet tank, tossing books into the ceiling when I opened the door.

"What do you know, Joe?"

Investigation Log
The Smell of Music
Entry #5 | 12:15 p.m. | Disused faculty bathroom

"Bert! I told you to leave this alone."

I hadn't noticed it before, but I was starting to see streaks of bloodshot lightning in his eyes. There was a shine in the sweat on his cheeks. He had the same look of exhaustion as that weekend when we'd staked out the old Welcker place. He thought it was ghosts; I thought it was mole men. Turns out, it was a pregnant raccoon.

He scrunched his face up before returning to his task.

"Pretty lonely study group, you have here." I propped myself against the door, trying to look cool and blocking his exit at the same time.

"It's not what you think. I had to get to these before you found out. I told you to leave this alone!"

Something stank, and I'm not talking about the locker room vent. I grabbed Joe by his unused belt loops and pulled him to the floor. "Spill it, Joe."

He started twitching. My interrogations tend to have that effect. Or, maybe it was the locker room vent.

"Things . . . Things have changed since you got the boot, you know? The school is worried about the budget, you know? The patrol, we've all taken on some extra duties, you know?"

"I do now."

"What was that? Do you hear that?" He jerked his head around like the teacher had just called his name to demonstrate long division on the board.

I didn't. "I don't."

He was clearly confused. Who knows why? If I hadn't personally witnessed Joe's iron stomach, I might have said he was about to toss his cookies. He even turned a little green around the gills. (I never understood that expression, by the way. Humans don't have gills. And I've never seen a fish throw up. I think my grandpa made it up.)

"At first, they just wanted our usuals. They'd be in for half a day and done. They didn't look great when they got out, but that's the way it was with Bennet too."

"You're talking about the kids in detention? Went has you *targeting* kids for detention?"

Joe swayed a bit. Things were getting intense. I could tell because my ears plugged up, and there was a distant ringing I sometimes get when I'm onto a lead.

"Went has a list, a type. The ones who weren't clever enough to avoid capture, weren't clever enough to solve the equation." He swallowed hard, and his eyes rolled into his head for a moment. I'm not a doctor, but that didn't seem like a promising sign. I was glad we were in the bathroom.

The ringing in my ears got louder. It occurred to me that I should've been worried it was Mr. Roth, but in that moment, I had more pressing concerns.

"Cut to the chase, Joe."

Trying to sit against the wall, Joe said, "He's got the patrol now, too." He lost his strength, and we both ended up sitting on the floor. Joe hadn't been there for me when I hit bottom. We didn't both have to be punks. "It's the music, Bert. We can't escape the music." He closed his eyes again, and I couldn't get him to come to. I figured the locker room smell was getting to him.

The whistling was still getting louder when I realized it wasn't Roth's version of "Puff the Magic Dragon." The sound kept getting louder and screechy, until it stopped like someone had pressed the mute button. My ears unplugged, and that's when it hit me.

The smell.

The vent!

The music!

I left Joe curled on the bathroom floor and pulled a U-turn through the door and into the boys' locker room.

I pushed the door, and there was a metal clinking, echoing

around the mildew-covered . . . everything. The echo lasted longer than it should have. There's something about this kind of all-encompassing tile that seems to alter the laws of sound. I got to the row of lockers closest to the shared wall and found nothing but a ground-level fog of shower steam. I whirled around, which parted the fog enough for the glint of something to catch my eye. It was a recorder, lying on the shower floor. It wasn't one of the plastic ones we all got in fourth grade. It was sleek, more pointed, and shone with more care than any student has ever given to their school-issued instrument. It was almost too clean, considering I'd found it rattling around a bathroom floor.

The recorder was warm when I picked it up. (Gross.) I began to worry about what that meant when footsteps echoed down the cavern of lockers. I tucked the recorder inside my jacket pocket. It didn't fit comfortably, but at least it was hidden. I blew through the door and nearly broke my nose running into the sweater-vest-clad skeleton of Mr. Went.

"Watch where you're going, young man! Have you seen Joe Wrigley? He's one of the safety patrol members, and he's late for duty."

Why don't adults seem to know how funny that word is?

"No." I covered for Joe on instinct before I actually decided it was the right thing to do—for the investigation, anyway. "He wasn't in the locker room?"

He eyed me, noting that I had asked him a question rather than simply replying to his. He's the only person it could have been in there. Unless there's something I was missing. He didn't know that I was on the case, but now I had become noticed.

"Just you," he said. "Who are you, by the way?" He stood taller as his suspicion was piqued.

"Pauley Marcus. I was looking for Coach Dodge. Message from

the office." I flashed the lunchroom napkin I'd been keeping notes on and hoped he wouldn't notice. It was a white piece of paper with scribbling on it. I've had less official-looking passes.

Went squeezed his lips together. He broke away, giving me the win in our staring contest. "Well, make sure you get back to class. Or you'll see me again . . . in Detention." He was halfway down the hall before he finished that last threat.

I turned, walked past the faculty bathroom and around the corner in case he looked back. I gave a six count (everybody thinks in fives) and slipped my head around the corner to see Went's shoes taking a right at the end of the hall.

Joe was right where I'd left him when I got back.

The bell to end recess rang as I finished stashing the books. Joe may have been trying to keep them from me, but at least I knew where they were now. And hopefully Joe was the only other person who did. It seemed like the one thing I wanted was for Went to not have access to these books. Not until I knew what was going on.

They were what I'd expected at first, a number of old music history texts that probably hadn't been opened since the school was built. Then I found a collection of mythology textbooks. Nothing I recognized, but based on the hybrid creature on the front cover, I assumed it was one of those Greek myths I'd never heard of. It looked like a bunny rabbit with spider legs was trying to eat some guy in a loincloth. Ancient Greece must have been crazy.

There were a few other books like that, but I stashed them all. I hoped to figure out what it all meant later. My first priority was to get Joe some medical attention. With a little luck, Nurse Hale might have some apple crumble waiting.

Investigation Log

Floating, Glowing Toothpicks

Entry #6 | ??:?? | A vacuum where the detention room used to be

Two steps out the door, and my plans changed with two big sixth-grader-sized mitts clamping down on my shoulder. "Trespassing in a faculty restroom, in the hall without a pass after the bell rings, and assaulting a member of the safety patrol. Went knew you were up to something, Bert."

"Nice to see you too, Frank. Still eating preschoolers to keep up your strength?"

Frank didn't respond well to my question, and the next time I had a conscious thought, I was in detention.

The room was dark. The lights were on, all buzzing in that way you only get in poorly-funded office buildings or public schools. Same thing, really. I'd read once that the sound was due to a misalignment of the bulbs. A slight loosening of the bulb is enough to produce a drone that could be used for torturing enemies of the state. Joe had always said they never get fixed because teachers are too old to hear it. They think we're all crazy kids, complaining about nothing. Either way, the lights were buzzing, but the room was dark.

The light couldn't travel in this space. It was like being under water or trying to see through a classroom window. The medium between the light source and your eyes was too thick. I couldn't tell for sure who else was in the room with me, but I knew there were other captives around. Maybe half a dozen silhouetted figures sat motionless in the desks too damaged to be in the regular classrooms.

It smelled. The detention room wasn't close to the locker room, but it had the same stench—fear and sweat that had been left to decay in one spot for longer than medically advisable. Probably violated the Geneva Convention, too.

Whatever was stinking up the air and stopping light from traveling, it was heavy. I felt the need to slouch under its weight. The dark outlines of the others in the room seemed to have a similar issue with the relative barometric pressure. They were all sitting low and hunched over. Only one figure was standing: Mr. Went. He stepped out of the gloom and stood closer than I was comfortable with.

"Sit," Went commanded, gesturing toward an empty desk at my side. I didn't mean to obey, but I felt my backside contact the empty chair even as I was preparing to refuse.

"What's this . . . "

Went cut me off with a finger to his lips. "This is the room where we take problem-causers and turn them into problem-solvers." He leaned over at the waist without bending his legs—just pivoted at the hips until he was a right angle, putting the skin-wrapped skeleton too close to my face. "Obedience is only the first tool you will need. I have ways of helping with that."

Went then stuck his hand into my jacket and brought out the second half of my sandwich. He sneered and tossed it behind him. I didn't see where it landed. That was the moment it became personal. He searched my pocket again and pulled out the fancy recorder from the locker room. He brought it to his mouth and began to play.

I've heard all manner of music in these halls, from the popular radio tunes to the fashionably unpopular ones. This school has more than one beatboxing group and one kid named Brady who insists he's figured out Mongolian throat singing. Mrs. Baker is constantly playing some insufferably old piano song she insists will help our test performance. Whatever Went was playing, on the other hand, sounded like all of those styles smashed together and filtered through his tiny flute.

The moment he started playing, the thickness of the air doubled, and the smell along with it. The salami resting in my gut tried to climb back out before I convinced it to stay. It wasn't the screeching on the chalkboard that I expected. This was more of a feeling than a sound. It wasn't an attack on my senses, but on my emotions. I had gotten the same feeling on the day Coach Dodge threw me in the deep end of the pool. Fear and panic, like I was suddenly in over my head.

The haze didn't lift, but I was able to pick out more details as my eyes adjusted. There was a teacher's desk near the front of the room, where Went had piled the books from the bathroom. The chalkboard had various tutoring prompts on it: English lessons, some science model, the correct pronunciation of "Sacagawea," that kind of thing. There was even a caricature of Mr. Roth that somehow hadn't been erased. All of it had been forced to the outer edges of the board by a circle made of the same symbols from Mikey C. and Joe's arms.

The markings were chalk but looked like they had been written over several times. They were thick and the clearest thing through the polluted air. At first, they looked like our back door after we'd gotten that new puppy. Riley didn't like waiting for his time outside. The longer I looked at the board, though, the more the symbols seemed to have an order. Like when you look at a math problem for long enough, it seemed to make sense. I couldn't tell you what the symbols meant (and I usually couldn't tell you how to solve a math equation), but it felt like there was a system being utilized.

I looked down and found the same kind of marks carved into my desk. The same chaotic symbols and equations. And not the usual cross-generational communication that typically occupied those types of desks. Then they changed.

The marks started to glow light green and rose to be three-dimensional. It was like someone had dropped a pack of neon-colored toothpicks. I looked left at the nearest desk to confirm that it wasn't just mine. That one was glowing too, right into Joe's unblinking face.

"What do you know, Joe?" I said with my lips, although no sound came out. I felt the vibration in my mouth, but there was no sound. I listened and realized that even the lights had been silenced. The only sound was Went tearing up his recorder solo. It wasn't loud, but it was ubiquitous.

My neck started to ache and stiffen. I turned back to my toothpicks, and the pain went away. "That's not good." The toothpicks kept rising until they hovered an inch above the wood.

"Good afternoon, class," Went said, the recorder touching the corner of his mouth. Somehow, the sound still bounced around the room. Then Went started monologuing. I know as a detective and captive, I should have paid attention, but I didn't have it in me. He started with, "In ancient Greece, the great mathematician, musician, and philosopher . . . " and I tuned out. A combination math and history lesson sounded like a unique kind of torture. There was something about a cage of math (which didn't sound right) that would only be revealed through a secret style of logical music (that sounded even less right). Whatever was going on, he'd decided to treat students in detention like his personal crew of code breakers . . . but for math. He closed with, "Let's continue where we left off before lunch. Solve the Arachneili!"

He began playing again while I tried to make sense of what he had just said. I looked at the glowing symbols over my desk. It was all Greek to me. Well, the one looked like a butterfly. (A butterfly as drawn by someone who has never seen a butterfly.) I looked around the room. The other captives poked at their desks like they were tablet screens. I made out the silhouette of Mikey C. He moved faster than anyone else. I was so impressed with his speed, I almost missed the way his head hung to the left, resting on his shoulder. His eyes were open, but I don't think they saw anything.

I turned back to the butterfly in the middle of my desk, and I swear it looked back. Then my head split with pain, and I nearly knocked myself out, bringing it to meet the shapes. Through squinted eyes, I looked up at Went. He continued to play his cacophony, but it was clear he was playing at me specifically. Like when the teacher warns the class that pets will no longer be allowed for show-and-tell the day after your bat escaped its box and was still roosting somewhere on school grounds. Poor Bill.

My right eye was level with the butterfly shape, less than two inches away. I stabbed a finger at it, halfway hoping I could impale it on my pinky. It was like lines of gelatin, cold and bouncy. I was grossed out for a moment before my body shivered, and something left. I don't know what it was, but I felt it leave my body. Like when you have a really good sneeze, and the thing that comes out is bigger than anything that should be up your nose, and then you take a breath and realize how little oxygen you've been getting along with all day, and you feel light enough to fly. It was like that, except that whatever left hadn't come from my nose.

(Looking back on it, the characters glowing from the desk might have felt more like something that comes out of your nose than gelatin. Maybe the lines were made of boogers. Maybe that's what it took from me. Maybe gelatin is secretly made of boogers? I'll investigate that later.)

My headache went away, and Went's playing faded into the background. I still heard it, but it was muffled, like it was playing through an old speaker. It was no longer the voice of the room. The butterfly was.

Investigation Log
What the Butterfly Showed Me
Entry #7 | What is time? | What is space?

I tried to look at anything else in the room, but everything was hazy now and farther away than it had been before. Also, as soon as I wasn't looking at my butterfly, the knife in my brain would twist. I figured out pretty quickly where my attention was wanted.

The butterfly didn't speak or even introduce itself, which I thought was rude. Instead, it was like jumping into a video game without the tutorial. You figure out the goal through context. The butterfly gave me context.

I started to see how the characters hovering above the desk fit together. I didn't understand any of it, but I was developing an instinct for what symbols to push and when—which ones connected. I was discovering the rules to this language, purely based on the feedback I felt from the butterfly. Pain meant it was a wrong answer. Lightness and freedom, correct answer.

Before I realized what was happening, my hands were corralling entire groups of symbols. Apparently, there was some kind of unifying relationship at work. I didn't know what I was doing, but based on the light feeling in my chest, I was pretty good at it.

Faster and faster, my fingers leapt from symbol to symbol. They started to blur, and the tendons in my forearms ached. I tried to stop but couldn't. There was some other momentum that kept my digits skittering across the equation.

My tendons leading to my wrists burned. I could feel them bulging out of my skin. I didn't expect that kind of carpal tunnel until I had logged many more years of gaming. Desperate to see how bad it was, I rotated my wrist as much as I could while keeping my fingers working. That's when I saw the green. The same symbols that I was becoming fluent in were showing up on the insides of my arms. It looked like they weren't going to stop there. I still didn't know what any of them meant, only what they felt like according to the butterfly. It was there too, staring at me from my own skin.

That's when I got lightheaded. The ringing in my ears came back. I became hyperaware of things happening in my body—my heart beating, my stomach melting away my lunch, the hairs on my arms stretching as far as they could manage. All of these systems were working overtime. I was concerned about something, but my brain couldn't tell what. My breathing had become the loudest sound in the room as my lungs struggled to find enough oxygen in the swampy air.

The space on the chalkboard at the center of the symbols turned black. It was the first time I had ever seen a blackboard that was actually black instead of green. The symbols around it rotated and rearranged themselves, while I recognized some of the groupings that I had worked on assembling. Everything I had done on my carved-up desk was reflected on the board. I could see the copy of my work in that circle of fluid glyphs. The space inside the arrangement got darker. It was uncomfortably dark inside the circle—like, too dark to be anything but nothing. The caricature of Mr. Roth looked as angry as ever.

Distantly, I heard shouting. I chanced a glance his direction. As long as my hands kept arranging the equation, the butterfly didn't seem to mind. Went wasn't playing on his recorder anymore. He was reading from one of the books Joe had pulled from the library.

As best as I could tell, the rest of the class was still hard at work. Joe was unresponsive in the lefthanded desk, but every other student diligently worked on their equation. I could feel the other students within the equation. It was like singing in a choir. Even though the point was to sound like one voice, the individual singers could sense the others in the group. I could feel other minds working on the equation that was coalescing on the board. Suddenly, I had a new sense of respect for my fellow detainees. Sure, it was by force, but they were dedicated to the task at hand. They didn't even change pace when the first leg articulated its way out of the blackboard.

At first, I thought it was a trick of the dim light. It looked like a hotdog with a point on the end had poked through the chalkboard. A black, furry, breakfast sausage. That didn't seem right. Probably just a hunger hallucination. Then another poked out. And another. The three pointy hotdog ends braced against the lip of the blackboard hole and flexed, putting pressure on the surface. They sent cracks shooting to the sidelined tutoring and Mr. Roth's terrified chalk face.

The pointy hotdog bits continued to leverage against the blackboard until a rabbit's head—as big as a soccer ball and covered in matted black fur—emerged from the hole. Turns out, the legs were much longer than a hotdog, more like several connected hotdogs (similar to what you see dogs chasing in old-timey cartoons). Each section was about a foot long and stronger than any hotdog I'd ever eaten. The ears stood straight up like on most bunnies, although one was missing the top third. The eyes were uncomfortably big, also like most rabbits, but they glowed yellow, like stars within its dark galaxy of a face. Its nose twitched.

The thing continued to pull itself through the hole as Went closed his book with a triumphant clap. At my desk, my butterfly gave less feedback and my booger symbols began disappearing.

It was suddenly cold, like that time Kyle Trickle had thrown me into the school's walk-in freezer. My hands shook, and my lungs couldn't take in enough oxygen again. My stomach told me I was starving. I thought about my half sandwich from lunch, but my stomach lurched. It wasn't ready for salami and onions yet. That is, assuming I could find where Went had tossed it. The way the silhouettes around the class had collapsed at their desks told me they had a similar reaction.

" . . . is here! I knew it." Went's voice slowly rose from the muffled sea it had occupied. "Think of the possibilities. I'll never write another lesson plan again!"

He walked toward the hole that was giving birth to the rabbit-spider thing and reached out his hand. "Arachneili," he said, followed by something I couldn't understand. The creature sniffed heavily, spraying some black goo across Went's sweater vest. Then it attached two legs to Went's shirtsleeves and pulled.

I wanted to drop at my desk like the rest of the class. I'd seen enough movies to know that if the monster coming out of the portal thought I was already dead, it might mean I would survive to the end of the film. Instinct told me that I didn't want the rabbit-spider to catch my eye (like when the teacher starts asking the class questions about the homework you didn't do). I figured the best strategy was to pretend I was invisible. I hadn't studied for whatever quiz this thing had in mind.

I was in it, though. Safety patrol meant putting the school above yourself. Usually, that responsibility didn't involve a bunny the size of a backpack with five-foot spider legs crawling out of a mathematical portal in a chalkboard that had only been revealed through ancient, ear-shattering music played through a child's instrument . . . but life is full of tests we didn't study for.

Went strained under the weight of the thing. I don't know if the creature was truly that heavy or if his muscles were that weak, but he couldn't hold his arms straight out. The creature gripped with its seven legs (I know, weird) and it made its way up to Went's shoulders like a pet monkey in a cartoon. Went seemed happier than I'd ever seen him before. That's not saying much, now that I think about it, but still.

I snuck up to the front of the room with all the stealth and grace of a newborn giraffe. The rabbit with spider legs from the portal didn't seem to notice. It scuttled along Went's arm and perched on his shoulder like a parrot on a pirate. It began sniffing him again.

"That's what this was all about?" I asked. "What, you're hoping to hold the school hostage with your new pet until the P.T.A. pays some kind of ransom? I'm guessing new music stands for the band room. Although, if I were you, I'd settle for a new wardrobe."

Went looked at me in a way I'd learned to recognize on many teachers' faces. He was disappointed and confused and not sure which was the dominant reaction.

"What? No," he said as the creature put two legs on his head for better stability. "Do you realize what I've done? What I've proven? Do you know how many research facilities will pay for my technique? What I know? I can finally get a university position! No more teaching theory in twenty-minute increments. No more pep rallies. No more worrying about budget cuts. No more trying to balance a band of twenty trumpets and a single trombone. I have rediscovered the musical key to other worlds! This little guy, the Arachnieli, is just the beginning. And to think, all you degenerates made it possible."

As he finished, the creature came around to the front of Went's sweater vest. It sniffed again and then speared one of its spider legs through Went's stomach. It retracted its arm with some of Went's insides stuck to the end. (I don't know what part. We haven't gotten to the anatomy section of our science book yet.)

Went's face reacted with surprise at this before melting into acceptance. "Of course," was all he got out before the Arachnieli rode him to the ground and started chewing on its prize. It even chewed in that kind of side-to-side way bunnies do.

I looked around for any clue about what to do next. There were enough bodies passed out at the desks, so I figured I could avoid being eaten a little while, but that wasn't my first option. Most of these kids were rule-breakers, but that didn't mean I wished them any harm. Well, maybe one or two if I'm honest, but I won't get into that now.

There was an empty bookshelf, a few toilet paper rolls ready to serve as facial tissue, and an overhead projector that might only be good for blinding or burning the thing. Maybe it was afraid of mirrors? I was just about to try to trap it like a mummy in the toilet paper when I saw the trashcan. That's what we'd eventually had to catch Bill in, so I knew the plan was sound in theory. Then again, an overfed and freaked-out pet bat wasn't much comparison to a seven-legged spider-rabbit from the chalk world.

I got to the trashcan just in time to see the creature slurp up the last of whatever it had pulled out of Went. (Liver? I think I read somewhere that some things eat liver.) It raised a leg to go in for more, and I crashed into the can. I might as well have dropped an entire clocktower worth of bells for all the stealth I was achieving.

We stared at each other for a bit. Its overly large, glittering almond eyes blinked. I probably blinked too. Despite the sheen of blood splashed across its twitching snout, it still looked kind of cute.

"I don't suppose you want to talk this out, do you?"

It made a trilling sound, like a bird. My stomach gave a lurch that I know it heard because its ear jerked.

"Gilligan." The voice was weak and scratchy. Not the voice I had expected to come from this adorable, portal-hopping monster, but I wasn't about to judge.

Then there was a hand on my shoulder. "You always did have strange friends," Joe said. He handed me my half-sandwich from lunch. Went must not have gotten much distance when he tossed it. "Give the dog a bone."

I'm pretty sure that last part was gibberish because he collapsed back into the desk right after that, but it gave me an idea. I unwrapped my lunch and held it out to the creature. My stomach growled again, and this time the thing skittered back a step.

"You must be hungry. I didn't follow everything that just happened, but it seems like you came from a long way away. Long time away, too . . . I think? I'm not sure." I was rambling. I had to focus on what I wanted to say, and I also had to remind myself not to eat the sandwich. "I get pretty crazy when I'm hungry too. Do you want some of my sandwich? It's not vegetarian, but I don't think that'll be a problem."

The Arachnieli looked down at Went's torso and poked it with one of its legs. The creature lowered its body so that its head was below its leg joints. (I hate it when spiders do that. Knees go below the head, always. That's a rule.) The creature sniffed again and then made its way, one creepy step at a time, to me.

I ripped the sandwich in two and tossed one into the can. The other one, I offered back. The Arachnieli came less than a foot away and then rose so its legs were almost perfectly straight. Finally, it looked me in the eye. (I hate it when spiders do that. Be one height!)

The thing smelled *bad*. It was like that time the kitchen staff had left a box of mystery meat out over a long weekend. Apparently, the Arachnieli hadn't been wherever it was before it had come through the chalkboard, and at that close range, I could see bits and splashes of leftovers (not just Went) poking out of its fur. Some of it must have started to rot. The creature flared its nostrils, tiny drops of mucus threatening to fly from the rim. I hoped that whatever it had smelled on me wasn't to its liking.

It reached out one leg and skewered the sandwich. It brought it close, blinked once, and started nibbling. It stared at me the entire time. This close, I could see that while it had the traditional bucked bunny teeth, they were flanked by the sharp daggers of a newborn puppy. It made quick work of the offering. I liked to think it was more because I'd made a dynamite sandwich than it being a ravenous eating machine, but who's to say?

"I hope you like mayonnaise."

I like dogs. You can always get a sense of what they're thinking. They can convey emotion and let you know how they are feeling. Are they happy to see you? Do they have to go outside? Are they going to leap up and tear out your jugular because they blame you for the death of their master? A dog will usually tell you. That's what the swishy tail, big eyes, and expressive jowls are for. Only an idiot can't tell what a dog is thinking. Rabbit faces don't do that.

The fact that I wasn't dead yet was reassuring, but Went had probably had the same feeling right before it was too late. The thing just kept staring at me while it ground my lunch in its odd combination of teeth. Its ears snapped into different directions as it tracked ambient groans from my collapsed classmates. Its eyes, though . . . They never changed shape, narrowed in relaxation, dilated, or so much as dimmed in their cosmic glow. They remained open and worried, like rabbits' eyes always do. Given the gloom of the room, the preceding few minutes, and the seven furry spider legs coming out of its body, those wide, worried eyes looked more like the unblinking craziness of a kindergartener who'd missed snack time.

It stopped chewing with a final gulp that shuddered all the way down its legs. Then it held out a leg that I chose to take as a non-threatening gesture. In retrospect, the creature simply existing seemed like a threatening gesture.

"Sure, you can have more." I tapped the garbage can. "It's right in here. You know how teachers get about eating in the classrooms." The can was just big enough for the creature to fit. Its legs might stick out over the lip, but as long as it kept them out of my body, I figured I'd be able to get it somewhere safe.

The Arachnieli leaned forward so that its nose was at the edge of the can. It looked at me, then back to the sandwich. It stuck its leg inside, grabbed the sandwich, and looked back to me as it started eating.

"Or you could just do that, sure. Why wouldn't you?"

It put a leg on my shoulder and hoisted itself up to sit there, its free legs dangling. One leg followed the line of my spine down from my neck. I shivered and tried not to think about how it had done something very similar to Went. The thing gripped tighter, bringing its masticating muzzle right next to my ear. Its stomach rippled over my shoulder as muscles tensed—preparing for what, I was afraid to guess. Then it let out the foulest smelling burp since Tommy Dickson's after he'd had too much free pizza at the third-grade fun fair.

"Onions do the same thing to me."

It nuzzled closer and purred.

Investigation Log
Renovations, Staffing Changes, and a New School Mascot
Entry #8 | Two days later | The wellness room

Explaining the state of the detention room to Principal Grenoble was a trick. She seemed more inconvenienced than surprised when she saw Went. "Where am I going to find a sub who knows music?" she muttered to the room. She called for the custodial staff and told them to bring the sawdust. The Arachnieli and I, meanwhile, tried to stay out of the way by sitting on the desk.

"Don't sit on the desk," Grenoble commanded.

The Arachnieli and I watched from the corner as the staff mopped up what they could and bagged what they couldn't.

Nurse Hail tended to the detainees and Joe. Soon, they were expected to make a full recovery. Most of them had already lost their green tattoos. Joe swore he didn't know what was going on until it was too late. I believed him. He had never been the brightest bulb on patrol.

There was a newsletter sent home the next day with an odd collection of stories. The truth was there if you read closely enough. Parents *never* read closely enough.

The old detention room is getting a renovation! Thanks to an anonymous grant and a forward-thinking parent group, the space is going to be repurposed into a mental health recovery space featuring soft music and at least one beanbag chair. This is all an attempt at a kinder, gentler approach to detention.

The school is saddened to report that, effective immediately, Mr. Went, the much-loved music teacher, had to be let go. Budget cuts. Coach Dodge will be taking over music classes. Coordinating football offensive plays and conducting a band can't be that different.

The school has adopted a new pet/mascot/emotional support animal: Neil, the bunny! The custodial staff discovered Neil living in the old tool shed, and after a much-needed bath, we decided that Neil will be the perfect addition to the Warburton Elementary community. Neil isn't any ordinary bunny, but that's why we are so excited to welcome him into our hearts.

The school is also thrilled to report that after many different strategy attempts, the rat infestation in the basement will no longer be a problem. Not that it ever was a problem . . . But it definitely won't be a problem moving forward.

As for me, I've been put in charge of the school's new mascot. They tried putting Ms. Markson in charge of it, but Neil took two of her fingers. I gave him an extra sandwich that day. So now, he lives in the new mental health recovery room. The students love it. Nobody makes a peep when they're in there. They just sit and stare at Neil's shimmering cosmic orbs.

So far, nobody seems worried that our new mascot is a seven-legged spider-rabbit with glowing eyes and fur like it just came out of an oil spill. For what it's worth, I'm not too concerned about it either. As long as the cafeteria keeps the salami coming, that is. If not, there's always the rats in the basement.

Case closed.

For Sam

Objects From A Past Life:
A Hollow Brook Story

The building door was propped open. Someone was moving in. Maybe someone was moving out. Maybe someone was waiting for a pizza delivery from Castinetti's. Whatever the situation, it saved Jay the trouble of finding a way past the locked door. Jay walked in like he was supposed to be there. At the time, he thought he was. The open door was a sign. The mail slots had said the apartment he was looking for was one of the four on the second floor.

The hallway leading from the two units on the east to the two on the west was tight. The architect had made spacious landings outside of the individual apartments without realizing that it forced the hallways to be barely more than three feet wide. Getting to the other side of the building was a test of claustrophobia. Jay didn't know it at the time, but it wouldn't be his last.

The girls avoided the hallway, opting instead for the bed sheet tent they had constructed against the half-wall next to their own stairwell. Plenty of breathing room. That's where Jay found them, cuddled under a worn, thin pattern of flowers and bunny rabbits. Jody was reading something about cats. June was coloring.

They were happy to see him, but they were not happy. They each wore the woven bracelets that they had made with Jay and Marie the week before at the rec center. Red and purple for Jody. Green and white for June. It was a simple braid that Jay had learned at summer camp years before. He hadn't expected to still be making friendship bracelets at twenty-five, but life was strange sometimes.

Jay entered the apartment. The doorframe was cheap.

When Jay left the apartment, June handed him a picture. He patted her on the head, folded the picture, and put it in his left back pocket. The right back pocket was occupied.

"Coffee, please." Jay smiles at the server. The muscles in his face are still getting used to this orientation. There are so many different ways to smile. So many different reasons to smile. It's all about the context. Jay knows a smile is the appropriate action in this situation, but he's not sure if he is doing it right. He isn't confident in matching the smile to the context. He's out of practice. If he's being honest with himself, it was never something he'd been good at, anyway.

The server smiles back. "Anything to eat?" He is young, probably younger than Jay was when he went away. Then again, maybe not. Age is a hard thing to gauge for Jay these days. Nearly everyone looks younger out here.

"Not right now. We'll see how long I'm here. Thank you."

The server—Devon, according to his nametag—closes his notebook with a little snap and nods his retreat, a stained towel flapping from his back pocket like the saddest cape a superhero ever donned.

Jay has never been to The Dining Car before. He's been to the railyards nearby and has even met people in the parking lot, but this is the first time he has ever been inside. Until today, he has never looked at the black and white photos of trains that used to pass through the town, never seen the silverware rattle from the trains that still did, never seen the ancient box of matchbooks still waiting at the register, and never eaten anything from the diner.

He doesn't know what to order. The options are all a combination of eggs, bread, and meat of some sort. Yet, it is still overwhelming. None of it appeals to Jay's silent stomach.

Jay hasn't developed an adventurous pallet yet, anyway. His cellie warned him about the eyes-and-stomach relationship before he got out. "Freedom pounds," York called them. Jay will stick to the coffee. It's stale and a little burnt. It is the closest thing he's found to the Woodson mud that he got used to.

The partially rusted bell above the door dings. It's not her.

The diner is emptying out. Dinnertime is over. There will be stragglers, late eaters, and the ones who took an hour to decide where to go rather than face their own cooking. He isn't alone, but there are fewer eyes on Jay with every ding of that bell above the door. If everything goes right, at some point the ding will increase his company. He's on the clock, though. He needs to check in with Spencer at the house by 10:30 tonight. Condition of parole. Jay still doesn't quite understand how it all happened, but it did, so here he is—waiting in The Dining Car, waiting for the right person to ring the bell above the entrance.

Jay takes another sip and stretches his arms to the sides. His lefthand fingertips graze the window. His righthand fingers reach into the aisle a good six inches. The booth is probably a bit over five feet deep. A guess of six feet wide. The aisle is about the same amount of space he's gotten used to over the past seven years. Five by ten, give or take. Of course, the airflow in this space is significantly better.

The partially rusted bell above the door dings. It's not her.

It's a man in a suit. Not a fancy suit, but a functional suit. Black and white and black. It's not a sign of status like the gray and pinstripes and pocket squares and patterned-to-clash ties of lawyers and "businessmen." It's a suit to be ignored. People who didn't wear suits would assume this man had higher affairs to attend to. People who did wear suits would dismiss this man because the suit was forced on him, not earned through pedigree. He isn't part of the club. He is dressed to serve those in the club without raising eyebrows. He simply won't be an embarrassment if they end up in the same taxicab. This suit is clearly something the man has to wear, not something he chooses to wear.

This man blends in by not blending in. He is someone else's concern, and so he becomes nobody's concern. At least, that's the way he explained it to me once. But that won't happen for a few years. I'm not sure I believe that it works as well as he thinks. Especially with that lapel pin.

Jay notices the lapel pin as the man sits in a booth along the south wall. *It almost looks like an owl,* he thinks but doesn't think more about it. Not yet. He is more concerned with checking for a badge on the man's belt. There isn't one. The man pulls a blue envelope and a small notebook from his jacket. It seems he's got work to do.

The waiter walks by again and replenishes the three sips Jay has taken with four sips worth of liquid. A few excited drops escape over the side of the mug. Jay has a subconscious worry that the sloppiness will reflect poorly on him.

"Decided what you want to eat?" The *"yet"* is implied. He's a good enough waiter to not articulate it, though.

"Just the coffee, thank you. I don't know how long my friend will be."

"Oh, you're meeting someone. I'll bring another place setting." He leaves, still with that towel flapping behind him.

Jay lifts his mug carefully and cleans the spill, making sure to wipe the bottom and sides of the cup as well. If there is still some on the bottom rim of the cup, there's no point in cleaning in the first place. He takes a second napkin, doubles it over, and puts the mug back down. One more thing to wait on.

The partially rusted bell above the door dings. It's her.

Her long, curly black hair has been too often exposed to the kinds of airborne chemicals and humidity that people don't get paid enough to work in—kitchens, factories, nursing homes. She keeps it pulled back and coiled in the hood of her Misfits hoodie. The same hoodie she wore every morning when they opened the rec center. It's too warm for a hoodie, but that has never stopped her. Her sleeves are rolled up, though, revealing the various tattoos along her arms that she always made a point of covering in front of parents. Nobody complained, but they treated her differently. The looks weren't even lost on the six-year-olds that were being dropped off. She couldn't do much about the ones poking up from her collar bone. She isn't quite as tall as Jay, which is to say, not tall at all. She isn't to be messed with, though. Again, if you work in kitchens, factories, and daycares for long enough, the resilience and toughness come through in your stride. She was always the one who intimidated the kids and scared the parents. Jay was the softy.

Marie hasn't changed. That's why Jay was always able to rely on her back then. That's why he can rely on her now. At least, that's his optimistic logic.

Marie's rolled up sleeves also reveal the woven bracelet—strands of black and green to match her hoodie. Jay is impressed that it lasted all these years.

Jay doesn't see the box.

Marie doesn't wait to be seated like the sign at the entrance tells her to. She sees Jay and sets a path past the empty buffet counter and around the aisle seemingly reserved for single dads and their disappointed kids. She smiles and waves at an elderly couple a few spots down from where Jay is seated. It looks like the man mouths "Marie," but it's hard to tell.

She is almost seated but freezes mid-crouch when the waiter appears. He's been waiting to pounce. Devon places a water cup, flips the second coffee cup up, and begins filling it with the same level of care as Jay's refill. With his left hand, he pulls a silverware roll from his apron and places it not quite squarely on the table. "Can I get you anything to eat?"

"I don't generally like to make those kinds of decisions in this position."

He stares for a moment, trying to make sense of Marie's response.

"Let me sit down first. Also, I'm going to need a menu."

Marie finishes sitting and settles into the booth, customizing the coffee and eating utensil arrangement. The waiter is still at the ready. Marie doesn't smile but gives the waiter a look of tolerant patience. Jay has seen it many times before. When a third grader thought it was time to rebel and not pick up before snack time, sometimes the best tactic was a simple stare down, forcing them to make the first move. The waiter doesn't seem to notice and only increases the intensity of his smile.

"No problem. I'll be back in a minute." He leaves.

"Cheery service."

"Yes. I don't trust it either." Jay takes a short sip and turns it into a sad half-smile. "Thank you for coming."

"Of course. God, it's good to see you. What, it's been five, six years?"

"Just shy of seven. Six years, ten months, two days. Leap year got me twice." He scoots his mug a bit, adjusting his grip. "I'm as old as you were when I went in."

Marie scoffs. "Maybe in the next seven, you can learn to keep yourself out of trouble."

"It's good to see you again too. How's Katie?"

Katie isn't the girl he really wants to know about, but respect and consideration for another person's family became more important recently. If you're looking to bond with someone, if you need them to like you, then let them talk about what they care about. It's a kind of calculation Jay was never good at before. It's also just the polite thing to do. The rules of politeness have recently come to mean more to Jay. Something of a hotter commodity.

"Good. She's good. She's a senior now. Asks about you. Swim team. Working at the craft store, looking at colleges. See if she can make a better thing of it than I did." Marie sips her coffee. It's hotter than she expected, causing her eyebrows to furl in anger for a moment like they used to when her swipe card wouldn't work at six in the morning. "Once she turned eighteen, things got easier. She could choose when to spend time with her dad, which fortunately hasn't been often. It's been better, being just the two of us."

"Good. I'm happy for you. For both of you." Jay feels the emptiness in his sentence but can't come up with anything to fill the gaps.

"Katie is excited you got out. We both are. Wanted to know if she could come tonight, but I told her what you said . . . This must mean they're finally clearing everything up, right? Are you really . . . "

"I think so." It isn't the answer to the question Marie intended to ask. Not directly. That's why Jay interrupted her. She would interpret it that way though, and it was easier than explaining the context. "I must be. That's why they won't let me leave."

"So, you're out, but you're *not* out?"

"Something like that. All I know is, one day I thought I was going to be gray when I got out. The next day, I'm out. I can't leave Hollow Brook as part of the deal—a deal I never negotiated or saw before they were asking for a signature. Until I know more, I want to use my time wisely. Productively."

They both lower their heads and scan the dining area. Neither of them knows what to look for, but it comforts them.

"I'm not with the rec center program anymore." It's a test. A prodding. A warm-up to see how Jay reacts.

He turns back to Marie and tries to look unbothered by the topic. Fortunately, he is. Distracting the children before the school bus picked them up had simply been the introduction, it wasn't the conflict.

"When you, um, left . . . they made me the lead. It wasn't worth the pay raise." They both chuckle. "How did you deal with some of those parents?" She freezes for a moment, realizing her mistake. This is what she was supposed to dance around. How Jay dealt with parents was the conflict. "I'm sorry. That's not . . . "

"No, it's fine. You're right. Parents make childcare difficult. That's one of the reasons we worked so well together. I made sure you didn't have to deal with them."

Marie rolls her eyes in agreement and huffs as the tension recedes.

Devon comes back, still with that corporately mandated smile and towel trailing behind him. "Decided what you want to eat?"

Part of being a waiter is always being in a rush but never acting like you're in a rush.

"You know what?" Marie spreads an arm on the back of the booth and turns. "Just give me two of the basics. Eggs, sausage, pancakes. The closest you have to that. I'm not feeling fancy, but I'm hungry. I get the feeling we're going to be here a bit."

Devon makes a few strokes with his pen that couldn't possibly translate to a written language and turns to Jay. He does not succeed in opening his mouth completely before thinking better of it and retreating into the wider restaurant.

The man behind Marie—the man in the suit, the man who is invisibly noticeable as part of his job—tucks the blue envelope into his jacket pocket and turns to his notebook. It isn't like the notebook you had in high school. It's not a notebook with loose, spiral binding or the lazy sprawling of notes in the first twenty pages, followed by many more pages of blankness that you could reuse for something but never have and never will. It's not that kind of notebook. It's smaller, smoother, made for class and discretion. The man fiddles with something in the notebook, pulls out a newspaper clipping, and begins writing.

Devon appears at the man's table and places a plate. Jay doesn't recognize the dish. There is a light-colored sauce covering two lumps of eggs. It looks fancy, like maybe there is even a bit of greenery included with the meal that you're not supposed to eat, but somehow the meal would be incomplete without it. Jay doesn't remember seeing the man order.

"Did you have much trouble?" he says, tethering back to the conversation.

Marie sips her coffee slowly and gives a shallow nod. It wasn't agreement but acknowledgement of a transition. "Not much.

They questioned me. I told them what we had both heard. What everyone had heard. They were more interested in finding out about you. I mean, turns out they already knew about him. That's why you're out so early, right? Because they already knew about what he had done?"

There is a small, sad grin at the corner of Jay's mouth. He doesn't know it, but Marie notices.

Marie is right. The authorities had known. Sometimes the authorities knowing isn't enough, though.

There had been phones called, reports filed, investigations initiated. There were never any visible marks, but if you looked into Lila's eyes, there was evidence. Without something on the inside changing, without someone pushing forward, the situation would stay the same though. The file of phone calls would keep growing, the neighbors would keep being concerned, but until something changed, nothing could be done. Not by the people making those phone calls, anyway. Certainly not by June and Jody, the two little girls with nothing but a blanket fort to keep them safe.

Then something did change. Then there was a choice. Then there was an action. Jay was able to do something. There was a seven-year intermission in which Jay learned some alternative cooking methods and the importance of stamps. Then Jay found himself in a diner on the edge of a town he's not allowed to leave, talking with Marie, waiting for the right moment to ask about the box with the candy cane pattern on the outside that she brought with her. Each of those steps had a certain level of difficulty.

"I meant getting here," Jay says. "It's what, a twenty-minute drive from Cedar Grove? Plus, I know you don't like coming here if you can avoid it. Weird town."

It's Marie's turn to smile. It's a slightly embarrassed kind of smile, like she would use when the third graders would beat her in Connect 4. "That was fine too," she says. "As long as my ex doesn't know I came to town, it'll stay fine." She sips her water, forcing a break.

Devon strides up and deposits Marie's meal in front of her. He tilts his head, pointing his chin in Jay's direction.

"Still just the coffee, thank you."

Devon's question still wants to come out of his mouth but gets held back as he smiles around his tongue and leaves.

"So," Marie begins, trying to recover. "I've noticed you're still clean, at least from what I can see. They didn't give you any decoration in jail?"

He doesn't bother to correct her. Prison, not jail. "You know me, I could never get the design right. If *you* couldn't convince me to get a tattoo, I don't know who could." It isn't the first time they've had this conversation. Just the first time in over six years. Marie is always looking for her next one, and after three years of working together, she had almost talked Jay into getting one. It never manifested, though.

"Still, now that you're out, you don't want something to mark it?"

"I've got marks." Jay cringes slightly at the clichéd turn of phrase. It's unimaginative. Then again, maybe that's what the situation calls for. "Lingering marks is why I asked you here, actually. You did find the box, right?"

Marie maintains her expression like the conversation hasn't shifted to her yet. "Yeah. I found the box. How did you know . . . "

"That it would be safe there? The rec center locker rooms have always had signs saying they don't allow overnight lockup. But in all the years we worked for them, did you ever see anyone go and actually check? Those signs are up just so they don't have to pay someone to check. I grabbed a half-size one so it wouldn't inconvenience anyone. Inconveniences get noticed."

"Right. Well, it's in my car. I can . . . "

"Not yet. I'm not ready. I appreciate it, though. Like I said in my letter, it's dangerous. I just need to know it's here."

The partially rusted bell above the door dings. A family of three leaves, the small child lingering to examine the pie display near the register. She's planning her next visit. She's so distracted, she doesn't even notice the fish tank on the way out.

"How are the girls? I wasn't able to contact them. They never came to visit." This is the question they both knew they'd get to. The package in Marie's car is important, but only as it applies to the girls. "Not that I blame them."

Marie stops preparing her food with cutting and buttering. She doesn't put the knife or fork down, but they are on break. "They moved away. Once Lila finished the nursing program, they went to live with a cousin or something in Madison. The whole thing was too much after the trial. Some of his buddies started harassing Lila, hanging around her work. She had a patrol come by the apartment for a while, for all the good that did." She forks a bite. "It was good they got away."

Jay takes a larger than average sip of his coffee. It's at a comfortable drinking temperature. He estimates about ninety seconds before it cools further and becomes a beverage that is tolerated rather than enjoyed. Such is the danger of tiny diner coffee cups. The temptation is always to drink as much as possible in this brief window, but that isn't part of the game.

"How are the girls?"

"Better, as near as I can tell. Those first few weeks were rough. They didn't come to the program much after Lila's sister came to stay with them. Maybe *that's* the relative in Madison. Not a cousin, a sister. Anyway, she could only stay in town to help for so long. After that, when the girls came back . . . Well, you know how kids can be."

Children are very good at gathering information. The quiet ones are quiet because they process their information, draw conclusions from it. The loud ones make sure to broadcast every misconception that flits between their ears.

"Like I said, it's good they got away."

"I just wanted . . . " *No!* That's what Jay came here to change.

"Hey, everybody knows what you wanted. We all wanted the same thing. Everybody knew what was going on. What he was doing to her. It was only going to get worse for all three of them. They have it better because of you."

June and Jody were good kids. Sisters. Half-sisters, as it turns out. They stuck together more than some of the full siblings in the program. June was older, Jody was smarter. June was tall for a third grader, but skinny. She had the biggest silver dollar eyes and a smile too big for her face.

Jody looked like her mom, Lila. Dark hair and round features. She didn't laugh so much as she chose to show amusement. About a week before the old Jay made his decision, she had been approved for the gifted program. That meant the sisters would be at different schools the next year. Lila wasn't sure she would be able to manage two drop-offs across town from each other.

They were always dropped off at the rec center around seven in the morning. Not as early as some families, but early enough to get breakfast.

When Lila dropped them off, she was always sad to see them go. She'd sign them in, make sure she was up to date on any paperwork or school holidays, and address Jay and Marie by name. She was exhausted—overworked with two kids, school, and a job. She was aware of what June and Jody needed, though.

Lila had a boyfriend that helped out. When he dropped the girls off, he'd sign them in, tickle them a little too roughly, turn around, and head back down the hallway. He had the same overconfident smile on the entire time. He always gave a friendly nod to Jay as if the two had been teammates back in some imagined past. In truth, he probably didn't know Jay's name. He certainly didn't know Jay would be the last person he'd ever smile at.

"Not everyone knew."

Marie nods a concession while she finishes her sausage link. Links were the exception at Woodson. Most sausages were overly seasoned disks they'd use to fix lopsided tables more often than anyone would consume them for nutrition.

"Nobody actually believed that stuff about you and Lila. Well, maybe some did but nobody that matters." Marie takes a sip of coffee. "It's never the right temperature, is it?"

Jay's diaphragm contracts with a laugh that he didn't expect. "No. But it serves its purpose."

She gives a considered grin back. It's in that moment that Jay remembers what it's like to have a friend. A friend forged from mutual support and experience. There was plenty of that at Woodson, but it was different when it wasn't forced by close quarters. Out here, the other person could always walk away but chose not to.

The partially rusted bell above the door dings. The elderly couple who smiled at Marie are leaving. She secures a wrap around her hair while holding the door open. He makes a joke to the waitress while trying to conceal his leaning on the counter. He feels his knee giving out, but he refuses to be seen in public with that walker. He fiddles with one of the free matchbooks on the counter, gathers his strength, and leaves. He even taps on the fish tank along the way.

"So, what's next? Where do you go from here? Katie and me will help if we can but . . . "

"You have. You are . . . helping." The Dining Car is nearly empty now. The tables aren't being cleared with the same gusto as thirty minutes before. The staff knows they've got time now. "What's next is why I asked you here. Why I . . . I need that box. I don't know what's next." He takes a sip from his coffee cup. The coffee is low enough that it doesn't reach his lips, but he acts like it does. "When you've finished, we'll find out together."

Marie continues eating. Jay has more coffee. They talk about the kinds of things strangers who used to work together talk about. Some of it isn't new, simply stuff that they never talked about when they worked together. Jay never knew that Marie played guitar. Marie never knew that Jay thought guitar was overrated.

Devon checks in more frequently than is necessary or wanted for two people clearly on the downslope of their meal. There is always a smile. Always an attempt to fill Jay's belly. Always coffee slopped over the side of the nearly full cup. Jay always cleans it up. It's the little acts of disorder that lead to chaos.

June didn't have a mark that anyone would notice. It was the way she carried herself that clued Jay in. She was a little more careful when she sat down, her head hung a pinch lower, and her smile was a beat behind coming to her face.

Some of the questions didn't need to be asked, because rumors and investigation of public records had already provided the answers. It never got to the girls, though. They weren't even in the apartment when it happened. Locked out, in fact, until it was over. Police reports verified this, as the girls were usually curled up, sleeping outside the door. "Camping out" was the story. The officers always left without much more than a report of the call. It was just a mistake. The TV was up too loud. Everybody argues. "She provoked him," more than one report claimed. It was the kind of thing that happens on TV, so we don't believe it when it happens in real life.

Something changed, though. "Jody forgot her math book in the apartment," was all June said when Jay asked. "She tried to sneak back for it." Something else changed in that moment. It's that change that brought Jay to this night.

"How was everything?" Devon is back.

"It's gone," Marie says.

"The coffee reminds me of prison," Jay says. For the first time, Devon's smile wavers. He nods and leaves the bill in the middle of the table.

Marie offers to pay. The $1.25 for Jay's coffee hardly seems worth quibbling over.

Outside, the air oscillates between the castoff grease coming through The Dining Car's vents, the raw mechanics of the railway, the lingering asphalt smell from the freshest strip on the north side of the parking lot, and the occasional curl of clean air asking if there is any need for its services. The Wendy's to the south is closing up inside. The drive-through will be open for a few more hours, but the floors inside can be cleaned now. Ketchup restocked. Napkin dispensers checked for things that are not napkins.

The north has a vacant lot carved into the hillside that guides the highway down past this little oasis. The lot used to contain a hotel. Then there was a fire. Then the lot was vacant.

"Remember Elijah?"

"Ha," Marie says. She glances at the lot. "Fourth graders."

Marie's car is parked between light posts on the highway side. Even though there is parking on all four sides of the building, this is the "back" of the restaurant, opposite the entrance on the railyard side. You could also tell by the busted picnic table and rusted coffee can on top. The cooks have to put their butts somewhere.

Marie's car looks new, but it's the same one she drove to the rec center on those early school mornings. There was a new malfunction nearly every week, but she stuck with it. Jay always figured it was something to talk about—not that either of them knew what they were talking about. Mechanics is an overlap of ignorance for both of them.

Marie opens the passenger side door. She won't find out for three days, but the window is broken. There is a fault in the clamp that holds the glass in place. The worker who inspected it was new to the job and didn't know what he was looking at. A few hundred vehicles had the same fault, but only a quarter of them will suffer because of it. The worker knows better now.

Jay and Marie stare at the box for a moment. It's a pre-decorated Christmas box, covered in candy canes to be passably a "winter box," but everyone knows what they mean. It is small enough to only be useful for a watch, a pair of socks, or something along those lines. Either something for which the expense would impress over the size, or something that isn't meant to impress on either front.

Jay liked these boxes because it saved him the trouble of wrapping—another overlap of inability that Jay and Marie share, although they don't know it. If he was feeling fancy, Jay could tie a ribbon around it. He mostly didn't.

It was the first box he found that night. He didn't know if he would be caught or if the event would even be reported as it had happened. A report would be made, of course. Filing a police report would be the easiest way to get rid of a body, should such be deposited in your living room or breakfast nook. Sometimes insurance would even help with the cleanup. They had to have a report, though.

The box seemed like a good idea to preserve the moment. He pulled one from his closet when he got home and filled it with objects from the night. Jay became a different version of himself in that event. An isotope of the base element "Jay." The box was where he chose to preserve that isotope. Jay thought it might be a valuable element in the future. A revolutionary element that would change the course of Jay's life and the lives of everyone around him.

Jay didn't understand the instability of an element like that.

"There it is," Marie says. "Do I get to see what's inside now?" It is said with a laugh, but she's nervous.

Jay reaches out, and his chest tightens. A shiver creeps from his wrists to his back like a fast-moving leech, slick and looking for a way inside. He remembers to breathe. "Would you mind?" He stuffs his hands into his pockets and heads toward the dilapidated picnic table.

Marie stares and considers the box. There is a tingle at the base of her neck that she hasn't had in a while. The kind of tingle that usually means she should lock the door and have Katie stay with her grandma. They are alone, as near as Marie can tell. What few cars there are left in the lot are out front. A couple employee cars are nearby, but this time of night, they won't be occupied until closing time. She ignores the tingle long enough to grab the box and set it down between herself and Jay.

"I'm here for you. I'll trust you. But if there are legal issues with what's in this, you need to tell me. I think I deserve that."

"The case is over. I'm out. It came as a surprise to me too, but here we are. This is the last thing, and I'm the only one who knows it needs to be addressed. You're clear. Legally." Jay still doesn't open the box. Looking at it makes his eyes dry.

Marie takes a deep breath and tastes the years of nicotine that have infused the area. It's in the bricks of the building, the blacktop underfoot, and the wood of the table (which, strictly speaking, isn't a legal distance away from the door). It's even in a slow cloud around the table that has never been allowed to fully dissipate.

It has been a long while since Marie's last cigarette. She will buy one more pack shortly after this meeting with Jay and consume a quarter of it before the morning. The rest will be because of Katie— the transitions to college student, then face painter with a traveling renaissance faire, then tightrope walker, tarot card reader, and then back to college student to study psychology. The last cigarette will be lit when Katie defends her dissertation. Mother and daughter will share it.

Jay reaches for the box and pulls it toward himself. It's heavier than he remembered. The corners are still sharp. He pulls his new pocketknife from the appropriately named part of his pants. The tape at the sides holds strong before he slices through it. The top slides off once Jay leverages one of his fingers between it and the base.

The folded piece of paper isn't old enough to be yellowed, but its original white has mellowed somewhat into a mild eggshell. The creases are soft, and the edges flop a bit with weight. The woven strands of string sitting on top are more or less new looking. There is enough plastic in their construction that they won't degrade for longer than either Jay or Marie will be alive. It's not high-quality stuff, but it was the best the budget allowed for when Jay and Marie bought the supplies. The clasp bead is a solid wood, painted red.

"Is that . . . " Marie starts, pointing to the bracelet of blue and green. She wants to reach out and touch it but knows better. She doesn't realize it, but she gestures with the hand bearing her own bracelet.

"Yes." Jay's heart is not racing; it's trudging. Every beat is strong and intentional, but isolated from the two around it. In one beat, Jay can't remember how long it's been since the last one, nor does he have any confidence there will be a next one. "I became someone else that night. No, that's not right. I opened a door to another version of myself. I thought I knew what he was doing. I thought that was the person I needed to be in that moment. I thought that was a person for the countless other moments like it. A person I thought I wanted to become. A person who defended the powerless. Spoke for the voiceless. A person I was going to grow into when I got out. These are his things."

Jay grazes the bracelet's big, wooden bead, and it's like sticking his finger in an electrical outlet. His body violently twitches top to bottom, rocking the table out of place. He can't identify the flavor that his tongue is drowning in.

"Whoa whoa whoa . . . You ok?" Marie braces herself, not knowing how far the table is going to shift. Jay didn't see her move, but now she is in a new position.

"Sorry. It's . . . It's just . . . a lot." Jay's voice is only partially present. What's left is shaky and cracked.

"Okay. I guess I just . . . Warn me if you're going to flip the table."

"Sorry," he says again. His voice is more complete already.

Jay grabs the bracelet. Marie grabs the edge of the tabletop.

"I wore this that night. They needed a friend that night." He drops the bracelet into the coffee can ashtray. Marie says something in objection, but it doesn't register in Jay's mind. He can only hear the intentional pounding of his heart.

He takes the folded sheet of paper from the box. He doesn't feel the same jolt as the bracelet. This time, it's cold. His fingertips are nearly numb, and his knuckles ache like an old man's as he moves the drawing to the can.

"Wait, I don't get to see it?" Marie's voice comes in as if through an old walkie-talkie—a little static and miles away instead of inches.

"I don't want to look at him. June did it. It's how she saw me that night, in that moment. It's how I wanted to see myself. I can't. I shouldn't."

A car lays on its horn as it climbs the highway. It's heading north, into the city, in a hurry. The driver is returning to eyes that disapprove of where he has been and what they think he has been doing there. He thinks the sooner he returns, the less judgement he will receive. He, too, disapproves of where he has been and what he has been doing. He hasn't figured out how to stop, though. So, he continues into judgement, wishing he could escape himself but not wanting to prove the eyes correct.

Marie and Jay stare into the coffee can. Any wind that was wandering around earlier has settled for the night. Distantly, on the other side of the building, the door opens and the partially rusted bell above it dings again. Jay pulls his recently acquired matchbook out and sets it on the table.

"You saved them," Marie says. "This guy was going to keep smacking her around, and June and Jody were going to keep witnessing that if it weren't for you."

"True. I think I did the right thing." Jay hesitates to go on. He's gone back and forth on this point a number of times. "But I can't admit that. I can't accept that as a possibility for me. I have to close that door."

The cardboard cover of the matchbook is stiffer than Jay expected. Folding the flap back and tearing a match is clean and firm. This might be the last diner still ordering new matchbooks. It lights with a dry snap and burns hot when the other matches spark.

Jay takes a deep breath and drops the fire into the can. The drawing by a nine-year-old catches first and is gone quickly. The bedding of cigarette butts and random candy wrappers goes next, giving the fire more points of contact to stretch its legs in the column of orange. The bracelet—at least, the parts that contain plastic—scorch and melt. They aren't gone, but it would be a challenge to make it resemble a bracelet again. It's a molten hunk of black, stuck to the bottom of the can. The bead that holds the two ends together has been turned black on all but the topside. It's too thick to be destroyed completely, but its purpose and utility has been removed, so the object has changed.

The smoke emitting from the can is heavy and dark. It's not campfire smoke. That is, unless you are in the habit of throwing your plastic fork on the campfire after you're finished with your meal. You shouldn't do that. It makes the smoke toxic and thick. It's an unnatural and malicious smoke. It doesn't look airy enough to function like smoke. It's not wispy. It's almost as if you could reach out and grab a solid twist of the smoke. Not that you would. Every voice in your head tells you not to touch something so contaminated.

"*Uhum.*" Marie coughs. "You know, I quit years ago." She continues to hack a bit.

Jay doesn't let the smoke into his lungs. He hasn't let go of his breath since he lit the flame. The whole point is to not let it in. His eyes are watering. Irritated and dry, they are fighting the corruption as well. He must watch, though. Watch the door close.

When the fire begins to recede and there is nothing left but ash and smoking plastic, Jay finally closes his eyes. He can still see his smile. It was the same smile every morning when he dropped them off. It's a smile that thinks there is shared understanding. He thinks they are two warriors, and he accepts the warrior's defeat. He accepts the honor in his defeat. He can't conceive that this is simply the removal of a tumor. The parasite has been removed from its host, cleaning up a mess that had been let go for too long. There is no honor in this defeat. There was nothing honorable about that situation. Nothing about that night was honorable.

But still, the smile persists.

The fire doesn't last long. Jay and Marie need a shower to get rid of the smell, but that will be the last lingering, physical trace.

There will always be that smile.

Jay lets out a breath for the first time since the paper started to burn. With it comes something else. He's not sure what, but he knows it has left him. He feels lighter, looser even.

"So, what next?" Marie is afraid to ask, but she's never let that get in the way before.

"I'm hungry."

Marie laughs louder than she intended. His voice is clearer, higher pitched.

"Think they'll give me something to go? I have to be back at the reentry building in about thirty minutes."

The bell rings above the door as Marie escorts Jay back inside, where he orders two skillets—one with lots of meat, one with lots of vegetables—and a slice of peach cobbler. The waitress, Shannon, thinks she recognizes these two, but that happens a lot if you wait tables for a living. She smiles like they are regulars and places the order. Marie and Jay watch the fish tank while they wait. There are no fish in it.

"You think they ran out of the Friday special and had to fry up flipper?"

"I've heard of stranger things." Jay flashes back to the meals they would be served in lockdowns. Sometimes, not much more than a peanut butter sandwich was passed through the bars. The cell door didn't open until the cause of the lockdown was resolved. Hours, days, some stretched beyond that. A fried goldfish might have been just the thing to hit the spot after a while.

Marie gives Jay a ride home. He doesn't have a car. They take a selfie so Marie can show Katie when she gets back. Jay waves at Spencer, waiting at the front door, with three minutes to spare.

Out behind The Dining Car, a man in a suit that is plain enough to not be noticed sits at the picnic table. His lapel pin—a simple geometric pattern that almost looks like it's staring at you—flashes in the floodlight above the back exit. The air is still laced with the toxic fumes of melting plastic. There is something else that the man can't identify. The man pulls out an unmarked box, about the size of a shoe box, and fills it with the contents of the coffee can. The bit of plastic is fused to the bottom, so he puts the can in the box too. With a little force, it fits well enough. He puts the pieces to the candy-cane-covered box in the larger box and wishes he would have known a box would be provided on this one. He ties the package with twine and makes a few marks on the lid that look like the result of an angry cat attack. The bead inside the box rattles against the can the whole way to the car.

For Willow

Ringo: Plush Companion

The raccoon continued on. The hill was longer than it had appeared at first, but Ringo only knew to head in that direction, not for how long. Basic navigation was a standard feature for any Plush Companion. Children were so often not where they were supposed to be. The raccoon hadn't been able to connect to the system since the mountains though, so all that was functioning was the compass. David had said that if they were ever separated or lost, they could always find each other at home. As near as Ringo could tell, home should be in this direction, so that was the line he would follow.

The sun had crept out from behind the horizon and taken all of thirty minutes to dry Ringo's fur. It was matted in odd clumps and thick with debris from the trail, but it was dry. Ringo had made a point of getting on all fours to allow the most surface area to face the sun. It also made the Plush Companion less vulnerable to the wind. Looking toward the cloudless sky and nothing taller than himself to offer shade, Ringo suspected dryness would be a plentiful resource. It was a welcome change of pace.

The wind helped. Of course, wind is how the fur had gotten so sandy and full of debris in the first place, but it was a fair trade-off for dry fur.

The matting had been a long time coming. Many nights nestled between David's arm and chest had turned the raccoon's once fluffy fur into something closer to flexible armor. Small clusters of fuzz had locked in David's scent, which was now being replaced bit by bit. There were new scents, scents the raccoon had not encountered before, and scents that were only *similar* to what Ringo knew. Something resembling a campfire was chief among the new pockets of aroma. Deep under it, however, if the raccoon focused, David's scent was still there.

Ringo continued on. There wasn't much to see. Nothing that triggered anything in Ringo's memory, anyway. All Ringo could do was keep walking. Comfort and protection could not be achieved without a child. The primary task, therefore, became surviving long enough to serve a child again. Ideally, it would be David, the child Ringo had been assigned to. With the sun shining bright and filling the small sensors running through the faux fur covering Ringo's body, there wasn't likely to be a need to dip into energy reserves until the mission of the moment was completed.

Ringo had started its current part of the journey staring into the sun. Over the course of the day, the sun had traced a contrary path to Ringo, sliding to be overhead, and then slipping to shine on the raccoon's back. The sun had been about the only thing that had changed in the landscape. The sun, the occasional tumbleweed, and the flat horizon were all the raccoon had to go on until near evening. That's when the first sign of civilization popped up.

Ringo made it to a road about the time the sun was firing as hot as it could, getting rid of its last bits of energy before hiding away for the night. The splendid diversity in color and texture that sunsets are known for had largely concluded its task for the evening, leaving a monochromatic glow that would last for longer than it seemed like it should. The light directed Ringo's attention to a squat building that had seen better days.

Or maybe not. Maybe the building was exactly as it was meant to be. The window frames glowed with the remaining sun, but inside the dried-out building, there was only gloom. An odd orientation of architecture. The exterior walls were little more than that. They held the roof up, protected the inside from the elements (mostly), and one side seemed designated for holding posters for entertainment that would not interest Ringo or David. Not exactly an inviting presentation, but it occurred to Ringo that maybe these kinds of buildings attracted people in other ways. Not everything catered to the attention of a seven-year-old.

The object in the doorframe only covered the middle third of the space. It wasn't a saloon door like in cowboy stories that Ringo had read to David. The two bits of wood swung freely in and out on saloon hinges, but they weren't the flourished panels with sweeping trim making the two doors appear as one. These were simply two doors, with the top and bottom sawed off in an efficient, splintery line below and above what remained of the original. *Benny's* was burned into the lefthand door, and *Bar* on the right.

The raccoon waddled through the doorway, paying no attention to the door whose bottom edge stopped inches overhead. Ringo's tail dragged behind, clearing a brushed path in the dirt, dust, and other assorted detritus that had collected since the last time it had been swept (a day closer to the day the floor had been poured than the day the raccoon walked across it). Ringo stood up on its rear paws and continued toward the first human it noticed.

The bartender watched the small figure, silhouetted in the sinking sun, as it followed its shadow to the edge of the bar. It moved slowly, much more slowly than any he had seen before. Of course, most of his examples were the creatures he'd chased out of the dumpster at night. Benny grabbed the baseball bat he kept under the bar and put a foot up on a crate, preparing to leap over the bar and deal with the intruder. The two other patrons in the bar hadn't noticed the raccoon yet, and hopefully Benny could have it outside before they did.

There was something about the figure that made Benny pause mid-leap. This creature did not seem frightened, agitated, or in any significant way energized. Benny had never encountered a raccoon that *wasn't* agitated. It was certainly dirty enough to be a raccoon, but there was something off about its calm, straight path across the floor. Again, Benny had never known a raccoon to travel in a straight line. He had seen a handful walk on their rear paws, but never for such a sustained amount of time. The raccoon made for the bartender and disappeared behind where Benny could not see it through the bar. Then there was a soft shuffling of wooden legs against the well-worn floor, and a raccoon head popped up over the metal guard.

Once closer, and under what served for good lighting in a place like this, the bartender could see the uneven condition of the creature's fur. Matted. Speckled with dirt. A twig or two. More notably, on the raccoon's left shoulder, under its chin and up that side of its face, the fur was deeply burned, some completely gone, leaving the skin exposed. It was blotchy, black, and explained what the odd smell was.

Not knowing what else to do (and having little training in the care of wild animals), the tender grabbed the shallowest dish he had, filled it with water, and placed it in front of the raccoon. With a narrow paw, the creature moved the dish to the side.

"Something stronger?" the tender asked.

The raccoon opened its mouth with some effort, but all that came out was a slow clicking sound like the bent tip of a fan hitting its housing. To be sure, in a long list of sounds the bartender had not expected to hear from a raccoon in response to his question, this was near the top.

The raccoon closed its mouth and considered the tender for a moment. Then its right eye began to glow light blue. From the now radiating orb, a projection was cast on the bar's surface. In focused light, *RINGO* appeared. The raccoon then pointed at itself. The motion was slow and had a shakiness to it.

"Benny," the bartender replied, pointing to himself. It then occurred to Benny that he was talking with a mechanical raccoon, and he was grateful there weren't more people in the bar. Then again, it probably wouldn't be the oddest thing seen in the bar that night.

The name floating above the counter broke apart and began to reassemble, line by line, into the head of a small boy.

Must be one of those plush companions, Benny thought. He knew bits and pieces from what news played on the screens around him in between sporting events. They were stuffed animals like there had always been, but robotic and programmed to protect the kids somehow. The way Benny understood it, there was some very specific programming that kept these machines focused on the child's safety. They could talk, play, and keep the child safe. One more everyday task given over to the robots.

Benny didn't have kids of his own and had no plans in that area. Babysitting his patrons was more than enough for him.

The thing must belong to the boy he's showing. These things were supposed to be pretty dedicated and rarely left their kid's side. The burns and weird voice took on a more ominous feel for Benny. The whole point of these companions was that they protected the kids. They were only small fluff balls with some advanced wiring, though. What happened when the kid got in over his head?

To the bartender, the face hovering over the sticky bar was little more than simply a boy's face. His line of work didn't often require that he interact with anyone that age. Ten, if he had to guess, but he wouldn't be surprised if he were off by five in either direction. On the rare occasion when someone who looked like that did come across his vision, it was the first step in getting them off the premises. Still, he hoped the kid was all right.

The projection collapsed. The raccoon waited for eye contact and then lifted its paws in a shrug.

It took a moment for Benny to realize that the creature's oddly human gesture was asking a question.

"Oh, um no. I don't know the kid. This isn't really the place for kids anyway." And then curiosity got the better of Benny. "Are you trying to get back to your boy?"

The raccoon bobbed its head up and down.

"Well, I wish I could help you, but like I say, we don't get many kids around here. Even if we did, I'm not sure I'd be able to recognize any of them. Do you know where the boy lives?"

Again, the robotic ball of fluff's eye began to glow, and the word RESTRICTED appeared above the bar. Beneath, scrolling text began to explain that any personal information about the child to whom this Plush Companion was assigned was protected under its primary guideline, to protect the child.

It took the bartender a minute to get through it all, his lips instinctively following along.

"Oh, but you do *know* where he lives, right? You don't have to tell me, but if I told you where you are now, you could use GPS or whatever and find your way back? Hold on a sec."

The bartender stepped into a back room and returned with an atlas. He unfolded it on the bar and pulled a pencil from the apron around his waist. "We're about here," he said, making a circle next to a line that was labeled 93. He put the pencil down. "Does that help?"

Ringo attempted to compare the map with his system, but again, there was a problem. *CONNECTIVITY ISSUES* hung over the map in glowing blue. Underneath, a scrolling list of technical readouts passed, none of which Benny could follow.

Both figures hung their heads.

"Bummer. Although, I might know somebody who can help out with that, or at least understand what the problem is. If you can wait a bit, I can give him a call. He's probably on his way already. It's euchre night."

Once again, Ringo was left on his stool as the bartender disappeared. It didn't know what to do in the current situation. There wasn't a directive that required any immediate action. Ringo could not protect its child, because Ringo could not locate the child. Ringo was attempting to return, but that required repairs if it was to be an expedient and successful journey. Protection required return, return required repair, and repair required waiting. Ringo waited, hoping the malfunctions didn't worsen.

Ringo again looked to the map and the mark of the current location. There was a compass rose in the corner. Ringo compared to the direction it had been following to get to the current position. The raccoon stretched a paw and pointed to the spot Benny had indicated. He dragged a digit along the line of the past few days— past the pond, beyond the flat sand and its wind, past the tree and Tiger, and ending where Ringo had started after the crash.

Ringo remembered David's face. David's parents had been there too. They were on a helicopter tour of the mountains. It was windy and loud. They hadn't been expecting the storm. There was a flash and then a louder loudness. The faces of the other three tightened, and Ringo could feel David's heart beating faster. Ringo's data log then said *REPAIR*. The vehicle began to spin and fall. Ringo left David's lap and climbed out onto the exterior of the helicopter. Ringo's claws weren't made for metal or high winds, but they managed well enough. Hopefully, Ringo could get back inside before too much water collected in its fur. The companion's internal systems were protected enough from the water, but Ringo's fur would soak it up like a sponge. The Plush Companion raccoon model joints had been stress tested with dry fur but were known to fail under increased water weight. Ringo's self-preservation was aware of this design flaw. It didn't usually come up though.

There was fire and smoke coming from the main rotor. Ringo didn't know how to fix it, but the internet did. Ringo smothered the fire, igniting himself in the process. It wasn't a smooth ride, but Ringo held tight. Ringo tightened or reattached what could be tightened or reattached. It wouldn't be perfect, but it would get them to safety. The mechanics stabilized, the dome bucked, and Ringo's claws failed in a situation they were not made for.

The helicopter was flying straight as Ringo fell farther from it. David would be scared but safe. Ringo saw the tops of trees, the internal log noted several systems requiring attention, and then sensory data stopped for an unknown amount of time.

Ringo clutched the pencil that Benny had left and sketched a small tongue of fire on the spot. Nearby, Ringo drew a pine tree. That is where Ringo's memory picked up again.

Ringo was reactivated by a cry. The raccoon dug out of the damp mound of dirt and pursued the cry's source. It didn't take long.

The cry was coming from a child about David's size. She was not in danger, but she was in distress. Her eyes were red, and tears quickly flooded her cheeks. She looked frantically around her but always returned to the tree she was standing under.

"Tiger, please come down. Be a good kitty!" she shouted up the tree. Ringo looked and saw a fluffy, cream-colored cat clutching a branch nearly six meters up the trunk. The cat's eyes were as distressed as the girl's, but that yellow dot refused to move.

"Tiger, please. We have to get home. I know the storm was scary, but we have to get home. I can't leave you here." The girl didn't notice as Ringo approached.

"Okay, Tiger. I'm . . . I'm coming up for you." Her face told Ringo she knew it was a bad idea. It was an unsafe idea. Ringo agreed. She was going to try anyway.

Ringo scampered between the girl and the tree. Ringo extended its gripping claws. They weren't the same claws as a biological raccoon, but they were much better suited for tree bark than the outside of a helicopter.

Ringo noticed two things on the way up to Tiger. First, the hooks in Ringo's paws were damaged, and one was completely missing. Whether it had been lost during the repair or as part of the fall, Ringo didn't know. Also, Tiger was not relieved to see a raccoon crawling toward him.

Ringo attempted to let out a soft cat purr that approximated the neighbor's cat back home. Maybe if Tiger thought Ringo was one of its own kind, the rescue attempt would go more smoothly. It did not work as planned. Instead of replicating the friendly vibrations of a seven-year-old striped cat named Bailey, Ringo let out a halting bit of static, causing Tiger to fumble its grip and nearly fall from the limb.

"No! You stay away," the girl shouted at Ringo. For a moment, Ringo thought to obey. If Ringo stopped, though, the girl would climb and put herself in danger. Ringo had to act quickly so that the girl knew Ringo meant no harm.

Ringo launched at Tiger with hydraulic legs far more powerful than a normal raccoon. The branch broke from the force of Ringo's impact, sending Tiger and Ringo into a freefall. Ringo made every effort to cocoon Tiger as the two fell, which Tiger was not pleased with.

Ringo's fur and soft underbelly—specifically designed for comfortable snuggling—also worked to cushion much of the impact of the fall. Ringo released Tiger, and the cat jumped high enough that it nearly reached the level it had just fallen from. Tiger darted to the girl upon landing.

"Oh, Tiger, I was so worried. Let's get you home." The girl then looked at Ringo. Fear and desperation replaced whatever relief she felt at Tiger's return. "Get away. You nearly killed Tiger. Just get out of here!"

The girl then ran away, down the hill, leaving Ringo alone. Ringo tried to call out, but again, nothing but static came out. The girl was as safe as she would allow for. Ringo could follow and ask for help in finding David, but it was clear the raccoon was not welcome.

Ringo continued along the map. The next thing it drew was wind.

It wasn't the desert. Ringo had seen pictures of the desert. The desert had hills of sand called dunes. Instead, flat, dry dirt stretched as far as Ringo could see, and then some. There was sand and wind but no dunes.

The wind blew and never weakened. Populations of sand migrated with its flow, never amounting to more than a dusting upon the cracked ground. The sun continued to bake the ground, taking any moisture there was until it was suddenly gone behind the horizon. The stars revealed themselves, and the wind kept blowing. Maybe that's how the stars moved, Ringo thought, like the sand, riding the whim of the wind.

"Maria," flashed in Ringo's mind. It was from the music file and had been often requested by David's father. He had downloaded the file onto Ringo for easy access. When David was younger, there had been a ten-day period during which he wouldn't sleep without hearing that song. Why the music section of Ringo's system was better protected than navigation was a question for the engineers.

The "Maria" file had been called up now through association with the wind. Ringo's sensors were programmed to collect data from the environment and check that data against past activity. Ringo had never been in this amount of wind or sand, but the description matched the song. The sensors recognized the environment as "Maria." This was "the West," "the frontier" as David's father had described it in cowboy stories before bed. It was vast, dry, and beautiful—a challenging terrain that would reveal the hero or villain at the core of any gunslinger. David had always liked those stories, almost as much as his dad had liked telling them while Ringo would softly play "They Call the Wind Maria," in the background. Ringo began to play the song called "Maria" to the stars and sand carried on the wind called "Maria." Ringo could see David's calm, sleeping face.

Ringo was protected enough from the sand, but at slightly over thirteen kilos and due to leg joints that had seen better days, Ringo was at Maria's mercy. The wind would wail before a big gust, and Ringo would tunnel into the dirt and wait. When the wind wasn't at full strength, Ringo would extend its claws, still weary of the missing one, grip the flaky dirt, and make progress at whatever speed Maria permitted.

Ringo followed the line of events created on the map and stopped at a strip of blue. Ringo knew where the blue was. Ringo had left Maria and found a rocky place filled with boulders twice Ringo's size. Ringo had scampered up and down the rocks, following the same direction as much as possible, when the sound of splashing came over the next row of stones. Ringo climbed on top of a rock and saw a boy playing in a hot spring with his dog. There was steam coming off the water in the early morning chill. The child was laughing.

The boy and the dog were alone. The boy was safe. Up a gravel path, Ringo saw the tip of a chimney. *The boy's home*, Ringo concluded. It was the only built structure that Ringo could see.

Ringo found a raccoon-sized divot in a boulder and rested. After how the girl had reacted, Ringo didn't want to frighten the child, so stealth became the preferred state. It wasn't difficult to maintain, given that the child was making plenty of distracting noises on his own. Ringo would continue before long. For the moment, however, the child and the dog were having fun, and Ringo's hydraulics could use the break.

A few shakes, and Ringo's fur sprayed sand everywhere. It was tempting to wash in the spring, but not knowing how long the journey to David would be, the water was too dangerous in this current circumstance. Ringo could splash some water through the more knotted bits, though. Being careful to remain quiet and hidden, the raccoon eased down to the water's edge.

Ringo saw the raccoon reflected in the water and took a moment to process the image. The bottom left quadrant of its face was devoid of fur, showing the charred pseudo skin and the occasional twinkles of metal poking through. Other patches of fur were blackened or frozen in an unnaturally windswept arc. Dirt, twigs, sand, and all manner of debris had begun to collect in what remained of Ringo's fur, making it look more natural than the animal Ringo was built to emulate.

Would David recognize Ringo upon return? Would David want Ringo back in this state? The damage would not be easily repaired. Would David's parents repair or replace Ringo?

No matter. Ringo must return to be of service to David. Fulfillment of any of the rules—protection, obedience, or self-preservation—required return first. Ringo dipped its paws into the water and began to separate fur from other.

It wasn't clear when the splashing changed, but by the time the sound broke through Ringo's cleaning, action was required. The boy was struggling. It was difficult to tell with children sometimes. Excited and scared often looked the same to Ringo. Yet, even through the erupting plumes of water, this time it was clear. The boy was scared. The boy was in danger. Ringo had purpose.

"Help! Star! Mom! Dad! Help!" The child repeated his calls between descents into the water. The dog was barking as well, unsure how it could help. There were people close by that could help. At least, the boy thought so. The chimney had seemed relatively close at first. Ringo was closer.

As the boy flailed, frantically calling out, one of his arms landed on a wet ball of fur. "Ah!" he screamed. Ringo tried to squeeze under the boy's arm to function as a floatation device, but arms and waves kept getting in the way. One descending arm sent Ringo under the water, where the problem revealed itself. The boy was kicking, trying to propel himself away from the bottom, but only with one leg. The other foot had become trapped under a boulder.

If the boy would remain calm, the water would not be over his head. Even Ringo knew that a trapped child remaining calm was unlikely enough to be considered an impossibility. The boy would tire soon and fall beneath the water level permanently.

Ringo dove into the froth, avoiding the darting foot and pebbles it was kicking up. The rock was no bigger than Ringo, but it would be far too heavy for a panicky boy underwater. The boy couldn't be pulled out for fear of injuring the foot, so moving the rock became the goal. Ringo braced against another boulder and wriggled tiny claws around the base of the problematic one. Ringo pushed and rotated slowly, sliding the rock away, which allowed the boy to kick free.

The kick was more powerful than Ringo had anticipated, and the raccoon was pushed deeper into the water, narrowly avoiding the recently freed rock. Ringo began to swim back but found that every stroke required more energy than the last. The weight of its now-drenched fur, combined with an already compromised system, made Ringo's survival probability minimal.

Self-preservation was a law, though, so Ringo paddled again. Paw over paw, every effort brought Ringo closer to a survival that was nearly impossible. The raccoon managed to get to the surface, but merely staying there was taxing. Ringo still had to fight to the shoreline. Ringo's internal system continuously ran the calculations, indicating that the probability of survival was dropping faster than Ringo could swim. Ringo did not see a variable that would prevent drowning, but the programs maintained the swimming motion.

Ringo kept moving and tried to keep the meniscus below the horizon for as long as possible.

Something sharp but gentle grabbed Ringo, and the water started to fall away. Ringo was bounced up and down in the grip before being dropped on the gravel shore. The dog looked down at Ringo, slobber and spring water dripping from its muzzle. Golden-red fur exploded in front of Ringo as the dog shook.

"Star, you got him! Good girl." The boy started petting the dog. Then the boy's face changed to concern. "He doesn't look too good. It doesn't look like he's breathing. Poor guy."

The boy grabbed a towel and shoes. His foot looked bruised, maybe scraped, but not permanently damaged. Ringo tried to rise, but the weight was too much.

Star prodded Ringo with her nose. Ringo's arm groaned under the water weight, but it managed to find Star and give her a weak pat on the snout. Star gave a bark in response.

"C'mon, girl. Let's get mom. She'll know what to do." Then he turned to Ringo, the wet, dirty, partially burnt lump of fur slumped on the rocks. "We'll be right back. Mom is really good with animals."

Star gave a last look at Ringo before following the boy away from the spring.

The raccoon stayed sprawled on the rocks, a soaked lump. The boy had his dog. The boy was protected. The boy was safe. Ringo's priority once again turned to survival and return. The signal was sent to Ringo's limbs to move, but nothing happened. The raccoon tried again, but the only response Ringo received was strain warnings going off in his head. Most of those were garbled and incomplete renderings of the code that should have been there.

Maybe some water had gotten into Ringo's system. Maybe Maria had snuck more sand into the Plush Companion's system than had originally been assessed. Or maybe a raccoon-sized robot couldn't survive an explosion and fall from a helicopter and walk away with its system still intact. Maybe Ringo's directive to return didn't take into account how ill-equipped the little raccoon was for such a mission.

Star and the boy weren't coming back. The boy's parents would see his wound and attend to him first. If the mostly drowned raccoon was real and not something the boy had made up, it was probably dead by now anyway. Ringo was alone.

Ringo stared at the clouds. The midmorning sun was there but offered little more than highlights to the rounded puffs of silver in the sky. Ringo's memory files stumbled onto an experience of cloud gazing with David. Ringo was programmed with enough abstract recognition to pick out bunny rabbits and flowers in the sky. David always saw dragons, though. Ringo stared at the clouds and tried to see anything in the formations. All the raccoon could see was David's face, floating away.

Ringo didn't want to, but the programming required return. Ringo once again signaled its limbs to move. They did. Small, twitchy movements at first, but gradually, the companion's claws flexed, and then paws and legs, all the way up to the shoulder sockets. The strain warnings still came, they were but less urgent. Maybe the sun was shining warmer than Ringo had realized. Ringo didn't want to move. Ringo needed to move.

Ringo pushed up on quivering paws and, stopping only to ring out its tail, searched for the path home again.

Ringo looked at the penciled-in splash now on the map. The water had been that morning. Then came the trudge that ended here, at this circle on the map. *Benny's Bar.*

"Ash is on his way," Benny declared, returning from the back room. "He says he should be able to clean you up. We'll get you on your way in no time." His eyes fell upon the map. "Looks like some of it's coming back already."

VISUAL RECORD SLIDES hung over the bar in Ringo's glowing blue script. Ringo then pointed to the markers on the map, and the words shifted to a slideshow of images the camera had captured. It was programmed to take a photo through Ringo's eyes every thirty seconds. It wasn't everything since the fall, because some files had been corrupted, but it was what Ringo could offer. It made for a stranger tale than Benny was expecting.

"Huh. Well, Ash will put you together again." Benny gave Ringo a soft pat on the shoulder and went about his bartender duties. Benny took orders, served what was asked, and made a space for enjoyment. According to the sign above the bar mirror, Benny also took responsibility to protect the place from any "brawlin'" that might take place.

People came in. Fewer left. The bigger the group that entered, the shorter their time at the bar. Ringo didn't know what to make of that paradigm.

The raccoon sat there, bottom paws barely reaching the edge of the stool, front paws resting on the lip of the bar. The fine lenses that served as its eyes did not move. Ringo stared ahead at the smudgy mirror and the raccoon it showed. It hadn't gotten much worse than the face in the spring water, but it hadn't gotten any better, either.

"This him?" came a high-pitched voice from behind the bar. Apparently, there was a back entrance for special customers. Next to Benny stood a figure that was more beard than anything else. Thin skin and a baggy set of overalls supported a tangle of brown and gray wires, broken up only by a pair of sunglasses where eyes should've been.

"Yep. This is Ringo."

"And payment for the part?"

"I'll waive your entry fee."

The talking beard named Ash dropped a tacklebox on the bar and opened its compartments. Screws, washers, bits of wire in a variety of gauges, and the implements to manipulate them were precisely assigned to their own trays.

A second tackle box dropped. This one was newer than the first, less scuffed and beaten. It was smaller but almost as heavy, based on the sound it made against the bar. There was a rainbow sticker smiling at Ringo on the left side.

"He reminds me of Champ," said a soft, clear voice from behind the rainbow box. Ringo stood up on the stool and peered over the bar. A girl in a long-sleeved shirt and overalls to match Ash looked back. Her hair was woven around her head, achieving the practicality of keeping it out of her face in the most intricate of methods. She wasn't smiling, but Ringo could still see that she was happy. There was a dilation in the eyes that meant she was excited. David had had that reaction when his parents first presented Ringo.

"What do you think, Emily?" Ash asked.

"Your beard has been dirtier."

"You're not wrong."

"If we fix it, the kid it serves will be happy."

"Right you are," Ash said with a laugh.

"Then we should help." She pulled a box over to stand on and opened her own tackle box. Inside, Ringo saw a picture of Emily, younger than she was now. She was holding a unicorn model Plush Companion.

"All right, Ringo, if you waddle onto the counter, Emily and me'll get you on your way."

Ringo got into position and felt Ash trip the switch hidden along Ringo's right hip. This allowed port access for maintenance. Ringo's system would tell Ash what was wrong and what could be fixed.

While Ash typed and tweaked at the electronic end of the situation, Emily grabbed a comb and a cup of water. She ran the wet comb in short swipes through Ringo's fur, careful to not force any tangles. She pulled out anything too big for the comb, including several twigs, some larger pebbles, and a couple clumps of fur that had fused together (but weren't entirely burned up). A spider had taken up residence in Ringo's tail. Emily didn't flinch when it scampered out. She simply cupped it in her hands and walked it outside.

After the comb, Emily rubbed some floral scented lotion into Ringo's fur. "This should loosen some of the matted parts," she told Ringo.

"Pseudo for the gaps in the skin?"

Ash looked up from the open door to Ringo's central processor. "Sure. That should hold long enough. Keep out anything that might undo our work. It's lucky more sand didn't find its way into the system."

The two kept working. A small hose was used both inside and outside. Ash spent time in several different systems, reprogramming, cleaning, and replacing what he could. Ringo was still missing patches of fur, but what remained looked much better. It was lighter, anyway. Emily gave Ringo a pat and packed up her box. "They aren't all as lucky as you, Ringo. Take care of your kid."

Ringo thought back to the picture inside of Emily's box. There were only a few reasons why the companion wouldn't still be with

Emily, and none of them were good. Ringo thought about the journey so far to get back to David. What if it all came to nothing? What if Ringo couldn't return? Like in the spring, Ringo's programming would keep pushing forward, but that didn't guarantee success. Like in the spring, there might come a time when Ringo couldn't fulfill the companion programming.

And then it came back. Ash was working in Ringo's chest cavity when suddenly Ringo knew where they were. More importantly, Ringo knew how David's home connected to where they were. Ringo had access to the system again.

"That must have done it," Ash said as Ringo stood upright. "If you hold on a second, we can close you up."

Ringo looked to the door but settled back down on the counter. Return was possible and the priority again, but Ash wanted Ringo to wait. The system indicated it would be a couple more days of travel anyway. Best to be sure the repair work would hold.

Ash secured Ringo's inner workings back together and unplugged. Ringo stood up once again and hopped down onto the stool, feeling the new lightness throughout its body. Ringo hesitated and turned to the two mechanics. "Thank you," Ringo said. It wasn't the usual voice that Ringo spoke with. There was static, and it was sharper by a quarter step, but Ringo had a voice again.

"Don't mention it," Ash replied. "We all serve in our way. Now get back to your kid."

"Wait. Wait." Benny hustled over from the other end of the bar. He tied a business card around Ringo's neck. "A souvenir."

"Thank you, Benny."

"He talks now? Nice work, you two."

"I couldn't do anything about the memory files, but it can talk and should be able to find its way now. If it stays away from sand and water, that is. Hear me, Ringo?"

"Yes, Ash," Ringo croaked.

"Cleaned out some of the joints. Emily did a great job on the covering too. Now it's in those little raccoon paws o' yours."

The four faces looked at each other. Ringo hopped back onto the counter, walked toward Emily, and gave her a hug. Ringo felt Emily relax into the embrace. "We all serve in our way," Ringo said to the girl.

Ringo released and scurried to the door. The sun was long gone, but Ringo's solar batteries had enough reserve as long as the pace wasn't too quick. The stars would be enough for Ringo to find the way. According to the map in the system, David was three states away, with a few mountains and lots of farmland in between. Ringo could return to its purpose. Ringo could be David's companion again.

The raccoon continued on.

For Justin

Animus

◢◢Very good, Martin. Look, he's coming 'round already."

Nathan Clarke felt hungover. The kind of hungover with dry scratchiness inside and outside of his body, the need for every light within two miles to be extinguished, and something akin to nearly hardened glue swimming around where his brain should be. That was all unfortunately familiar to some degree. What made this one notable was that he couldn't remember what he had done to earn this caliber of a biological "I told you so."

All the light in the room seemed to have coalesced into one bright orb directly above him. There might have been someone between him and the light, but it was too glaring to make out any detail. Sounds were echoey and difficult to focus on. There had been a voice just now—a clear voice with annoyingly precise diction—but Nathan couldn't guarantee where it had come from or even if he hadn't simply imagined it. It wouldn't be the first time he'd heard echoes of the night before. Granted, the echoes were usually less articulate. He tried to move his limbs and was met with such resistance that he concluded he had been dipped in honey at some point. Cold honey.

"Welcome back," said the precise voice. It belonged to a long, blurry shape, probably a woman based on the pitch, who was leaning over Nathan. "Jonathan Clarke, correct?"

"Yes," Nathan's brain began automatically. It was the start of a long and well-rehearsed introduction, in which Nathan explained that he actually went by Nathan because Jonathan was too boring, and Jon was even worse. It was how Nathan had introduced himself to everybody he'd met since he was thirteen, and it was a speech he could give in his sleep now, more than a decade later. He felt the familiar signal pass from his brain to his jaw, which prepared his teeth to form the words, but his lips would not separate.

"Take your time," said the woman, gradually coming into focus. Her hair was pulled back, and her Kelly-green coat had a high collar that came up almost to her even higher cheekbones. The word "vampire" flashed across Nathan's mind. "Your fine motor control might be a bit sluggish coming back. You're also probably a bit dehydrated, so that won't help. Anyway, your tag says you're Jonathan. It's good practice to check, though."

"Tig?" The misshapen word clicked out of his mouth. Nathan turned his head, heard popping along his neck, and had to close his eyes again from the dizziness.

He didn't see any tag, but the room was becoming clearer. Lots of metal, less light except for the one right above his face. There was a desk on the far wall, next to the door. A wall to the side had a large display screen, although it was turned off at the moment. There was a series of square drawers coming from the wall to his left. He had seen enough procedurals to put the context clues together. There was a sheet covering him up to mid-chest. That was the only fabric on him.

"I'm dead." It was the first intelligible phrase he had managed, but the words still felt clunky tumbling over Nathan's dried out tongue. He needed a drink. Water would probably be all he was offered, but he would need something stronger before long.

"Yes. Well, you were," said the maybe-vampire. "And you will be again. I've re-enlivened you in the hopes that you can tell me how you died the first time. I, along with my partner, Martin, am investigating the specifics of your rather unique demise, hoping to intervene before it happens to someone else."

Nathan's mind attempted to process several things, but nothing took any clarity. "You . . . re-en . . . *what-ed* me?"

"What? Oh, yes, sorry. *Re-enlivened.* So, magic is real, and sometimes it's employed for more than love spells and card tricks. Sometimes, magic is the device by which crime is inflicted on our society." She paused and straightened her spine. "In those cases, the authorities contact me."

"Or Nelson," chimed a second, smaller form standing next to the first. Presumably, this was Martin.

"Yes, or Nelson." She gave a sharp glance and eye roll combination. "Bernadette Stephens, Mystic and Law Enforcement Liaison." She bowed her head and paused. "Yesterday afternoon, you were killed in what evidence suggests was a mystic manor. So, tell me, what do you remember about dying?"

"I don't . . . It was dark . . . " The memories came, but they were like the answers to a test he had studied for in seventh grade. Distant and not entirely there. Nathan didn't feel anything about them. They were just bits of information that hadn't gotten lost, connected as reactions to prompts. Nothing he actively remembered. "It was a loading bay, um . . . off an alleyway. Behind the coffee shop."

The man beside Bernadette began scribbling in his notebook like a reporter from a black and white. He was the round and mustachioed Hardy to Bernadette's statuesque and slight Laurel. He carried his shape well, though, and had eyes on the moment.

"Wait. Magic?"

Bernadette sighed. "Yes. It's more common than you know and usually less spectacular, trust me. But it is a unique skillset and one not often responsive to the more brutish and pedestrian tactics of most law enforcement. Now, I know I told you to take your time, but we actually do have a bit of a deadline. So, let's be simple. What's the last thing you remember?"

"Cold. I felt cold."

"Yes, that's probably from the blood loss."

"What?"

"Blood loss," Martin offered. "Whoever this person was, they slit your throat and drained your blood. Presumably for the location spell, based on the sigils around where your body was found."

"Sigils . . . " Nathan brought a hand to his neck and found a bumpy texture he had not been expecting. It started near the middle and ran across the right side of his neck. It wasn't tender, but it was tight. He could feel thread and knew it was the series of stitches holding him shut. Once again, too many procedural crime shows filled in a lot of the blanks.

Bernadette put a hand on her partner's shoulder. "Drawn around you. That's why this person needed the blood. It was actually a very simple spell, but there are several factors that may be of interest. Well, three factors to be specific. First, the strokes were crude, indicating a novice. In other words, someone new to the discipline who hasn't developed the elegant muscle control. Second, it shouldn't have required *all* of your blood, especially considering that it was fresh. I, myself, have achieved similar spells with less than a cup of the medium. This, too, indicates a novice." A thought slowed her momentum, and she turned to Martin, the notetaker. "Or possibly someone unconcerned with leaving a trail or a body count. Make a note of that, Martin. We may have been thinking of this all wrong. That still says novice to me, though. Why waste such a valuable resource?"

She glanced over at what Martin had written, conferred, and looked back to Nathan. Nathan looked back, not sure of anything he had just heard—let alone what it meant.

"The third factor?"

Bernadette seemed to jolt to life like someone had just flipped the switch on a fan. "Third, and this is the curious part, is that the writer crafted a spell without specifying what it was trying to locate. They could direct the spell en route, as it were, without a map. This indicates a considerable source of power and control. Far more than I would expect from someone with such sloppy strokes and sense of resource conservation."

Martin nudged Bernadette and offered his watch.

She nodded. "I'm sorry. I'm sure you have many questions, but we only have a few more minutes before the charm preventing us from being disturbed fades. Attention is so difficult to command. Away or to something. So, please, anything you can remember before or after your throat was opened would be potentially useful in finding who did this to you."

Both figures stared at Nathan, eyes wide, pen poised in Martin's case. Again, Nathan's brain was thick. His throat didn't seem eager to produce anything the brain came up with anyway.

"Voices," Nathan croaked out. "Uh, a different voice from the guy that attacked me."

"Good. Was there anything distinct about it? Accent, word choice, a deep and inexplicable pit in your stomach when it was intoned? Anything like that?"

"It . . . it was a strong voice? Commanding. But quiet. I'm not sure I was supposed to know he was there. I never saw the second guy. He was there, though. The guy that attacked . . . um, killed me . . . He was talking to someone, and it wasn't me."

Bernadette moved closer, along the side of the gurney. She traced the line across Nathan's neck. It was only then that he realized the line itched like that time he'd gotten into the poison ivy at summer camp. "The man who killed you," Bernadette began. "Was he wearing any jewelry? Bracelet, ring, even so much as one of those pandering flag pins?"

"He had a kind of goth necklace. Uh, choker style, with a crystal or stone of some sort in the middle. Purple, whatever you call purple crystals."

"Amethyst, seems most likely."

"What?"

Martin thrust his notebook at Nathan. "Draw it."

Nathan sat up slowly and took the pad and pen. The dizziness came again but receded quickly. He tried to translate his foggy memory into a serviceable sketch. It was like his fingers were frozen. They still functioned, but like everything else so far, they were slower and heavier than he remembered. They were his, although maybe a shade or two paler. All the same spots and cracks. The scar on his left index finger from an errant nickel during a game of "bloody knuckles" was still there.

"I think, something . . . like this." Nathan returned the pen and paper. Martin and Bernadette looked at what he had drawn.

"Bernie, does this mean . . . "

"I would think so."

"But she's supposed to be . . . "

"Apparently not. And now we know how."

"Antiquity?" Martin held up a business card with a stained brown color scheme and an overly flourished script running across.

"He either overcharged for it or knows who did. That also gives me two theories as to what the location spell was used for." She buttoned up her coat and tightened the built-in belt. She then shuddered as if someone had dropped an ice cube down her back. "Well, the charm just failed. Let's go see what Antiquity knows and how much it will cost us." She was already out the door. Martin began to follow, then turned back.

"Um, so, normally we would put you back." Martin glanced over his shoulder, where Bernadette had left. "She has to be the one to do it though. So, um . . . Welcome back? If you could not tell anyone about this, that'd make it easier for both of us." Martin patted the table, gave a self-satisfied nod, and retreated. "Sorry for the inconvenience," was all he said before vanishing down the hall.

Nathan was left in silence with dim light bouncing off the reflective contours of the room. Presumably, there were also other dead bodies around, but Nathan couldn't see any from his gurney. The hum of the lights overhead slowly established its presence in the space. Somewhere, a fan was running, ventilating the room. But that was it.

Nathan sat up, his back muscles resisting the whole way. The sheet sloughed off as he brought his legs around to sit on the edge of the table. He was still cold, but it didn't bother him. Nor did the news that he was apparently dead. That one, he suspected, might take a minute to settle in. Same thing for the revelation that magic was a thing and he had that to thank for his ability to move around while dead. Yep, there were a lot of things that would hit him later. Not right now, though.

Clothes, he thought. He would need clothes if he was going to make use of his mobility. He'd draw less suspicion anyway.

He dropped his feet to the floor. Nathan felt the sharp crinkle under his foot as he stepped on his own toe tag. There wasn't much on the tag that he didn't already know. Looked like an autopsy was deemed unnecessary. The cause of death was probably pretty obvious. Nathan reached up to the pragmatic stitching holding his throat flaps together. He was going to need a scarf or something.

Most of the drawers and cabinets around the room were locked. Must have been to keep the controlled substances and sharp objects safe from the corpses. There was a file on the desk with *Clarke, Jonathan P.* written on it. Like the toe tag, it was a pretty straightforward document. Dead body was found, loss of blood, positive I.D. His clothing had been disposed of, although if his manner of death was accurate, he probably wouldn't want them back anyway. There was a note scrawled at the bottom, in a box for law enforcement notes. The investigation was being handled by the M.I. unit. Nathan didn't recognize it from any *Law and Order* spinoff, though.

Getting his legs moving again was slow work, but they woke up eventually. Opposite the door to the hallway, there was an opening that led to a narrow bathroom, complete with shower. The examiners probably didn't like the smell of the chemicals either. Next to a shelf of towels—like the poorly stocked cubbies at a slightly upscale hotel pool—there was a stash of maroon scrubs. Nathan was tempted to grab a stack and get out, but if the shower was available, he might as well wash the dead guy smell off.

The shower was a shining silver box, big enough to turn around in but not much more. It reminded Nathan of the showers at the campground his family had spent summers at when he was a kid. He didn't expect to have to scare a bat out of this one, though. The water came and heated up quickly. When the steam worked its way into Nathan's body, his stiff muscles relaxed, and he began to feel the familiar quirks in his limbs. His left big toe clicked when he raised it. His right knee had felt off center ever since that flag football mishap during junior year of high school. Even his ears seemed to pop in the right way as the shower worked its magic.

There wasn't any blood circling the drain when Nathan shut the water off. He reached up to his new scar. It wasn't sticky or tender. It just looked like he was getting an early start on Halloween. He stepped out and looked at it more closely in the mirror. It was noticeable, but somehow, knowing that he was alive (or maybe re-alive) made it seem less severe.

The rest of him looked more or less how he remembered. Not muscular, not fat. Not tall, not short. He could use a shave. His hair was short enough that it was hard to tell it was wet. He was a little pale, but that had always been the case. In fact, wait until the end of February, and he'd probably have been that color anyway. He didn't feel like a zombie. He didn't look like a zombie. He looked like himself. He felt like himself. He wasn't sure what that meant now, was all.

Nathan toweled off quickly, dropped the towel on the floor, and grabbed the first pair of scrubs he saw. They were baggy and wouldn't cover his neck, but it was better than what he had. He slipped his toe tag into the chest pocket and made for the door.

The light was more than he was prepared for, but the adjustment was quick. The hallway was empty, which only meant there was nobody around to see Nathan looking completely lost as he fumbled for a way out.

Nathan found his way to a garage-looking area with two ambulances in a sunken loading bay. This was probably where he had been dropped off. The EMTs looked like they were resupplying. One of them glanced at Nathan but barely gave a nod before returning to his work. Maybe that charm had some lingering effects. Or maybe they simply had better things to concern themselves with. People so often did.

"Dr. McCallum have you cleaning up?" It was one of the EMTs entering the garage behind him. Maybe that charm wasn't still in effect. Maybe there was no charm. Maybe the woman claiming to be capable of magic was just a crazy person off the street. Or a hallucination. Maybe Nathan was having a vivid dream as his body slowly died from blood loss. Either way, another person was staring him down, expecting an answer.

"Yep."

She smiled. It seemed like her attention was out of camaraderie rather than suspicion. At least, that's how Nathan preferred to interpret it. "It's his way of breaking in the new hands. Make sure they can handle the less glamorous end of looking at dead bodies." She leaned back against the pipe railing that marked the boundary between person and ambulance territory. "You all have the same look. A little lost, a little tired, not to mention pale and smelly from all the time in the labs. No offense."

"None taken. If the shoe fits, right?"

She moved the boxes she was carrying to one side and extended her hand. "Ellen. Welcome to the trenches."

"Thanks," Nathan returned the handshake. He saw her noticing the stitches on his neck. She either was too scared or was too polite to ask. It was clean, just fresh. Maybe she had simply seen worse. Still, Nathan would have to look into covering it before too long.

"Cold hands too." She laughed. "That why you wanted to work in the morgue? These patients don't complain about a cold touch."

"I just kind of found myself here."

"I know what you mean." She stood straight and started toward her crew. "Well, I'll see you around before too long, Mr. . . . . "

"Clarke," Nathan replied on instinct. "Jonathan Clarke. People call me Nathan, though."

"That's obnoxious," she said. "I like it."

She waved, and Nathan turned to the bay door. The supersized garage door for the ambulances had a pedestrian person-sized doorway cut into it, complete with that inexplicable trip hazard left at the bottom. It was like somebody had cut a space for a person-door in the garage door but decided to put it four inches off the ground.

The daylight didn't hurt as much as Nathan had thought it would as he stepped outside. The flanking buildings rose high enough into the sky to filter much of the intensity. The traffic noise was more intrusive than he had expected, though. The same walls that kept the light out kept the sound in.

A survey of the options before him left Nathan feeling lost. He knew where he was. He had never been to the morgue before, but he knew it was on the back end of the hospital—the wing that touched the least trafficked street the building had access to. The hospital was roughly the center of the city. It was a small enough town, you only needed one landmark to find your way to any other. It also meant that getting anywhere meant you were probably going to come within spitting distance of the hospital. Nathan could get wherever he needed to from here. He simply didn't know where he needed to go. He couldn't even tell where he wanted to go.

Should he go back to the coffee shop? That's the last place he remembered being. That's what he would do in a video game. A list of names scrolled through his mind. Friends, coworkers, his landlord, but none of them stuck out as the right choice. In fact, they all seemed equal to one another. They were just names. Home seemed like the best option. He could find clothes that fit there, at least. He grazed the sutured cut along his neck. It was too warm outside for a turtleneck, but Nathan thought he had a light jacket with kind of a high collar buried somewhere in the closet.

On the other hand, there was the scent of oils and spices that Rico (Erik, to his mother) used in his bowls. When the wind was blowing right, or the pressure from a pending storm kept everything in the air at ground level, Rico's could be detected from a mile away. Anyone visiting the city would find themselves at Rico's. It wasn't the best place in town, but it was the only one that actively called out, seducing anyone with a nose. Nathan couldn't see the shop, but he knew how to get there from the hospital. (Head east to the post office, drop a block to the south.) He should follow the scent and fuel up for what was likely to be a complicated day. His stomach had to be empty, but it wasn't growling yet. Nathan knew he should be hungry, but he didn't feel hungry. He cycled through the menu options, and nothing made his mouth water. Maybe whatever magic had rejuvenated him was also squashing his appetite. Food could wait.

Instead of heading east to Rico's, Nathan headed south and hoped he'd have more of a plan before he got back to his apartment.

Rico's didn't want him to go, it seemed. The farther away Nathan got, the more persistent the smell became. He passed the unfortunately named craft store, Handsy's. When Nathan was a boy, he would go there for diorama supplies with his dad. He could remember countless experiences in that building, long conversations, and heated debates. Which dinosaur was best, how many vertebrae a giraffe had, what color they should use for the

Loch Ness Monster. It was a slideshow of his memories, but the only thing his senses knew was that Rico's Rice Bowls was a simple change in direction away.

Nathan continued. He needed clothes. He needed a quiet place to sit and think—decide what parts of the last hour he believed, what he had hallucinated, and what it would all mean moving forward. His apartment wasn't anything special, but it was his. If the timeline was right, the landlord probably didn't even know Nathan had been missing. If he had really only been dead for less than a day, it should be like he had never left.

About a block farther, on the right, was the flower shop Nathan had stopped at twenty minutes before the winter formal, junior year. He'd bought the last corsage in the case. His date knew when he presented it but was kind enough to not say anything. It was a blind date. They had both been happy the other one showed up. Ever since that night, any time Nathan walked by the Billy's Blooms he could feel his cheeks flush as he remembered the embarrassment of youth. This time, all he felt was curiosity about how Rico's was overpowering the smell of fresh flowers.

Two doors down was First Bean, the coffee shop where twenty-four hours before, give or take, Nathan had had his last cup of coffee. The thought occurred to him to walk by and see the place where he'd died. Who gets the chance to look at the space of their final breath and know it for what it is? Barring that, he could go in and see if anyone remembered him from his last day. He remembered the barista, even the table he'd been at. Maybe there was something to follow up on.

Nathan stared into the alley, past the caution tape, at the gravel and asphalt path still darkened with his blood. The dumpster was full. There was a security light, but it wasn't shining this time of day. He knew he should feel angry. Or sad. Or vengeful. Or just weird about the spot. But there was nothing. His brain took in and organized what he saw, compared it to what he remembered. It was just information. The only desire, the only tug on Nathan's will, was from Rico's. The smell was a secondary sensation now. It had turned into an intuition, a calling that was simply packaged in the familiar pepper and starchy steam. The farther Nathan got from the calling, the stronger it became.

Nathan decided a costume change could wait and followed his gut back towards Rico's. Once he committed to the path, the smell took over. It became a feeling, an intuition. Whenever Nathan changed direction, it was at the guidance of this new, invisible path. He was a grain of sand being relocated in the river. He knew he was moving, but how, why, and where were decidedly removed from his command. He was vaguely aware of the nouns he passed—the people, the individual locations, odd objects, and decorations of the downtown streets. None of them registered as more than a blip in his mind as he maintained his stride.

Then, he was at Rico's.

Then, he was passing Rico's. The smell was present, but the feeling that Nathan had come to recognize along with it had separated. That feeling was still calling. It wasn't Rico's—it was using Rico's as a mask. Nathan kept walking, leaving the thick, floating blob of oil and spice to be discovered by some other wanderer. He couldn't place the exact sensation for this secondary impulse, but the path it laid before him was clear and distinct. It brought him three doors down to the Grinding Gears repair shop.

The shop had never seemed to be open. Not that Nathan had ever checked. It was one of those old shops in a downtown with a faded sign and inexplicably dusty doorway. It must have been popular enough in its day, but now, it was surviving past success and the assumption that it would always be there. They handled anything mechanical that wasn't electric. Nathan had never required its services, but his grandparents had spoken of it with the familiarity bestowed on a community institution. They remembered it from their childhoods and so assumed everyone else did too. Surely everyone in town knew that Grinding Gears was where you went to repair any mechanized device, just like they had for decades. His grandfather had gone there for pocket watch inspection. His grandmother for typewriter repair. Never mind that Nathan had never used a typewriter or owned a pocket watch.

The windows—well, the places in the bricks where windows should go—were boarded over and covered with murals of silhouette figures from a time when typewriters and pocket watches had been the rule. A time when the shop had been a necessity, rather than an oddity. What life had been like before the sign had faded, and the entryway had become gray with disuse. This was the doorway that the indescribable feeling in Nathan's gut, masquerading as Rico's, had led him to.

Nathan looked up and down the street. It wasn't empty, but what people were out and about were trying to be somewhere else (Rico's, most likely). They had their own affairs to attend to. The man in scrubs with no shoes and an odd scar along his neck staring into a shop that none of them could remember using was someone else's problem.

Nathan touched the handle and felt warm for the first time since he'd woken up. The sensation drawing him to the door smoothed out, like he'd finally fully submersed himself in the bathtub. The door opened, pulling Nathan with it like he was entering a pressurized room. It closed behind him with a soft *chunk*.

Piano music came from the far end of the room. Nathan couldn't see anyone playing or even quite identify where the piano was, but the result was everywhere. It rested on the soft couches in the corner. It poked into the private, fabric roofed cubbies that populated the walls. It inspected the shelving of books and collected objects that bridged the gaps between private booths. The music connected everything in the room but came from beyond it. It twinkled in the low light of the lounge that Nathan had discovered instead of the Grinding Gears repair shop.

There weren't any tables in the room—just the dark booths, the couches that nobody used, and every inch of available wall space was filled with shelves of books and antique-looking boxes. The only break in the wall of bookshelves was on Nathan's left-hand side, where the bar was. It was small, with stools enough for only half a dozen people. Two were occupied.

The man standing behind the bar, figuring something on a notepad, was surrounded by the usual glass containers of colored liquid, although Nathan didn't recognize any of the labels. There was also a windup monkey figure nestled near the center of the bottles. Nathan wondered what would happen if someone drank out of that. There was even a collection of black and white photos chronicling the bar's past, like in every similar establishment Nathan had ever ventured into. Bordering the photos were countless business cards left with the most optimistic of intentions. Or maybe just someone trying to expense out a liquid lunch. None of them showed a typewriter. Not knowing where else to go, and having no guidance from the feeling that had led him to this spot, Nathan claimed a stool across from the two who were already there.

"What can I . . . Shit."

Nathan hadn't received a greeting like that since he'd shown up to his ex's birthday party. The bartender dropped the notebook on the counter and turned to the display of bottles. Nathan tried to follow what the man was putting together, but when he tried to look at one bottle of an almost (but not quite) orange color, he got dizzy and had to look away.

The two others at the bar gave Nathan long looks. One man with a twirly mustache and undone bowtie raised his glass in acknowledgment of the new arrival. The other woman dipped her finger into the glass in front of her and left it there without blinking. The liquid started to recede, and she smiled. At least, she smiled as best as she could, considering she had no mouth.

The bartender returned and set a shallow bowl of orange liquid down. "Drink this," he commanded. "Then we talk."

It was direct and forward—just what Nathan had been looking for. It was the first moment lacking confusion since he'd woken up. He took the bowl, which was cold to the touch but somehow still had traces of steam coming off it. With nothing to lose, Nathan lifted the bowl and drank it like the remains of morning cereal. It was thick like a milkshake and tasted like raspberries that had been too long on the vine.

The scratchiness in his throat smoothed and the itch running along the left side of his neck (roughly in correspondence with the zigzag tattoo he had acquired) cooled. It wasn't gone, but it was further away in time—like an injury that had happened in his youth rather than yesterday. As he got to the last drops in the bowl, Nathan's ears popped, and the intangible lure was back. It didn't pretend to be Rico's this time. The mask was off. It wasn't leading him anywhere, but simply making itself known. It was a stationary wind. An energy, a movement in the space around him, that had yet to be activated.

The bartender moved the bowl to the table behind him and leaned back. "So, how did you get here?"

"There was . . . something in the air. I could feel, I still feel . . . "

"Yeah, yeah," the bartender cut him off with the wave of a well-used dishtowel. "I know *what* brought you here. Magic. We'll get to that. What I want to know is *how*."

Nathan blanked for a moment. The bartender held his disgruntled stare. "Oh, um . . . Someone was trying to find something, I think? And used my blood, I guess. All of my blood." At this, Nathan gestured to the mark on his neck.

"You're the one Stephens was in here asking about, aren't you? Shit. Not bad enough somebody went off-book with a little necromancy, but now the detective isn't putting away her toys when she's done. Ah . . . How are you feeling?"

"Itchy? Cold. But better. What was that?" Nathan asked, nodding to the bowl on the counter.

"Magic." He chuckled. "Alchemy, if you want to get specific. We're not going to let something like a little blood loss stop us. We can keep your pieces running long as you need 'em. Welcome to the world, kid. I'm Lyle, and this here is Reverie." At this, Lyle gestured wide to the piano lounge that was supposed to be Grinding Gears. "Even magic users need a place to get away and turn their brains off."

The bartender shrugged and turned his attention toward the patrons at the end of the bar, the one with the mustache and the one without a mouth. Nathan's face had not changed by the time he returned. The bartender leaned back against the bar wall and scratched his beard, burying his fingers in the fur. Nathan wasn't sure if "fur" was a metaphor for Lyle's thick beard or a weird bit of magic that he would have to get used to.

"So, let me guess," Lyle began. "She brought you back, had you answer her questions, and took off without so much as a 'thank you.'"

"She seemed like she was in a rush."

"Yeah, well, that might be. She was in a rush when she left here, too. Probably right before she came to you. Still, no excuse for rudeness. Sorry, kid. Probably been a rough few hours for you. On top of, you know, getting your blood drained, of course."

"Thanks. It's actually not that bad. I suppose it should be, but it's just . . . not. I mean, I'm still trying to figure out if magic is real and what that means, or if this is all some hallucination as I lay dying in an alley. It's pretty distracting."

Lyle stared off for a moment. The mirror behind him showed the booths to Nathan's back. They weren't much to look at, with their walls and fabric ceilings like an ancient bazaar, the insides shrouded. Probably the point. There was a flash of purple in one. Nobody seemed to notice. A frog levitated out of another before a hand that may have also been a tentacle pulled it back in. Nathan wanted to turn and see if the world presented in the mirror was just some trick, but his reflection shrugged at him, and he decided it didn't really matter.

"I'd expect a magical tavern to be livelier than this," Nathan offered.

"You're one to talk." Nathan didn't notice the joke. "Magic isn't all it's supposed to be. You ask around the room, and they'll all tell you the same. It's just another set of rules." Lyle could tell from his scrunched-up face, Nathan wasn't following along yet. "You ever have a friend who, I don't know, learned to fly a plane or got a blackbelt while they were still kids?"

"A buddy of mine was an Eagle Scout."

"Sure. Whatever. They had an experience and training in a very specific discipline outside of school and other usual hobbies. They still did normal person things, probably, but there was this separate set of abilities that you caught a glimpse of sometimes, right?"

Nathan thought. "He was the only one of us who knew how to use a compass."

Lyle laughed. "Well, that's just embarrassing. But magic is the same thing. Those of us who find a door to the skill set aren't different. We aren't smarter, and life isn't easier, on the whole. We just have different tools for a specific set of tasks that most people would avoid anyway. We have the advantage in some things, but we have a unique set of everyday annoyances too. Case in point, blood isn't as easy to come by as you might think."

"I wouldn't think." This time, Nathan heard the two at the end of the bar chuckle too.

"We have a handful of answers, but we have more complex questions too." Lyle fidgeted with something below where Nathan could see.

"And this place is all . . . "

"Magic users, yeah. Or at least, people who have been exposed to magic. Everyone here knows about the magical world, even if not all of them have equal skills. Isn't that right, Alicia?"

The mouthless one at the end of the bar lifted a middle finger in acknowledgement.

"It's nice to be around people who share knowledge of the world. It's like an after-school club. Only here, sometimes animals start talking, or you walk out with different appendages than you came in with."

Parts of several questions tried to escape Nathan's head but only made his mouth stall out in half formation of each one.

"That's mostly a joke," Lyle reassured him. "It's my experience that most magical mishaps are self-induced."

Nathan looked around the room. There wasn't any thick smoke. Nobody had a cauldron going. As near as he could tell, nobody had a pointy hat. Even Lyle looked mostly like every other grizzled bartender who had ever served him a round. The only odd thing was that most of the rest of the room didn't really look like a bar. It looked more like a members-only library . . . that happened to serve drinks (apparently, drinks that could boost one's health, even if one had recently been dead). Then there was another flash of purple from one of the shrouded nooks, which shifted Nathan's assessment a bit.

"Are you sure I'm not just dead, and this is all my brain shutting down in random, although intricate, images?"

"Pretty sure, yeah." Lyle took a moment before crossing closer. "Once you take a peek through the magical lens, it becomes hard to be sure of anything. I mean, what is real?" He laughed, but even Lyle knew it wasn't a good joke. "Don't misunderstand, you are dead. That detective reanimated your body. She gave it motion again. You're animated by magic, is the only difference between now and before. Your body wants to repair itself, and it will. The magic just gave it a jump start to trick it into not realizing you were dead. Near as I understand it, anyway. I'm only an alchemist, after all. And between you and me, one with a specific talent for the more bibulous concoctions. Hence this place." He spread his arms again, indicating Reverie with his impressive wingspan.

"The detective was here. So, what did you tell her? Do . . . do you know who killed me?"

"What, because I run a lounge for the magically inclined, I know all mystics?"

"Well, I mean, maybe. I'm pretty new to this, so maybe." Nathan surprised himself with his frankness. It was a response of impulse, but for whatever reason, he hadn't refined it before it left his mouth.

Lyle cracked a smile. And bobbled his head a bit. "I suppose that's fair. And I did tell you this was a gathering point for magic users. I guess it makes sense. I can't tell you who did this to you. *Why* is simple, though. You had a valuable resource. Your blood."

"Sure used a lot of it."

"Yeah, that's what the detective said." Lyle paused and pointed a solemn gaze at Nathan. "You're not going to do something stupid like try to find your killer, are you?"

Nathan considered. It hadn't occurred to him. There was a part of his mind that said it would be the logical thing for him to focus on. Every other part of him didn't care, though. It didn't feel like a big priority. He had bigger things to take care of first. Like, did he still have an apartment? If there was a record of him being dead, could he keep his job? Was he technically a zombie now? Still, he was curious. "I can't say I'm not curious."

"Listen, whoever did this is new to the world, like you. They don't know the rules of the culture yet. The job they did on you was sloppy, not to mention rude." Lyle gestured to Nathan's neck with a dismissive wave. "They got some taste of power—likely some witch thing, life force stuff—but they don't know how to control it yet. That makes them dangerous. That's why, as much of a mess as she makes, we're lucky to have people like Stephens. She'll track the novice down and set 'em straight, one way or another."

"Me," Nathan muttered. "The mess, you're talking about. I'm the mess, aren't I?"

Lyle dropped his head and laughed a moment. He looked back to Nathan and held up a finger, asking for a minute. He turned and picked up the windup monkey from between two bottles of glowing liquid on the shelf. It was about a foot tall, and all crouched over. It had a fez and vest in what was probably an antiquated form of racism. Nathan had seen similar mechanisms before. If you wound the key, it would do a backflip and land on its feet. Nathan wondered how physics compensated for the tail that curled behind the toy.

Lyle set the monkey on the bar, wound the tarnished key sticking out of its back, and took a step back. The mechanized monkey curled deeper into itself and then sprang up, nearly completing its flip before landing face-first on the bar. Then the thing picked itself up and stretched like it had spent too long sitting in an office chair. "I'm gonna land that one of these days, I know it." The creature's voice was that of a thirteen-year-old still navigating the chemical waves of adolescence. It didn't crack so much as rattle, like taking a bike down a gravel road. "Busy night?"

"Nah. He's new to the world," Lyle said, drawing the toy's attention to Nathan. "We have a few things to discuss. Watch those other two, will ya, Dave?"

The monkey (Dave, apparently) threw a glance at the end of the bar. He tipped his fez with his tail. He walked in their direction, calling "Alicia, Pete! You two don't work hard enough to need this place." He walked side to side like the monkeys in the zoo. Nathan wondered which Dave had been first, a monkey or a toy.

"One of the regulars a while back—a witch, if I remember right—was much better at charms than paying his bills. We worked out a trade." Lyle's explanation didn't help a great deal, but it was better than nothing. "Anyway, where were we?"

Nathan couldn't remember right away either. "Cleaning up messes. I don't know if the monkey's going to be much help."

"Ha, probably not. This will, though." Lyle ducked behind the counter and came back up, holding two bottles with rounded bottoms and long necks, each with a cork at the top. They were like if wineglasses had been put together upside down. They would have fit better in a chemistry lab than a bar, but Nathan thought that was appropriate upon second thought. The liquid was golden and suspiciously inert. It didn't smoke, didn't sparkle. It sat there, which struck an ominous chord.

Lyle pulled the corks and slid one to Nathan. "You're going to need that." Lyle tipped his own drink back and finished half of his glass.

Having never been one to turn down a drink (and having already survived the bowl of spoiled raspberry milkshake when he'd come in), Nathan took Lyle's advice. The liquid had a biting smell and tasted like smoke. Nathan wondered what this new concoction was doing to his insides as he felt the tingle spread to his limbs. Shortly, he decided he didn't care.

"Like I said, magic doesn't have all the answers."

Nathan furled his eyebrow as Lyle pulled a tall bottle from under the counter. *Lagavulin* was inscribed on the label.

"This is the purest of alchemy," Lyle declared with a sip. He gripped the glass by the bottom of the globe, which seemed inconvenient, but it worked. He tapped a finger on the name on the bottle. "I've seen this magic word do more for a person than half the books on these shelves." Lyle waited for the swallow to settle before putting his glass down. "What's dead should stay dead. You don't have to be familiar with any of the magical skills to know that tampering with that law can get messy very quickly. When someone is reanimated like you, standard practice is to put them back. Sorry kid, but you shouldn't still be around."

It was a heavy statement, but not terribly surprising. Nathan had seen the movies. Assuming he wasn't hallucinating, which he still wasn't sold on, it made sense that he would be on borrowed time. He took another sip and let the liquid smoke permeate his abomination of a body. He looked again at the glass in his hand. His ears started to ring, and he felt his heart become slow and deliberate. A chill ran up his spine.

"So," Nathan began, his voice scratchy again. "Is this where you tell me I have to die again? For the good of humanity or something cosmic like that, I have to be put down? Did you just poison me? Why would you help me and then poison me?" It seemed like he should be louder than he was. Nathan felt an urgency to what he was saying, but when he heard his voice saying it, it was the casual pace of a summer afternoon's musing, rather than a potential identification of impending doom. "Or maybe the spell has a time limit, and this is all some sort of miscalculation. I just have to wait out the clock to see when I stop moving? The detective's assistant said something about usually cleaning up after the spell." Nathan took a breath and noticed himself in the mirror. "How is my face doing that?"

The face staring at Nathan in the mirror was red and purple. He wasn't a biologist, but it seemed like that shouldn't be possible, considering he had recently misplaced a good deal of his blood. Come to think of it, there were a number of things he had been doing since before he'd found himself at the bar that should have been impossible. Only then did Nathan recognize the color change as what usually happened when he got nervous and talked too much to cover it up.

Dave the monkey and the two at the end of the bar were staring at Nathan at an angle through the mirror. They didn't seem upset or surprised by Nathan's rise in color, but definitely interested. Shamelessly, considering that none of them turned when Nathan caught their gaze.

"You're not a zombie," Lyle said. "Not the way you've seen in video games, anyway. Your body was restarted. Considering how fresh you were, uh . . . Pardon the expression, but your body didn't have that far to come back. Your lungs take in oxygen, you'll be able to digest most anything I can serve you, and you're generating blood to cycle around your body and replace what you lost. What Stephens laid on you is like a defibrillator, blood donation, and adrenaline injection all rolled into one magical ball. Even any brain damage you suffered from your timeout was shocked into repairing itself. Probably took a bit for your body to catch up while the detective and her scribe were watching you, but that's the best way they could make sure your memories would come back with you. They needed access to your brain."

Lyle grabbed the bottle full of orange liquid that he had first poured for Nathan. "This stuff picks up where they left off. It replenishes the building blocks your body needs to fuel all of what that first spell kickstarted. It's really just a fancy sports drink, but, you know, magic." He raised his hands and opened his eyes like he had just made a coin appear from behind a kid's ear.

"Does that mean . . . " Nathan reached to his neck. The scar didn't feel any smaller. He felt around his shoulder. He still had the contours from scraping against a rock face on that camping trip four years before. It had been Andy's fault for not securing the line. Nathan hadn't spoken to him since. The two thoughts were connected, but Nathan couldn't see why in the moment.

"You're not brand new, and you don't have superpowers. In fact, that magic has probably faded by now. It was a temporary supercharge so they could get their questions answered."

Nathan dropped his hands and found his drink again. It was comforting just to hold. It was comforting to drink too, but that was unsustainable. "Then, why . . . Why would you put someone like that, someone like me, down again? If I've essentially just been reactivated, why can't I just say, 'Thank you,' and go on with my life?"

"Are you religious? Do you think there's a soul somewhere at the center of every person?"

"I'm not drunk enough for this conversation." But Lyle just looked at him, patience in his eyes. "I guess I do. That seems to be the consensus. It feels like I do, but I don't know how I would prove that. Are you going to tell me that's the secret to magic? Channeling soul energy or something?"

"What? Oh, no. It just makes for a good point of reference, I find." He glanced at Dave, confirmed the imp was doing his job, and rested both hands on the bar in front of Nathan. "What do you think running looks like?"

It was too obvious of a question to not be a trap, but Nathan couldn't figure out what the trap was. He couldn't find the real question. It reeked of tricky teacher language. Nathan froze, trying to unravel the riddle. He barely noticed Dave shuffle up and perch on his boss's shoulder.

"Humor me," Lyle prompted after a few unblinking moments.

"When someone moves their legs quickly? Uh, quickly and in a repetitive manner, so that it propels them forward. Distinct from dancing, somehow. Or maybe it is dancing, just in a straight line? Is running just dancing in a straight line?" Every time Nathan answered, he felt there was something he had missed. It was like answering a test question with a sentence and then realizing the entire page was blank because that's how long the expected answer was.

"It's cute watching him try so hard," the monkey chided. "Dancing in a straight line is called line dancing."

"Be nice, Dave," Lyle commanded. "Okay. So, that's what it looks like when someone, when a person, is running. Now, take the person out of it. What does running look like?"

"That's nonsense," was out of Nathan's mouth before he realized it. He didn't regret it; he just wasn't prepared for it. "It's the annoying kind of nonsense your stoner, armchair-philosopher friend would bring up to kill a party. You can't have running without something doing the running. You can't have a verb without a subject." It still felt like a trap, but Nathan had decided to dive straight in and see what sprang. To his surprise, he was enjoying himself. It was the clearest path he'd had since the morgue. He took another sip, partly in celebration, partly in preparation for when the other shoe would drop.

"Good." Lyle seemed to think the conversation was a lot simpler than Nathan did. "We're on the same page, at least as far as basics. We have a framework. Now, do you agree that a subject can exist without a verb? We could assign something general, maybe like 'existing,' but not an active verb. It's not difficult to think of a person absent a verb, absent running. Fair?"

"I don't see how this isn't a trap . . . "

"It is," Dave goaded.

" . . . But yes? That seems fair."

"You are the subject without a verb. You are a person without action."

"Well, that's still just nonsense. Of course, I have a verb. I'm sitting, I'm talking, I walked here."

Dave made a motion that Nathan thought was obscene at first, but then he realized he was miming reeling in a fish. In the end, he decided it was probably a little bit of both.

"Yes," Lyle said. "But those are all new actions. The echoes of your previous motion have stopped. It's not that you're missing *all* action, just one very specific action."

Someone—Alicia or Pete—tapped their glass. Dave waved dismissively at them, but the tapping continued. Lyle popped his shoulder up, jostling the faux primate. Dave bared his teeth before swinging back to the other end of the bar.

"You're going to have to run that by me again," Nathan said, absentmindedly taking the last from his glass. "I'm not sure if it'll hurt or help, but I'm going to need more of that, too." Nathan pointed to the tall bottle on the bar.

Lyle obliged, topping off his own. "I love these glasses. A little impractical, but the long neck traps the aroma, so it all hits you at once."

A commotion from down the bar drew their attention as Dave refilled drinks with the care of someone who had turned in their two-weeks notice thirteen days before.

"Dave, I still have the number of the oddity show that came through last month. We can always make another one of you."

Lyle caught the dirty bar rag Dave threw by way of response. "Where were we?"

Nathan put his hands up and shook his head. "I honestly couldn't tell you. Some weird English-slash-philosophy hybrid that I did not sign up for. We were talking about verbs and subjects and magic and my death all tied in there, somehow. Shit, I don't even understand what I just said, let alone what this all means."

Lyle nodded. "That's probably fair. Like I said, my primary discipline is alchemy. I'm just a fancy chemist. I never had much patience for the lectures of wizards either. Let me see if I can break it down the way I understand it." He paused, took a sip, and let it rest in his mouth. The burn smoothed out, but he didn't swallow until the smoke smell left his nostrils. "All right, we're talking about the difference between animate and animus."

Nathan dropped his head into his hands.

"Stick with me, now." Lyle tugged gently on Nathan's color. "*Animate* is the ability to move. That's why we call cartoons animation. I think *animus* is the potential product of animation. It's the result of action."

Nathan lifted his head. His eyes were bloodshot and droopy, although that could have been from anything.

"The animus is like your personality. Not all humans do generate it, but most of the books on these shelves would say they can. We on the magical end of things have even found it in all sorts of animals. I think there was even a caterpillar that was supposed to have it, but that might have just been a story. We don't know what specifically generates animus, but it's an energy, a verb that, once it's generated, can exist outside of its subject."

"It seems like you're putting a lot of effort into not calling it a soul."

Lyle let out a sigh that carried bits of something from his beard with it to land on the bar, barely missing Nathan's right hand. "That's fair. I am, I suppose. I don't know souls. I know the twenty-one grams thing is bullshit, but that might only be the beginning. Had a wizard in here trying to explain it as 'phenomenal consciousness.' He talked for another forty-five minutes, and I was still trying to make sense of just those two words. I know magic. And alchemy isn't a discipline that worries about souls too much. For all I know, it could be the same thing. Like I said, it's a close enough idea. I've found that word, or at least the concept of a soul, makes these conversations a little more manageable."

"So, you have a lot of conversations with formerly dead people who've wandered in?"

"Three, including you. Places like Reverie are like that. When you're new to magic, you pick up its traces like fresh-baked cookies. The more cookies, the more magic that's concentrated in an area, the stronger the scent."

Nathan knew his line but didn't want to ask. "What . . . what happened to the other two?"

"The one didn't believe his eyes. Walked out of here before I could even introduce myself. The second was more open-minded. After a bit, she understood the situation."

"So, what is the situation then?"

"That's what I've been trying to get at. You stopped living. When you died, your animus was released. Don't ask me where, because I haven't the foggiest. Maybe it was trapped by a necromancer and has already been burned off for a spell. Maybe it dissipated. Maybe it's possessing a monkey toy on top of a bar somewhere?" He pointed his eyes at Dave, who was picking something from his fur and flicking it into the room.

"So that's what he is?"

"Heh, with his personality? He's not a golem, and I don't know why anyone would want a robot like that."

Dave looked in their direction mid-scratch, decided he didn't care, and continued putting a little extra effort into the movement.

"Dave is actually different. He's not possessed by someone else's animus. He was a thrift store find that I put on the shelf for character. The witch gave Dave animation, the ability to move and talk. He was only supposed to be a service robot to help out when things get crowded. The personality, the animus, is the byproduct of that animation and interaction with the environment."

Lyle and Nathan considered Dave for a silent moment. Nathan found himself wondering how many more animate tchotchkes were out there with more animus than he had.

"Anyway," Lyle continued. "You're back now, but your animus isn't. It doesn't just float back to you like in the movies. You're a painting with all the color washed away. You have your memories, your physicality, your materialness. You have the whole of your parts, but not the sum."

"That's the most sense you've made so far." Nathan didn't like the idea, but it felt right. That lack of context he'd been encountering, the lack of interest or disgust, even in situations that had distinct feelings attached to them. The craft store. The flower shop. He knew what they were, but he couldn't *feel* what they were.

"No." Nathan changed his mind. "No, I'm me. I don't know how I'm here, but I am. 'Magic' is a usefully vague word for it, but it could have easily been a medical mistake. I have my memories. I remember what foods I like. I know how I'm feeling. Angry, at the moment." The thought made him stumble. Was he angry? Or was he simply animating angry because that was his role. "This is all nonsense."

Lyle shrugged and took a step back. Dave swung himself up and perched on a shelf over Lyle's left shoulder, dangling one arm in a somehow menacing posture. Nathan felt a knot catch in his breath as the monkey toy stared him down.

"This will all go quicker if you're honest with yourself." Dave didn't bother to look at Nathan, opting instead to pick at the dirt under his fingernails.

"I know," Lyle began. "It's a lot. The way the process works, you have all your memories, like I said. There are biological, neurological, and probably other science-logical things that I don't understand that store those in your brain. That's what Stephens was after. But, what they mean, what those memories imply, how they take you from a collection of biology and turn you into a person, that's lost. You have no guide through this new life you've stumbled into. That's why folks in your shoes don't usually stick around. Everything they loved, everything they hated, every face of a friend and every sound of family, it all becomes equal, insubstantial weight. Your life is just a book you read once. For most, when they realize they can't feel the world anymore, it's not hard to talk them into having the spell reversed. They're happy to be returned to rest."

A curtain rustled behind Nathan as someone either left or came. Pete and Alicia clinked their glasses, and Pete mumbled something to his drinking partner. On a shelf to the left, a painting of a secluded cottage became a painting of a wooded glade as the dimensional anomaly it contained was returned to its prime deviation. It hid something specific from a specific person who was no longer a threat. Nathan noticed none of this.

"I'm just a marionette without a cricket." It seemed the most apt description. "What do I do then? Is there, like, magical witness protection?"

"Most of the Mississippi Valley," Dave said. "But you didn't witness, you experienced. We can't let that go. You threaten our existence, the entire magical community and beyond. A soulless wanderer who knows enough to be dangerous but not enough to be a person. That's why we have psychic assassins. They've probably already locked onto your brain waves and are slowly building a fatal stroke in there now. I've heard it's pretty painless."

Nathan stared at the monkey for long enough to forget to breathe. When Dave then leaped at him, teeth bared and paws out, the scream was weak and raspy. His freshly revived lungs and throat muscles twisted until he wasn't sure if they would ever feel right again. The monkey scrambled around his head a few times before darting back to Lyle's shoulder.

Nathan's heart was racing. He supposed that was a good sign. He still wasn't sure how long his new life would last, and a strong heart seemed like the bare minimum of requirements. He did a quick feel of his scalp for anywhere the creature might have drawn blood but came back with clean hands.

"If it hasn't been made clear yet, don't trust the monkey," Lyle said with a disappointed eyeroll.

"Even I follow that advice," Dave commented with his monkey grin.

"Nobody's coming to kill you. There are two things to know, though. One, you might rub some people the wrong way. You're a living broken rule. The detective may even come looking to clean up her mess, although I wouldn't count that as likely. It probably won't amount to much, but you might get some looks. Most of us have our hands full with our own tasks. We certainly don't have a team of psychic assassins, or whatever the monkey was chattering on about."

"Oh, good. Nobody is *actively* trying to kill me. My lucky day." Nathan took the last of his drink. Maybe it was the empty stomach from not eating while being dead, or maybe there was some heavy incensing going on behind him, but Nathan noticed that everything was getting a little hazy. Something was working, and in that moment, he didn't much care if it came from a glass or mystical chanting. His nose was more alert but had no idea what it was detecting. His ears focused but gave no importance to what they heard. "What do I do now? Since I don't have to run for my second life, do I just go back to my first one and hope nobody notices that

I've been dead for a day? How does someone who has come back from the dead occupy their time?"

"Anything you've ever wanted." Dave's eyes were wide. "Hedonistic debauchery. Rob a bank. Cut in line at the coffee shop. You don't have the voice in your head telling you you're wrong anymore. You are base impulse with no regulation but a lifetime of knowledge. Live it up."

Nathan's eyes got wide as ideas occurred to him. Maybe this wouldn't be so bad. It didn't sound right, but he couldn't find the fault with the monkey's logic.

"Let's hold our horses a minute." Lyle saw the look in Nathan's eyes. "You do that, and you *will* attract the eyes of the community. That kind of anomaly draws attention and creates more headaches than are generally tolerated. You'll have a bounty collected on you before you know what happened."

Nathan shrank on his stool.

"The real answer is what I was trying to get to before Dave graced us with his opinion. You're a fledgling person again. Your animus left, but you can generate a new one. You will generate a new one, at least to start with. It's already happening. As you experience things for the first time again, it shapes how you relate to them. You are stoking the fire within you. The bigger it gets, the more it shines through you as a personality. It's what makes you a person. But, it took you a lifetime to create it the first time. The only difference now is that you know what you're lacking."

Nathan's face was blank.

Lyle let out a huff, then mumbled something to Dave. The monkey sprang up onto the shelves and scampered away. Lyle continued, "Your animus is more than a moral compass or your emotions. There are people walking around every day who have emotions but no animus. Even people who don't have the excuse of having died. Not many, but it happens. When you are just moving—not living, not generating—that fire inside isn't fed and burns out. Nothing means anything. You still feel, and you know what to do in situations, but not strongly enough to act on it. You aren't fueled by anything other than the fact that you haven't died again yet."

"How do I stop the fire from dying out? You said it was hard, but I did it once, and I can do it again."

Lyle nodded slowly as Dave returned and handed over a leather notebook. Lyle took it and unwound the leather strap. "The woman I mentioned, the one who had been reanimated like you?"

Nathan nodded.

"This was hers. She found her way here, like you. She had cancer of some sort. Died younger than you care to see. Her father pulled on the right threads and found his way to the spell that would bring her back. Probably something similar to the one the detective used on you. Cost him more than he realizes, even now, but that's another story. She was happy to be back among the living, of course. She liked coming in here too, once she was the subject of magic. It was hard to adjust to the world of the living again, though. She said it was like being a robot. She had these memories that told her how to react, how to behave, what people meant to her and how lucky she was to be back, but it was all in someone else's voice. They were her memories, but she hadn't written them. She didn't feel them." He flipped through the book a little before putting it on the table.

Nathan went to reach for it, but Lyle placed his hand down, nearly covering the entire book. That paperweight wasn't going to move.

"She tried to pick up where she'd left off. It's amazing what people will overlook out of relief to have someone back. Medical miracles and all that. It was more of the same. She changed jobs and tried making new friends, but knowing how far there was to go was too much. She had nothing to cling to in the future or in the past. It was all pantomime that her brain told her would turn real, but her gut promised it wouldn't."

Lyle took a moment. Even Dave seemed to have sobered up a little. "She started coming in here more often. I think it was the only place she felt any connection to. Everything's off in here. We're all lost in Reverie. She would scribble in this book and then leave it for next time. Until the time she never picked it up again."

The room was still with the unanswered question. A soft clinking came from around the room as glasses were shuffled. The air hung slightly heavier in the way that dive bars always seem to be thick with memories. Nobody moved, even the ones in their booths, absorbed in their own affairs. Nathan didn't know if it was a product of magic, but it seemed supernatural no matter how you cut it.

"So, she . . . she decided . . . "

"No. That's just it," Lyle cut him off. "She didn't decide. She actively made no decision. They found her lying on the couch. She'd dehydrated and sunk into herself. She lost the will. She couldn't find a way to keep that new fire alive." He held up the notebook. "She said she knew what she was missing and how different it was from what she'd had. That's what made the journey back seem so vast. She couldn't find the motivation to find the motivation."

Lyle handed the book back to Dave, who took it and slowly returned it to its place among the shelves.

"Nobody is going to come after you, not if you keep your nose clean. And, hey, now you know magic is real. There are plenty of things to learn and experience. But most people never climb back up that mountain. There's a good chance you'll want to track down the detective before too long and have her clean up."

Dave returned but was making a point of being occupied with something behind the bar. Pete and Alicia had become oddly quiet. Well, it was odd for Pete. Even the draped nooks on the opposite wall seemed to subdue themselves.

"Where . . . where is the detective?" In that moment, Nathan didn't know if he was asking to find or asking to avoid. Nor did he know if the ambivalence came from genuinely being in over his head in a new world, or the dwindling ember of an animus that he was apparently working with. He knew that he had to know, though. Whatever his next move, he had to know where the detective was.

"That I couldn't tell you. She's got a place next to Smoky's Bakery. Second floor, up a staircase that's difficult to find even if she didn't camouflage it with magic."

He walked to the corkboard in the corner and selected a business card. It was holographic, like one of those rare trading cards they get middle school nerds to hunt for. *Bernadette Stephens* appeared to rise from the mustard background, along with an address and a magnifying glass. Some symbols were universal, it appeared. For the business card of a magical detective, it was underwhelming.

"She's probably out working your case, though. She stopped by here, which is how I got that. She didn't have much to go on. Then she came to you. What did you tell her?"

"Only what I could. My memory is still jumpy. It's like a DVD that keeps skipping." It was still odd for Nathan to think about his own demise. "The guy that, that killed me, was pretty nondescript. I never saw the other guy, just heard his voice. The first guy had some kind of weird necklace that Stephens seemed interested in."

Lyle bit down on his tongue to think for a moment. Then he decided and cleared the bottles from the back counter in front of the mirror. He turned back to Nathan, all worry and consolation in his eyes replaced with focus. It was the same look Nathan's grandmother got while doing the crossword.

"You have the guy's face?" Lyle asked.

"Like, did I bring it with me?" It was a silly question, but given the reanimation, levitating animals, and talking inanimate objects of the recent past, it seemed like a fair question.

"No. In your mind. Do you remember the face?"

Nathan nodded and tried not to take Lyle's disappointment personally.

"Okay. You know that old superstition about a mirror trapping your soul?"

Nathan nodded again.

"Well, this one does that, but with the images it captures. Like, the mirror has memories. It can replay the images it has reflected." Lyle paused mid-gesture, his hairy arm sweeping toward the surface in question. "It's like a security camera. I guess it would have been easier to just say it was a security camera." He shrugged. "Anyway, look at the mirror and think of the guy's face. Try to imagine him reflected back, like he's sitting next to you."

Nathan tried. It wasn't the silliest thing he'd ever tried. And the smoky alchemy he had been served was working its magic. He was willing to see where this trip would lead.

The guy's face was plain. Round cheeks, kind of baby-faced. No beard. Brown eyes. Probably brown eyes. It had been hard to tell in the dark. His hair was dark and floppy, like he'd recently been sweating. That, combined with the weird necklace, made him look like every goth kid Nathan had avoided in high school.

The mirror started glitching into long, thin columns. It was like a beaded curtain that had been disturbed. The individual strands were the same scene, but column to column was chaos. Vertical made sense, horizontal was visual gibberish. The columns shuffled like a new deck of cards being broken in. Nathan kept trying to remember the man's face, but the kaleidoscope of images pulled his focus in a myriad of directions.

It didn't hurt. He didn't feel anything mystical or foreign entering his brain. The only side effect was a bit of dizziness from the rapidly changing image fragments before him. Each image was a different scene, and he didn't know which one was going to ring his memory.

The shuffling slowed, and the resulting reflection was nearly unchanged from what it had been when Nathan first sat down. The shelves, the booths, and even Pete and Alicia were reflected. It was only by checking by the genuine article that Nathan confirmed Pete's bowtie was a different color—blue in the mirror, yellow and orange striped in person. Some of the incidentals on the counter were missing. Nathan was different in the reflection as well, in that he wasn't in the reflection. This was the reflection from a previous night.

And there, two seats down from where Nathan's reflection should have been, was the baby-faced, mop-headed stranger that had drained Nathan's blood away. Or *would*, maybe was the right way to phrase that. There was the choker, too. Dark, tight, and elaborately constructed, with a purple stone in the middle.

"Oh, that guy. I didn't like the look of him. Remember, Lyle, how I said I didn't like the look of him?"

Lyle rolled his eyes and stepped back for a better look. "You're right. Not much to go on. I remember him, though. Wasn't sorry to see him leave. Got the sense he was new to the world, but not like you. He was scared by it. Whatever magic he was practicing, you could tell it was taking its toll on him." Lyle looked closer at the temporally displaced reflection. "That necklace, though, there might be someone who can help you with that." He went back to the corkboard with the business cards and came back with the least flashy one. "Calls himself Antiquity. Runs a magical artifact emporium. It's guys like him that keep the theatrical flair alive in the magical world. Lots of smoke and dramatic lighting. He has an obnoxious wardrobe, like he's the lord of a seaside mansion in 1922. Anyway, you tell him about the necklace, and he might have something for you."

The card's ornate flourishes in the corners and the strategically dingy color of the cardstock gave it the appearance of age. From far away it had looked ordinary, but someone had gone to a considerable amount of work to make this mass-produced card appear old and unique. A false claim of mundanity to justify a mystique of the ancient. Yet, the sharpness of the edges betrayed the illusion. It took a moment, but then Nathan remembered why the name was familiar.

"That's where the detective went. I drew a picture of the necklace, and she said something about Antiquity. It didn't make sense at the time, but not much else did either. Her partner had one of these cards."

Lyle and Dave shared a glance. It wouldn't have been hard to predict with only one solid clue to cling to, but it was different knowing the actuality of the situation.

"So, what? Are you going to solve your own murder? I think channel twenty-three has that show on Wednesday nights."

"Dave, considering you were charmed to be an assistant, you are consistently unhelpful." Lyle flicked the monkey on the head. "Antiquity might know something. It might not be what you need, and it will take three times as long to get out of him as it should, but he'll know something. Even if he doesn't recognize the necklace, he'll know where Stephens went. If . . . *if* that's what you're after."

"I'll let you know when I find it." Nathan took the card and got to his feet. His head swayed a bit, but he recovered. "Am I going to be able to find this place again?"

"The address is on the door." Lyle paused a moment. "Oh, you mean because it's magic. Your senses recognize magic now. It will find you in more places than you realize. A place as concentrated as this, it won't hide from you anymore."

Nathan nodded. His muscles tensed to leave, but he paused. He had an impulse. "Thanks," he said, almost surprised as the words left his mouth. "I'm new to the world. Again. You didn't have to take the time you did to introduce me to it."

"That's the gig." Lyle shrugged. "I only wish I had better news for you. Magic isn't a way around the rules so much as a set of new ones. I'm not saying your book is closed, but it's rare to see one that ends different."

They both averted their eyes in mercy. They didn't realize it, but they also both bit their cheeks as the silence hardened between them.

"This place will always be here," Lyle offered. "If you find you have no reason to go anywhere else, this place will be here."

"You'd really open up to an animus-lacking zombie?" The attempt at a joke failed to relieve any of the conversation's weight.

"Sure. Place like this," Lyle gestured wide with his eyes, "we could always use a new stock boy." This attempt had more success. "Dave may be magic, but he can still only lift so much."

Nathan offered the card up as a thank you and made his way to the door. He paused at the threshold, half expecting to walk through and wake up from a weird trip or a medically induced coma. Instead, it was bright light he walked into. He was quickly reminded that he was only wearing scrubs as the hot cement got to work on the soles of his feet.

He could still feel the trail of magic that had led him to Reverie, but it was more diverse now. He could sense it spreading out in weaker but plentiful form. It was like seeing with new colors all of a sudden.

He checked the card against the nearest street sign. He knew where he was, and he knew where he was going. He didn't know why, but maybe something would occur to him before he got there. He picked a route and then modified it slightly. Nathan would stop at Rico's first. It was on the way, and a Rico's number-four sounded just about perfect.

For Pappy

In the Box:
A Hollow Brook Story

The Dining Car has never had enough light bulbs. Not working ones, anyway. All of the sockets in the fixtures are filled, though, even if they are all different models. Some LED, some curly. The oldest bulb in the restaurant was screwed in nearly thirty years ago. Nobody knows this. Nobody who works here now was here then. It is rare to find a complete set of working bulbs, so the lighting is always about twenty-five percent less than it's intended to be. That's about twenty-five percent more than it should be.

"More coffee?" asks Leslie. She has only worked at The Dining Car for nine days but has already waited on this man four times. She has seen him two additional times, but not in her section. He's easy to pick out in his nondescript suit with the little lapel pin shaped like an owl. Leslie figures he's part of some kind of club, like the Rotary or Kiwanis. Those clubs for old men who can't understand why nobody knows about their secret club anymore. She thinks she heard her grandpa mention something about it once. She has seen two or three others come through with that same pin, but this one is different. He always has a little puzzle from the newspaper to work with over his meal. Eggs benedict, no matter the hour.

"Yes, please. Thank you." The puzzle man makes a quick pencil scratch on his project before returning to his mostly completed meal.

Leslie nods politely and pours, bouncing her wrist to control the liquid spills. It isn't a difficult skill, and it's one Leslie learned quickly on the job. The fewer spills she makes, the fewer she has to clean up. Also, the tips tend to be better. The man appreciates it but doesn't say that he appreciates it. Leslie glances at the puzzle before continuing on her way. She wonders what the rules are. What the challenge is.

Leslie's eyes are nearly acclimated to the dim light. She still stumbles on occasion but never in a way that anyone would notice unless they were watching. Part of being a waitress at a place like this is that, while someone is always watching, it is never beyond the snow globe world of an individual table. Every three feet is like twisting into a new reality, with a new set of laws. She likes the job. She plans for it to be a "getting by" job until something unique pops up. Things will not go according to plan.

It's a strange town, but that's part of what drew Leslie here. It was close enough to other places that options were plentiful. It was far enough from those places that it was ignored by the people who lived there. People know the name Hollow Brook, but nobody makes it their destination.

Leslie grew up in the next town over, Cedar Grove—the "normal" but smaller town that collectively decided as long as they don't have the reputation of Hollow Brook, they are doing all right. Lawns are uniform. The downtown is ten percent too cheery. There is an agreed upon "that side" of town. And they can all get together and spread rumors about Hollow Brook.

None of them like to admit how frequently they come to town, though. Hollow Brook is where you can find the better grocery store and only movie theater within a half-hour drive, so it becomes a necessity at times. Besides, the annual tube-a-thon down the river makes it a cultural necessity to be somewhat familiar with the town. Leslie has never participated but grew up watching the tubes race along the water. Now that her class has graduated and gone their various ways, she won't know many of the participants come spring. She might still watch.

"There's nothing to do," she's heard some say about Hollow Brook. "That's where all the criminals from Woodson end up," said others. It was difficult to tell which was intended as the worse insult. A number of Leslie's friends had a less pedestrian theory when they'd heard that she was moving. They imagined a deep state, secret government kind of organization. CIA testing, backup Area 51, a giant witness protection city—the variations were never repeated but always entertaining.

Leslie didn't buy any of it. It was a weird town, sure. Weird in the quietest way. That quiet begged to be filled with something, so people filled it with the first thing that formed in their imagination, the most useful single piece that would connect all of the facts they *thought* they knew about the town. That didn't make any of it real.

Still, it gave Leslie something of a reputation on the occasions when she went home to visit. She doesn't correct any of their assumptions. She has the independence and the freedom to decide what to do with it. Everyone who knows she's there is too afraid to ask for details, which keeps them from meddling.

Leslie finishes her route around the restaurant and gives a perfunctory nod to Carlos in the kitchen. He's focused but never too much to acknowledge the front of house staff. Devon, the only other waiter for this shift and the one who trained Leslie, once said it was his way of making them think they were being watched. Whether or not it is true, she hasn't decided yet.

Leslie replaces the carafe on the hot plate and grabs the turkey and mashed potatoes Carlos has placed on the window. She's vaguely aware of a phone ringing somewhere in the restaurant and makes a note to be annoyed about it later. She takes the plate to table thirty-one. The woman in the kitten sweater that reminds Leslie of her third-grade teacher. It's not her, but it helps to keep the connection in her mind. She would never forget an order if Mrs. Graham was at her table. She only wishes she had a better opinion of Carlos's turkey.

The plate clanks down, and the Mrs. Graham impersonator dismisses Leslie with a smile. She's ready to dig in. Leslie glances around her section. The puzzle man is gone. She walks to the table and sees that his eggs benedict is not entirely gone. His coffee is still half full. Under the cup is the usual amount, including a considerate tip.

Leslie likes the predictability of this restaurant. Even in its chaos, it has a pattern, a rhythm. The regulars are usually regular, though. The puzzle man not finishing what he ordered doesn't fit the rhythm. It's the right note, but a different relationship to the notes around it. The song has changed. She glances around, but there is no further sign of the man. He didn't even finish his puzzle.

Outside The Dining Car, the air is cold, and the ground is wet. It hasn't rained recently, but somehow, the ground is still damp enough to have a different color than it should.

"Are you sure?" the man who did not finish his meal asks into the phone.

A voice on the other end answers. The two voices have spoken many times before, but only once over the phone. The man didn't know who the other voice was at the time. He only has a slightly better idea now.

"Yes, I know where it is. As long as she is still there, we can clarify the situation. That's what the boxes are for."

He has walked around to what serves for the back of The Dining Car, due to its reduced lighting and location on the opposite side of the main entrance to the building. The nondescript door next to the dumpster and break time picnic table complete the atmosphere. With one hand, he tosses the phone into the dumpster that should be closed to deter raccoons (but it isn't). The phone makes a thud as it ricochets its way to the bottom, but the man doesn't notice. He's already in the car he brought to the restaurant and is planning his new route for the evening.

The car starts with a sputter. The man wonders if it is some trick to the vehicle that the previous possessor either got used to or learned a way of avoiding. The man didn't notice the stutter the first time he started it, nearly forty-five minutes earlier, but his attention was divided among multiple concerns at the time. *Is this the right vehicle choice? How will the traffic be in this part of town over the next three minutes? Is the lawn mower loud enough to block the sound of the car's engine from notifying the owner that it's doing so without his consent?*

The sputtering start may also be a uniqueness reflecting the difference between the man in this moment and the man that started it forty-five minutes prior. Forty-five minutes ago, he was simply obtaining a new resource for work. Moving a piece around a board that he imagined he understood the rules for. It was routine.

Now is different. Now is a reaction to an anomaly. The events of now have sent the man off balance. He wasn't able to finish his meal. That always made him a little jittery. There was also the call from Management, but the man dismissed that as the source. Her attention sharpened his focus. She only attended to situations that required focus. She only attended to situations that were sharp.

The engine sound smooths out as the man guides it to the access road, past the car wash, past the Wendy's, and into the night. He may not realize it, but it is the first time in years that his mind doesn't fall upon the blackened rectangle to the north, which is all that remains of the merger between a hotel and box of matches. It will occur to him later, as he finds something to fill the empty place in his stomach that should have the other part of his eggs benedict in it. The thought will unsettle him.

The man doesn't like driving. People become extreme versions of themselves behind the wheel. The man doesn't enjoy engaging with people at the level of intensity they think is appropriate for the world. Accent those personalities with a mobile-controlled explosion, and you might as well arm squirrels with switchblades.

The man doesn't like riding either. He doesn't like being steered by anyone he doesn't understand. It's a very short list of people. It recently got shorter, in fact. Understanding and respect are not the same thing. Being driven does give him time for puzzles, however.

He usually has someone else to drive him, but the woman who recently acquired that role is assigned elsewhere this evening. It wasn't a coincidence, but the man who is reluctantly driving only knows that now.

It isn't night. Not yet, but the sun has left. Nothing but its meandering tails of light break up the gray-blue canvas of almost night. The moon will appear sometime. The moon tends to keep its own hours in the fall. The sky will darken and then lighten when the moon clocks in for work. Until then, it is neither night nor day. There's probably a word for that.

The man turns through the intersection and up the highway that runs along The Dining Car. He glances down toward where he was less than two minutes earlier. The waitress, Leslie, is stepping out with a bag of garbage. He likes her. He is curious about how she will react to the curiosities of the town.

Gary always parks in the faculty lot. He's not supposed to, but nobody checks on game nights. Actually, he's not sure how often they check during normal school hours, come to think of it. The biggest lot is also the one closest to the football field on the opposite side of the building. The faculty lot is secluded, quiet, and protected from congestion by a walk too far for most spectators on a midautumn night. On the off chance Gary is still around when the game lets out, there is little traffic from the faculty lot.

He latches his trombone securely in its case and sets it in the trunk of the car that cost less than the instrument. The plume and helmet are already tucked away in their case. If the team loses tonight, Gary has already worn this regalia for the final time. He didn't think to look at the score when he was dismissed after halftime, so he doesn't know how likely that scenario is. He won't miss the activity of marching, the simplified musical arrangements, or the struggle of corralling the freshmen players. He will miss the packaging, though. The uniform, the horn moves, the glances from the younger marchers as they check their position against his.

Gary isn't the best player, but he's the surest marcher. The marching band relies on that security, from the freshman bass drum to the senior drum major. Gary is the unspoken center that the rest of the band orients around. He's also the tallest member of the band, so it was a bit of natural selection. Depending on the decision-making of Gary's more athletically inclined classmates, that may be a responsibility Gary never fills again. He'll have to settle for playing at tube-a-thon, come summer. It won't be required once he graduates, but he thinks he'll still show up. Gary likes watching tube-a-thon.

He looks up at the ornate entrance to the school. Schools built in the early twentieth century often look like a castle on a budget—a grand doorway flanked by towers of stone. There is usually a bell tower, although those have since gone out of fashion. The bells that govern the buildings are automated now. This school has a bell tower that, ever since the bell was removed, has served as the band room for a few years. What they did in the winter, Gary doesn't know. Now the bell tower is used for storage. What they do if they need something in the winter is unknown. Some mysteries persist.

The grandiose framework is connected by straight lines of the cheapest brick they could find at the time. Hollow Brook High School even has two gargoyles, one near the top of each tower, although they are shrouded by the well-intentioned pine trees on each side of the entrance. The gargoyles previously shot out water that fostered the trees, which now keep them hidden. If they were to ever come alive, they could touch the needles of their work. Similarly, it would take little effort for someone in the tree to reach one of the creatures and grab a small package that was entrusted to the statues years ago.

A man drops to the grass along the main entrance, catching himself with a knee and an outstretched hand. A half moment later, the sound of rustling registers in Gary's brain. It happened before, but it had no context, and so his senses nearly overlooked the phenomena altogether. Now both pieces of data—the rustling and the sudden appearance of a man from the sky—rush together as if they are simultaneous occurrences.

A second sound echoes against the brick of the school building, but Gary doesn't recognize it. He's not used to hearing himself scream.

The man from the sky stands up. He's holding something small enough to be concealed in his hand. He brushes his knee before he sees Gary staring at him from behind the car. Gary feels the breath leave his body as every word he knows fails to show up to work. The vacancy in the air is broken by a commotion from the other side of the building. One of the teams must have scored. It's the away team, but Gary doesn't know that. The two men stare in assessment, each of them determining if the other is a threat or a coincidence.

"It's a tough game tonight." It's the only thing that Gary can manage to say. It is the unofficial greeting Gary overheard from everyone who was concerned with the result of the game.

The man squints a bit. He is shorter than Gary, but most people are. He's older, though. There is enough stubble and definition to the man's face that he could be a teacher at the school. He has the same cold look in his eyes as most five-plus year teachers, as well. The man's suit has a functional look to it—not fashionable, especially with the pine needles and sap speckling. He wears it with a purpose, not a perspective. What that purpose is at a football game, let alone up the side of the school, Gary can only guess at.

"The band played well tonight," the man replies. "Too bad the same can't be said for the team."

Gary doesn't recognize the man. He still looks like he could be a teacher, but Gary would recognize him if he was one. The man apparently doesn't feel the need to defend his presence up the tree, which probably means he feels that he's supposed to be there. Whatever the case, he's lying. The band was garbage tonight. They hadn't expected the team to get this far in the season, so many of the freshmen have stopped practicing the marching music.

The man holds up his hand and reveals the canister that he's been cradling in his hand. The body is black, with a thin, gray lid. Gary recognizes it but can't think of where it is from. Gary can't focus on retrieving the memory, either. As the man raises his hand to display the canister, the light from the parking lot catches the lapel pin. Gary has no trouble recognizing the symbol. It's sketched in every textbook and carved in every back row desk he's seen since fifth grade. He knows what the pin is supposed to mean. He doesn't think it actually means that.

"Night photography," the man says. "Need a good vantage point." The man begins to walk away.

Gary doesn't think of himself as brave. In the future, he will often start this story that way. But in this moment, words leave his mouth before his brain has time to be afraid. "Photographing the owls?"

The man stops and stares back at Gary. He pockets the canister. Whatever is inside rattles in a way that film does not. "They're around. But you have to keep your eyes open." He nods slightly. The man takes out a notebook, draws something on a page, and rips it out.

"You're real?" Gary's mouth operates on its own for the second time on this night.

"Only when we can't help it." The man comes close and sticks out his hand, offering the torn notebook page. Gary is too afraid to not take it. The man breaks away and disappears to where he left the car. Gary doesn't watch him go. He's afraid to. Nobody will believe him when he tells the story, especially when he gets to the end.

Ike remembers when the city pool was just a muddy hole in the ground. When he was a boy, he would walk the three blocks with his sister from their house to the pool every summer day that didn't have rain. And even a few that did.

The hole was later paved and turned into a certified pool. Then it was turned into a park and named after the second wealthiest family in town at the time. Now, they are only the third. A brick utility shed was built where practice canoes and innertubes for the annual river race could be stored. A diving board was added to the pool and lap lanes for friends or those who claimed to be friends of the family the "aquatic center" was named for. Then new names started using the lanes. A slide was added and a concession stand. It's been years since anyone with the same name as the park has set foot in the pool. What was the point of having a building named after you if you couldn't recognize the people inside?

Ike lost his taste for swimming shortly after the war. Still, he likes living in his house—two and a half blocks closer to the pool than the house he grew up in—with the big bay window, where he's been able to watch the entire nine decades of history unfold from his memory. The location was good to his children and his grandchildren, too. His living there sent the right message.

Obviously, the pool doesn't get much attention this time of year. The water is drained to the three feet mark, where a line of leaves and then snow will gradually collect until it's opened again in the spring. The only activity is when people come to the utility shed for the odd piece of equipment or to make sure the roof hasn't collapsed. Still, Ike watches. He's too old to get a new hobby. Somebody should be watching, at any rate.

A few years ago—Ike can't remember if it was three or five—the shed had a visitor. There had been a few fancier-than-average cars in the neighborhood around then. He didn't think much of it. Maybe the neighborhood was coming back. This specific expensive, low-to-the-ground, and needlessly loud vehicle wasn't park district issued, that was for sure. A park employee wouldn't have missed the turn and ended up taking out the corner of the brick utility shed and the headlight of such a fancy vehicle.

The driver (crasher?) was coming around when Ike got out to him. There was blood and broken glass, but the car was still running.

"Are you all right?"

"Fine," the crasher mumbled.

"I called it in. There should be someone on the way."

The crasher looked at Ike with fear that was transitioning into anger. Blood made its way down the right side of his face. He didn't blink. The crasher reached for something in the passenger seat but changed his mind. Ike knows what it was now, looking back on it, but at the time, he thought it was a phone to call for help. The crasher huffed a few times before slamming the car into reverse and speeding off.

When the police arrived, they inspected the damage outside and inside the utility shed. Someone had noticed that the shed didn't get much attention and had started using it as a drop point for some new narcotic. There was a loose brick near the back, where they could gain access to the inside. "You're lucky to be alive," one of the officers told him. "These new dealers have already killed two people that saw something they shouldn't have." That's when Ike remembered the object that was not a phone in the passenger seat.

"Thank you for letting us know, but if you see anything else suspicious, please let us handle it. We can't have you getting hurt."

The officer then gave Ike a pat on the shoulder that was more patronizing than he realized. Ever since, Ike has watched. Someone should. It gives him something to do. And tonight, it looks like he has still more to do.

Ike doesn't know what Phil Dooley's car is doing at the shed. He doesn't know why Phil isn't the one who gets out and opens the shed door. Ike *does* know that he's not going to take the advice of the officer or his wife of too many years and let someone else handle this. He'll call later.

He grabs the jacket that's too thin but comfortable from years of use. He grabs the scarf that's too scratchy but warm as the dickens. They were both a gift from his son. The cane was a gift from his daughter. He doesn't want to take it, but there is nobody around to see him and say, "See how much better that is?"

It isn't late enough in the season for there to be snow, but the layered leaves are nearly as treacherous. It would be better if it were a few degrees colder. Then they would be frozen and provide at least some temporary structure. Ike is careful. He's not afraid of falling, but he doesn't want to listen to his daughter if he does. By the time Ike makes it down the front steps and across the yard to the shed, the man who is not Phil Dooley is coming out the front door.

"What are you doing here?"

In his younger days, Ike would have said, "Can I help you?" but with the same tone. He's found that age has made him less prone to pleasantries. No time for it.

"Good evening, Mr. Donaldson," The man who is not Phil Dooley locks the shed door before looking in Ike's direction. His breath is visible in the air. It's colder than Ike thought it would be. Or the man has recently been drinking something warm. The man puts the key into a film canister and closes it up. It's black with a silver lid. Ike doesn't remember the brand, but he always preferred the one with the clear canisters.

Ike doesn't recognize the man, but that's not terribly strange. Ike doesn't recognize most people anymore. He recognizes isolated features but not the collected picture. It's like recognizing a parent's features in a child. The more he thinks about it, that's exactly what it is. Ike doesn't know any of the children of this town, but he probably knew all of their parents. He often recognizes faces of his past jumbled up in the faces of the present.

Ike doesn't recognize this man.

"What kind of clandestine foolishness brings one of you to my front yard? The cops cleaned this place out two, three years ago."

"They only confiscate what they know to look for."

Ike hangs his head a bit too dramatically. "Just answer the question. This is why nobody likes you people. This 'move in shadow, speak in riddles' boogeyman stuff is nonsense. We don't have time for your dress-up games. We have real issues in this town. You want to help, sneaking around at night scaring folks, then talk some sense into that new mayor of ours."

The man with the film canister looks off toward the garden and smiles. It looks painful. "We hid an object here a while back. It seemed fitting, given the name of the park. Turns out that tonight is when this object is required."

"What object?" Ike can see the man's hands. They are empty except for the film canister he put the key into.

"A memory."

"Back to talking nonsense. I've got a whole box of 'memories' in my attic. Haven't looked at 'em since my wife passed. You want to make yourself useful, quit playing spy and come bring it down for me."

"I'm sorry, Mr. Donaldson. You're not the assignment tonight."

Ike looks at the pool with gritted teeth. He glances up the road, into the park, where there is a bench that looks over a neglected public garden and drainage ditch, which the garden was intended to disguise. Ike can't see it in the dark, but he knows it's there. He doesn't know there is a boy sitting there tonight. The boy's heart is broken, and so he has come to this spot to mend it. It's his first time, so he doesn't know. Hearts can't be mended. They simply mend.

"What kind of a memory?"

The man with the canister isn't supposed to. He knows he's not supposed to. The man in the suit that still has pine needles sticking out of it should not. The old man deserves it, though.

The man pulls a box from an inside pocket of his jacket. It could be a small shoe box, except that it doesn't have any brand markings. It is simply a brown cardboard box, tied with twine and too small for the shoes Ike wears. Judging by the way the man brings it around, it isn't heavy, but he's careful enough that whatever it is must have weight. The man cuts the twine and lifts the lid off with the short *ffft* sound of a snugly placed top.

Ike looks. He isn't surprised by what he sees. It isn't what he expected, but he gave up on being surprised a few years ago. The tension in his shoulders releases. The object inside is only special because of who it had been given to. The only time in the town's history.

"They always won, you know," Ike thinks out loud. "They own most of the property along the course. Home field advantage. Not to mention the overtime they paid employees at those properties. One Saturday a year, those factories were open. Didn't produce much on those days, though." Ike gives the man a knowing look. "My first job was brushing crumbs off her granddad's shirt after lunch.

Sloppy eater. I had other duties, but the most important one, or so he told me, was keeping his shirt clean." Ike smiles with a mouth full of crooked teeth. Braces were only for the wealthy when he was a kid. A few kids tried to bend paperclips to imitate the look. Ike was never one for putting on airs. "Now, she's mayor. I don't suppose you're her crumb boy."

"No, sir," the man laughs.

"Well, it's a cold night. Looks like you've got business to take care of." Ike turns and shuffles back up the frozen yard.

"The city owes you, Mr. Donaldson."

"You bet," he calls back. "But I'm the only one still alive who remembers why."

The man watches Ike Donaldson march back to his home. Donaldson has been with the city longer than almost anyone else the man is aware of. There was a moment, years ago, when Donaldson was the most important person in the city. He never knew it. The organization the man represents knew it. The man and his organization remember it.

The whole point of owning warehouses is that you never have to set foot in one. Jordan Kane's grandfather made sure that the only people in these places were the people making money for their family. It worked for generations. Now, it is up to Jordan to renew that arrangement. With any luck, she will be the last Kane to come within one hundred yards of this place for another generation or two. If that means she has to burn one or two of them to the ground, so be it. She grabs a small brown box, secured with twine, and tosses it into the barrel fire. She likes the way the maroon of her jacket absorbs the glow. It's a sort of camouflage.

The overhead lighting is strictly functional, the old kind of yellow from bulbs lasting longer than they should. Their light is directed wide by the open cones hanging from rusty chains on the ceiling. They are probably the same lights from when her grandfather first built the place, or so she thinks. When he *had* the place built, would be more accurate. Of course, when the building was constructed, it wasn't filled with thousands of small brown boxes bound in twine. The only shift in the dim yellow comes from the orange whisps that rise from the barrel every time Jordan throws another box in. Flames sparkle in the eyes of the woman sitting cross-legged on top of the car that seems blandly familiar.

"How many is that now?" the woman on the car asks.

"Not enough, apparently," Jordan parries. She grabs another box from the pile nearest her. She can feel that it's empty but refuses to let it show in her face. Most of the ones she has grabbed have been empty. She can't let that slow her down, though. Into the fire it goes.

"I know you're bored, but if you could not, I'd appreciate it. You're getting to be an inconvenience."

"You know how to make this stop."

The woman shrugs. "Maybe there's traffic."

The woman sitting on the hood of the car is too relaxed for Jordan's liking. Jordan is used to a certain level of nervousness, or at least caution, when people are in her presence. If they aren't intimidated by the Kane name—and they almost all are—then the "mayor" title that comes before it usually imposes a respect debt that most are all too happy to pay. On some level, that's what has brought these two women to this warehouse in what used to be the center but is now the edge of town. A disagreement over respect.

The woman on the car has a name, but it never seemed important enough to find out. More specifically, everybody Jordan knew to ask came back with a different answer. Maybe before the night is over, Jordan will grab her fingerprints. Mayoral authority makes fingerprint data easy to obtain. Still . . .

"Really, you're going to make me call you 'Management' all night?"

"You have your titles, I have mine."

The woman is working on a crossword puzzle. Jordan doesn't know where it came from. It wasn't found when Jordan had the place surrounded and her team searched 'Management.' It must have been missed, either through deliberate or incompetent negligence. Either way, Jordan will have to fire someone for it. As far as weapons go, a newspaper isn't high on the threat list, but that isn't the point. And it has been a while since she's had reason to fire anyone.

Jordan sighs and checks her phone. Nothing from the units on the perimeter. They are a collection of dedicated citizens from around town. Some off-duty officers looking to serve Jordan directly. Some country club friends who needed an excuse to use the tactical gear they picked up at the surplus store. Jordan watches them through the open loading door, comparing gear and generally wandering aimlessly, trying to convince themselves it all fits comfortably. They don't know why they're here, but they know what to look for. Anything. They get to play soldier, and Jordan has a small private army. Win-win.

Management puts the crossword down in her lap but does not let go. She glances up at the rafters like she knows exactly what she is looking for, just not if it is there.

"Something I should be concerned about?" Jordan asks, mainly to fill the space.

"Probably," Management says with a shrug. "But that's the problem, innit? That's the thing about you people. You're never concerned with the right things. And you're overly concerned with the wrong things. That's why you require us." She returns to her puzzle with a dismissive wave.

Jordan doesn't know what to make of the comment. The woman talks like a conspiracy theorist finally venturing beyond her bunker. If Jordan didn't have a filing cabinet worth of incidents that this woman was responsible for (allegedly), she'd dismiss the whole thing.

"I require nothing from you. Specifically, I require the absence of you. As long as your agent delivers, you can do nothing, and I will thank you for it. I need *exactly* nothing from you." She tosses another box in the barrel. This one has something in it. Something the fire enjoys.

"What? Oh, no. I didn't make myself clear. You don't need us. Your presence requires our activity. Our watching."

Maybe she is just a nut who's gotten lucky a few times. Jordan checks her phone again. No messages. It's the phone she uses for these kinds of issues. It's supposed to be a secret number, a number that she has had since her parents set it up for her when she turned fifteen. "For family business," they said. Enough of the wrong people have gotten it over the years that it's only slightly harder to find than her official personal number. Still, it's never seemed like a big enough bother to have it changed. If she's honest, Jordan has forgotten which number is which so many times, it might be her fault that the number got out. Either way, no messages. More waiting. She tosses another box in.

"Will you at least tell me what you people are after? For the amount of attention I've been advised to give you, I gotta say, you all just seem like loons."

"We want the same thing you do. The same thing everyone wants." Management's eyes don't leave the puzzle. "We want you to mind your own business."

"I'm the mayor. Everything is my business."

"Funny how that worked out, innit? How someone with your name just happened to find yourself in a position with a legitimate reason to stick your nose anywhere you like?" She briefly flashes a smile at Jordan, making the latter's knees wobble.

"What's that supposed to mean?"

"You know a six-letter word for hostility? I tried "attack," but it doesn't work. I forgot the double *t*. Pretty sure it starts with an *a*, though."

Jordan stares at the woman and holds up her hands in disbelief. Her hands are still in her coat pockets, so she looks like she's trying to flap a set of maroon wings. She flaps once and turns to check her phone again. Nothing. "If this is some kind of stall tactic, it's going to be so much more trouble for both of us. You want to be left alone, give me what I'm here for. Now!"

Management squints her eyes, like Jordan is a blurry Bigfoot photograph. "You interrupted his dinner. Besides, he has to get to it. We don't leave our boxes just lying around."

Jordan gestures to the boxes that have formed their own elaborate architecture around the two women. She grabs one. It squeaks on the inside. When it burns in the barrel, what looks like a dog's chew toy melts down the side.

"Well, sure. Except for all of these."

"I feel like you're not taking this seriously. The only reason my family tolerated your little spy club all these years is because you had blackmail on us. They were too comfortable or maybe just shortsighted to do anything about it, but I'm not. There are going to be some new ways of conducting business in this town, and none of them involve you or your creepy warehouse of boxes. I am going to burn this place to the ground. If you don't hand over the file on me and my family, you get to watch the fire from inside rather than from a safe distance."

Management lowers her puzzle. "We don't have any blackmail."

"Don't try and play me! This isn't game time. You're surrounded by a bunch of trigger-happy public servants who don't know if you're my friend or my enemy. I know what you have, and thanks to one of your agents seeing reason, we know how you operate. That's how we figured out where you were stashing everything. In one of our own warehouses! I'm about ready to kick over this pit just to be done with this conversation. Looks like this place will go up real fast."

Management returns to her puzzle. "Things are simple if you let them be simple. He complicated things. *You* complicated him." She sighs with disgust, remembering the night she confirmed the order in this exact warehouse. "You made a complicated night for me. It was rude. I'm sure what's left of him would agree."

Jordan's body wants to collapse into a chair, but she didn't think to have one provided. Where should she even start to salvage coherent information from this conversation? "What is your agent bringing, if not blackmail? If you're telling me that you have nothing, this night is about to get a lot messier. The only reason you aren't already dead is because I need what you have on me."

"Well, that's just it. It's simply something we've collected. It's not blackmail. It's *you*. Or at least, a version of you. People . . . " She breaks off, glances around, and decides she's done with the puzzle for now. "People just leave things. Parts of their identity that they think they're done with. It's important that an individual's variations aren't completely lost. We, all of us, make subtle decisions about what version of ourselves we are in any given moment. Decisions based on where we are, who we're around, what song was playing in the elevator on the way. Sometimes, these decisions are more extreme than others. More unique and temporary. Sometimes, people need to be reminded of who they chose to be once upon a time, even if it was just for an afternoon. Don't you think?"

A noise vibrates from the direction of the sectioned-off office at the front of the building. Jordan can't place it, but it's not natural. It's not the wind. It's artificial in a way meant to sound natural. Like a recording of a moose mating call. Jordan doesn't see anything moving in the office.

"When the boxes start talking," begins Management, "I find it's best to leave them to their conversations. Best case scenario, it's all in your head."

The noise calls out again but at a different pitch. Jordan warns Management with a look. Through the loading door, Duncan (the de facto leader) casts a glance at Jordan, realizes she's watching, and stands taller. Poor man. No matter how much he puffs up his chest, it doesn't extend beyond his gut. He insisted she should carry a gun with her. Jordan didn't think he knew who she was meeting, but she refused anyway. There was power in showing that you didn't need to arm yourself. It was a lesson from her father. In this moment, as the troops start stirring, she wishes she didn't learn it so well.

The office hasn't been used for its built purpose in years. It's clean. That's how Jordan knows. Any office like this—an office meant for working, not meeting—should show signs. There should be stacks of papers, errant office supplies, and fast-food detritus, some of which would be containing those office supplies. This one is too clean. There are no fingerprint smudges on the bay door control panel. All of the tiling is intact. There's no calendar with cars and women fighting for attention. There's not even dust on the counter running along the walls. Nothing but a few boxes placed on the counter to the left of the door.

The boxes are nondescript and simple. Lids are separate pieces from the rest of their boxes. They aren't the same size, but they are on the same scale. These have yet to be tied.

The noise sounds again, but Jordan registers it only distantly. It's not coming from the room after all. It's coming from the loading door. Her impromptu army can attend to whatever is making that noise. Jordan is engaged with the boxes.

All of the boxes have a sequence of markings stenciled along the lids, but Jordan doesn't recognize the characters as letters or numbers. If she had seen any of the *Predator* movies, she might compare these markings to the alien language used in those films. She hasn't seen the movies, however, so the comparison doesn't occur to her. It's not the best comparison, anyway.

Jordan reaches out to the nearest one, hesitates, and lifts its top off. Inside is a wooden rattle like something a child who grew up in a log cabin would have. The handle is a natural wood coloring, but the sound-making end is colored in a flat purple. There is a place where a bell should fit snugly, but the bell has fallen out. It's hiding in a corner of the box.

The next box has a high school yearbook from a town Jordan doesn't recognize. The book is stained with something in the bottom left corner.

Another box contains the skull of a small mammal. *Squirrel*, Jordan thinks. It's not a squirrel. It's also cleaner than it should be. It has been treated for preservation. Jordan recognizes the signs of care from her grandfather's trophy room.

Another box has another box inside of it. The box is covered in candy canes. Inside the candy cane box, there is ash, cigarette butts, and a charred bead of something that rolls around when Jordan lifts the box for a better look.

The last box has a handmade scarf. It's not her colors, but Jordan doesn't see anything wrong with it, which strikes her as odd. She holds it in her hand—the overly dry, cheap yarn from a craft store. She owns nothing like it.

She knows she has missed something but can't place it. Jordan doesn't even know what she has looked at to be missed. She walks to the barrel, still holding the last box. The flames have gone down a bit, but they still flick above the rim. She tosses the scarf in, and it half burns, half melts. Draped on the rubbish at the fire's core, the grays and blues char until the entire thing is black. It doesn't lose its form until a piece of wood gives way, and the entire structure shifts. The scarf becomes little more than dust disappearing in the flames. The box goes in as an afterthought.

When Jordan looks back to Management, there is a man standing beside the car. He's hard to make out in the flickering light, but the owl pin on his lapel tells her all she needs to know. He's not as tall as Jordan expected.

"That scarf was made by a girl who thought she was a woman. She started it for one man but finished it for another. The second man knew that provenance but thought wearing it was a show of appreciation. What he didn't realize is that it became a mark of ownership. Even after he broke free and tried to change what the scarf meant, he was always someone owned by someone who had betrayed him." The man in the suit steps toward Jordan, stopping to form an equilateral triangle with her and the fire. Management is no longer part of the geometry. "You're probably right to burn it," says the man in the suit that is, for some reason, covered in pine needles. "That version of that man doesn't have many uses in the world. We didn't need him taking up space on our shelves."

"I will burn every weird story in this warehouse if you're here emptyhanded." Jordan catches a glance at Management over the man's shoulder. She has completed the crossword, apparently, and is now folding the paper. "I don't know why my family was always so cautious around you, but it's done. You freaks either give me the one box I'm here for, or I destroy them all. Whatever voodoo people think you have won't survive that."

The sound that isn't coming from the office is back. It's brighter this time and moving. Not moving emotionally, the way music is supposed to. It is moving physically, to the left, past the loading bay door. They can't track it in the dark, but it's moving through the trees at the water's edge. The eyes of Jordan's troops outside attempt to locate the disturbance. It is moving musically, hitting multiple notes up and down the scale.

Jordan sees a boy emerge from the shadowy trees, running as fast as he can while playing the trombone. It's not a very fast pace, but he is outpacing the agents that Jordan brought with her. As soon as Jordan figures out what is going on, she will have to deal with that as well. Maybe there will be more than one body found in the burnt remains of this warehouse.

"I thought your supporters could use some entertainment," says the man "And it leaves the three of us to settle this."

The man steps closer to Jordan. The boost that the fire got from the scarf is diminishing, but the heat is enough that, with his suit jacket and tie, he is starting to sweat. She doesn't notice, but he worries that she might. He opens his hands and twiddles his fingers slightly, hoping any moisture will dry itself.

"Where is my file?"

The man reaches into his jacket. He pulls out a box like the one that held the scarf, but smaller.

"That is not what I asked for."

The man turns to look at Management, who is still working on folding her paper. "I tried explaining it to her," she says.

The man turns back to Jordan. "This is what we have on you. It may not be what you thought you were asking for, but it's what you want. And you seeing what's inside, that's what we want."

The man opens the box, flipping the lid around and using it to hold the bottom. He doesn't hand it over but rather, waits for Jordan to come to him. To come to it.

She peers inside. She doesn't see any pointed objects or hidden hinges ready to snap. All she sees is a strip of maroon cloth. The cloth is familiar, but Jordan can't place it. It occurs to her that she once knew a child with a shirt that color. It doesn't occur to her that she *was* that child. Even as she subconsciously brushes her fingers over her jacket of the same color.

She picks up the cloth, and with it comes something solid and heavy with a ribbon attached. The ribbon is red but brighter than the cloth. Shinier. Cheaper, but meant to look fancier. The heavy thing it's attached to is a circle of metal, cheap brass. *Tube-a-thon* is engraved around the bottom border. The number *87* is centered in relief, with a stylized river crossing over the *8* and under the *7*.

"What is this?" Jordan mutters to the medal. She knows the answer, but her mind refuses to connect the dots. She is unfamiliar with this collection of sensory memories.

"This is . . . context," the man offers. "When it is in this warehouse, it's simply an object. The same goes for where we have preserved it for all these years. A hunk of metal and ribbon, nothing more. When it is in my care, it is a package, something to be delivered and protected. When it is in her possession, it is leverage." The man isn't looking at Management, but he pauses as she waves the newspaper, now in a triangle shape. "But it is only leverage because of what it is when it is in your hands. A memory. It is an identity. An identity that is a previous orientation of the components that make *you*. A version of you, which we think is the most valuable to Hollow Brook."

Jordan knows now. As she rubs the cold medallion between her fingers, she accepts. She feels who she was when she won the award. She had been expected—assumed—to take first place. Before then, a Kane had never lost. Hell, Grandpa Kane had started the tube-a-thon back in '45. Good for the community. Good promotion for the city's economy. Good for any business that sat on property owned by the Kanes, which was most of them.

Jordan knew why they always won. The whole town knew. An awfully high number of tubes seemed to experience structural problems right around the Kane properties along the river. Never the tube with a Kane on board, though. A little overtime pay and some strategically placed obstacles below the waterline made for a path that only the Kanes knew how to safely navigate. Either the tubes sank, or the riders took too much time avoiding catastrophe.

Sure, there were years when a Kane didn't race. The family was only so big, and it was only open to teenagers. If a Kane was competing, though, a Kane won.

Nobody was going to rock that boat—or innertube, as the case might be. Not until Jordan's junior year of high school, that is. The year Jordan told Allison Shaw the path. Allison was the only person who didn't seem to care what Jordan's last name was. Allison was also the only reason Jordan had passed Calc I that year. Allison deserved a shot. That wasn't the point, however. The point was, Jordan needed to know that any victory was hers, not the family's. Jordan earned her second-place finish.

Then came the summer of isolation. The summer of retraining. The summer her father and her grandfather explained her part in the future of the town. It was also the summer that she first heard about the secret group of watchers, as more than just little-kid superstition. The group was the local version of the illuminati. Kids would draw that stupid owl symbol in their notebooks as some kind of local inside joke. Yet, her father and grandfather spoke of the group with such seriousness. Until recently, Jordan believed that the grown-ups were simply more superstitious than the kids.

"Where did you find this?"

"Where it was left," comes the nonanswer from the man in the pine-scented suit.

Jordan places the medal back in the box, the smell of the river still filling her nostrils. "What do you want from me?"

The man shrugs. "Right now? Nothing. Remember, you called this meeting. Your choices are yours. Sometimes, people in your kind of position think there is only one path from a crossroads. We are curators of alternate choices." The man closes the box and walks with it back into the stacks, blending into the shadows.

"He's a little dull for my taste," Management says, hopping off the car hood. "But he gets the job done." She steps closer to Jordan and puts the newspaper, which is now folded into a pirate hat, on Jordan's head. "You're the captain. Don't make us sink your boat."

They stare at each other for a moment, both confused but for very different reasons.

Management pops her eyes at Jordan a bit. "This is my warehouse. Please get out."

Jordan blinks. "What? No, this my . . . "

"Is it, though?" Management interrupts.

Jordan shakes her head a bit before turning to walk out the door. She brushes the hat absentmindedly from her head. The night is immediately colder as she walks past the boundary of the warehouse. She got so used to the contained warmth of her fire, she forgot the time of year. Jordan pulls her jacket tight and sleepwalks to her car.

Upon seeing her, the guards scramble to look like they weren't punked by a trombone player. She dismisses them and drives home. She'll deal with them in the morning. An enemy who wants something is usable. An opponent that doesn't want anything is something else entirely.

Leslie refills the matchbook tray at the counter. It's something menial but productive that can make her look busy for the remaining seven minutes of her shift. The Dining Car is the only place she knows of that still has customized fire starters, but people seem to like them. That's why she has to restock them. And it makes Devon and Carlos cut her some slack.

A man—well, a kid who is undergoing the change into a man—walks in. He's tallish, slightly flushed, and it looks like there is at least part of a tree in his hair. He's wearing black fabric overalls with a white stripe going up the sides of his legs, and a white T-shirt underneath that probably didn't come with those mud stains. The trombone in his hands makes him stand out. He stares at the pie display next to the counter.

"A table and pie for two?" Leslie looks for acknowledgement of her wit.

"Heh . . . We could both use a place to sit," Gary says with a wide-eyed airiness that doesn't tell Leslie if he thinks she is funny or if he's just crazy.

The waitress grabs a menu and leads the trombone player to a booth one space away from the corner. He props his trombone up on the inside of the booth and sits down next to it for protection. His window faces Wendy's, which is the cheeriest view The Dining Car has to offer. It's a view of one of the places a kid like him should be patronizing after a football game. He even recognizes a few of the cars still in the lot. Somehow, the Dining Car felt like the right choice, though.

"Did the team run out of players and have to pull from the marching band?" It wasn't a hard deduction for Leslie to make.

"Something like that."

"Well, the team lost. So, you don't have to worry about it for a while." She places the menu and pulls out her notebook. "Pie?"

"Pie sounds great," Gary says, collapsing a bit into the booth. He smiles at Leslie. She smiles back and leaves.

Leslie grabs a slice of peach. The trombone player didn't specify which kind, but he doesn't seem like he's in a picky mood. The peach is pretty good. It's also the only fruit pie left in the case. Everything else is crust filled with different orientations of sugar and butter.

She meanders back to the trombone player, grabbing the carafe on the way. "Peach pie, and I thought you might like a cup of coffee. You look like you could use it."

"I don't drink coffee."

She nods and begins to leave, but he stops her.

"It feels like the night to start, though. Thanks."

She flips his cup and fills it shy of the edge.

"Thanks," he says again. "Do you have a pen I could borrow?"

She laughs to herself. "If there's one thing a waitress has plenty of, it's pens. Nobody remembers to put them back, and they are always needed." From her apron, she pulls out a blue one with the logo of a local bank on it and hands it over. "Keep it. I've got five more just like it."

Gary smiles and nods his appreciation as the waitress returns the coffee and does one last round of her tables. Gary pulls out a scrap of paper and looks at the symbols printed on it. They aren't new or difficult symbols. He sees them every day. In this order, though, they are nonsense. He scratches lines with the pen, more to feel like he's solving something rather than actually making progress.

"I'm almost . . . You're one of them?" The waitress is looking at the puzzle in the trombone player's hand. She sits down beside him and pulls out a piece of paper from her apron. It, too, is lined with letters in combinations that don't make any sense. They are the same symbols as Gary's but in a different order. Leslie's is half completed.

"A man in a suit left this earlier."

"He gave me this one after jumping out of a tree at the high school." Gary reconsiders this. "Falling. He might have fallen. I'm not sure he jumped. This was wrapped inside a map of the warehouses south of town. He wanted me there to distract some people down by the warehouses. At least, I *think* that's what he wanted, but he never actually said. That's what I did, anyway. I guess I wasn't ready to give up marching." Gary takes a sip of his coffee. It's too hot, but he fights hard to not show it in front of the waitress. "He didn't tell me the people would be armed. I think I saw the mayor, too."

"My guy didn't finish his meal and left this with the tip. Your story is a lot better."

The nearly rusted out bell above the door rings, but neither of them turns to see who is coming or going. They didn't even hear it. All they can hear is the ringing in their ears and the weight of their breaths.

"I think it's about substitution," Gary says.

"Transformation," Leslie offers.

Leslie pulls another pen from her apron, and they begin working. They split the pie. Gary's coffee is replenished by Devon. They leave together, just before closing. It's only then that they think to exchange names. They will have use for them in the future.

There is only one other car in the parking lot when they leave. It's nondescript but sticks out due to its solitude. For the evening, it belongs to a man in a suit that needs to be dry-cleaned. A man with a slightly tarnished lapel pin, which, from the right angle, looks like the head of an owl. A man who can finally finish his eggs benedict.

Backword

Everything you have just read is true
Except for the parts that I made up . . .
Though most of that turned out to be true, too.

A Song To Dream By: As a former Boy Scout camp counselor, I have a backlog of songs that I have very little use for. That all changed when my daughter was born. When confronted with a newborn, I found myself relying heavily on that catalog of camp songs. I quickly taught my wife some of these songs because, for a time, they were the only way to get our daughter to sleep. Every time one of the songs worked, it felt like an unstable kind of magic. I happened to be taking banjo lessons at the same time and tried to merge the two skills whenever I could.

As most parents will tell you, the psychological torture of trying to get a newborn to sleep is matched only by the paranoia once they do finally shut their eyes. Sometimes, those songs from camp worked so well (and I was so sleep-deprived), I worried I might have tapped into something extra. What if she didn't wake up? What if something else woke up?

There is also a bit of *The Ballad Of Black Tom* by Victor LaValle in here. That's where our protagonist got his name.

An Exchange was heavily inspired by the podcast *Welcome To Night Vale*. Specifically, this story is an attempt to replicate the unique tone and perspective of episode 45, "A Story About Them." I was fascinated by how evocative a lack of description could be. The drive of the characters that are so clear about what they are doing but without the reader's awareness was something I wanted to experiment with. It wasn't the plan, but that seed of an idea grew into three of the stories in this collection.

For the record, I really did used to live in that house, on that street.

A Moment Of Time is the earliest story in this collection and based on the idea of time travel becoming banal. If we ignore paradox, assume that kind of thing is safeguarded against, what would it be used for? The answer that seemed obvious was tourism. I have a degree in history, and so I would like to visit some key moments of discovery and decision. But, the more human answer seemed worth exploring. We all have moments that aren't in any history book while still being pivotal to our own development. A moment that maybe we are the only ones who know the importance of. A moment or an experience that seemed to stretch forever that we'd like to revisit. See if the magic is still there. This is an attempt to showcase one use of that perspective.

I still get to hear Al play sometimes. He's still got it.

The Case Of The Green Math: I've always liked detective stories and stories where the main character thinks they're in a different genre than they are. Throw in some other dimensional monster and my experience as a substitute teacher, and the result is this story. In both high noir and Lovecraft stories, I always get the sense that we are being told a very heightened version of the actual events. The only other place I've experienced that kind of unreliable narrator is when dealing with students. It would be a terrifying place if half of the stories some of my students told me were true.

There is also a *Codename: Kids Next Door* reference in this story that I should have removed in the interest of streamlining the narrative. But, it made me laugh, so I kept it.

Objects From A Past Life started when I was listening to the podcast *Ear Hustle*, a show about life and the lives in prison. Specifically, the episode "The Christmas Boxes" features recently released individuals describing what it was like to interact with objects they owned before they went into prison. How that object, for better or worse, represented a different person. Some of them had a visceral, physical reaction to it. It was an experience so divorced from my own that I wanted to explore what it would be like to have an object in the world that you needed to destroy because of what it meant to a different version of yourself.

I was about halfway through this story when I noticed a familiar scent on it. It took little effort to make it rhyme with "An Exchange." And so began the Hollow Brook Stories.

Ringo: Plush Companion is largely based on seeing my daughter interact with her stuffed animals. It's such a pure relationship, and I wanted to interpret that relationship through Asimov's Laws of Robotics. Robot stories are usually about adults. If kids are involved, it's either a horror story or we get a very watered-down version of robots. "Ringo" is an optimistic version of the laws of protection applied to those who most need that protection. I wanted to offer something closer to a non-romantic love story. What would it take for a stuffed animal to return the dedication a child gives it?

Star is named after the dog that watched over me and kept me warm when I was a baby. She was a good dog.

Animus is based on a note I made to myself while reading a book about sorcery nearly fifteen years before. It's common to have magic users wake the dead to find some key piece of information, but they almost never put them back. What does the reincarnated person do then? They aren't really a zombie because they have to be valuable to the magic user. This is my best guess as to how that would work. This is also the most purely philosophical piece in this collection.

The early draft of this story got one of my favorite reviews from my wife: "Is that really what it's like inside your brain?"

In The Box came about when I realized "An Exchange" and "Objects From A Past Life" needed a closing note. I didn't want to answer all of the questions, but I wanted to establish a third side to the Hollow Brook triangle. I was thinking about the boxes and this clandestine agency collecting Jay's bracelet. I don't know why they did it when I wrote it. It just seemed like a fun thing to toss in at the end. But then, if I was going to continue that story, I had to figure it out.

There are objects around my house that are "mine," but they represent achievements of an earlier version of myself. A version of myself that might as well be a character from a book. To be human is to evolve. To become different than you were. Certain objects have the terrifying power of shifting us back to earlier versions of ourselves.

I was in the middle of putting this story together when my Pappy began end-of-life care. Ike is a direct manifestation of that grief. Pappy is gone, but Ike's stories are just beginning.

Acknowledgments

There are so many people who helped this work find the light, and so many people who helped me on my journey from reader to writer.

Thank you to Mr. Copley, Dr. Frech, and Dr. Monroe for reading some early scribbles, even if they weren't the assignments.

Thank you to my rough-and-tumble early readers, who were kind enough to offer early notes and corrections. First, the infamous members of my role-playing group: Jason, Brian, Tom, Ed, and Colin. Also, my speech, theater, and trivia compatriots: Becky, Erin, Justin, and Julie. Thank you, also, to my always optimistic and ready to roll sister-in-law, Jen.

Thank you to Granny for encouraging me to be a reader at an early age. I couldn't always get her to buy me candy, but she was always willing to buy me a book.

Thanks, Mom and Dad. Early trips to the library and the summer reading program set the early foundation for everything here.

Thank you, Willow, for inspiring some of these stories and showing me what real creativity looks like. The way you see the world will always be something I try to emulate.

Thank you, Juliet. You believed in me when I didn't, read early drafts at all hours, and were always willing to tell me when I was too full of myself. You put up with my mountains of books and my thinking out loud when we're just trying to get to the next episode. As I promised you long ago, I will never stop trying to impress you.

Photo by Erin Kuntzelman

About the Author

Adam Moderow is an Eagle Scout with degrees in philosophy, history, and teaching. He teaches developmental reading and G.E.D. courses for Highland Community College. Adam also serves on the Stephenson County Board, plays trumpet, and takes on the occasional voice acting role. He currently lives in Freeport, Illinois with his wife, Juliet, and their daughter, Willow. *Songs To Dream By* is his debut work.

www.ingramcontent.com/pod-product-compliance
Lightning Source LLC
Chambersburg PA
CBHW071428260626
47170CB00008B/2631